I0726698

Moon Dust

Joseph J. Christiano

Moon Dust, © 2012, Joseph J. Christiano
2nd Edition, 2018
Tell-Tale Publishing Group, LLC
Swartz Creek, MI 48473

All rights reserved. No portion of this publication may be
reproduced, stored in an electronic system, or transmitted in any
form or by any means, electronic, mechanical, photocopy,
recording, or otherwise, without the prior permission of Joseph J.
Christiano. Brief quotations may be used in literary reviews.

Printed in the United States of America

For Amber, Alyssa,
Hailey and Bryce

Chapter 1

An Unscheduled Visitor

No sooner had Hansen's head hit the pillow than the comm chime sounded. He groaned and lay there for a moment, hoping he had imagined it. There was a pause, just long enough to make him think perhaps he had, then it sounded again. He rolled onto his side and thumbed the button on the bulkhead next to his bunk. "Hansen." He tried to disguise the fatigue in his voice, failed miserably. Whoever was on the other end of the line would hear it loud and clear. He instantly regretted the last round he had bought at the Gemini.

"Sir." The voice from the small speaker seemed to fill his quarters. "It's Wright. Can you come to the con, please?"

Of course it was Wright. He was the only one who addressed Hansen formally. Nearly four hundred-thousand kilometers from anything resembling military authority, Wright still insisted on maintaining protocol when addressing a superior. Hansen had tried to break him of that habit, unsuccessfully. It would not be so bad if Wright hadn't insisted the rest of the personnel address him in the same manner. In the four months since Wright's arrival, Hansen had noticed the stress level rise among the base personnel. It wasn't something he felt he needed to address, not with the GSA, anyway. He had tried subtlety, addressing Wright by his first name, but the major had not taken the hint. He had, in fact, seemed somewhat offended. Hansen abandoned that course of action. He was certain Wright's attitude kept Mikhailov busier than usual. She had probably not gotten the chance to lock the hatch to her quarters in four months. God knew he had been tempted on several occasions to schedule an appointment with her himself.

"What is it, Mr. Wright?"

His second-in-command's reply was immediate. "Sir, there's a vessel on approach. She just cleared the outer marker."

Hansen's brow furrowed. He knew without checking that the next supply drop and shift change was not due for another two months. He knew this specifically because there was a secret countdown going on among some of the crew members who looked forward to Wright's hopeful departure after a single tour. He would not admit to it, but he was counting down with them. "Who is it?"

"We don't know," he said. "They haven't replied to our signals yet."

Hansen heard the slight tremor of irritation in the man's voice. Naturally. An unscheduled visitor, especially one who did not announce his identity, was not how things happened in Adam Wright's world. Hansen wondered, not for the first time, how such a man had ascended to the rank of major, let alone in near-record time.

Hansen sat up in his bunk and reached for his shirt. "I'm on my way." He thumbed off the intercom without waiting for Wright's customary "Yes, sir."

A few moments later he stepped through the hatch into the main control room. Aside from the three hanger bays, it was the largest room on the base. It had been built to accommodate a staff of thirty. The tiered work stations that ringed the room, as well as the rows of terminals and monitors that made up its center, were largely unused. Some, Hansen believed, had not been activated since their installation. To Hansen's knowledge, Armstrong had never supported more than twenty-five people, and even that had been in its earliest days. Since then, the number of people that made up the base's personnel had fluctuated between seventeen, when he had first arrived, and its present eleven.

Nevertheless, the room itself was impressive. In addition to the workstations was the main monitor screen, which took up most of the forward bulkhead. At the time of its construction, it was the largest video monitor ever built. Hansen's office was to his right, the hatch still closed. A staircase stood to his left, stretching toward the loft area where the engineering systems were controlled and monitored. He did not have to look to know that Duncan and Narita were not there. He had left Duncan in the Gemini, quite drunk. Narita, he had been informed, was busy adjusting the environmental controls in B-ring.

Wright stood at the forward-most row of consoles. His stance was wide, his hands folded behind his back, at parade rest. He looked at the main monitor screen and gave orders to McKnight. The part-time systems analyst, part-time base pilot, worked the console in front of him like a concert pianist. His movements were practiced, precise. Lines of telemetry scrolled up the left side of the main monitor as, in the distance, a small silver dot grew in size.

"Report," Hansen said as he joined the only other men in the room.

Wright turned to him and moved aside. "She's coming up on the inner marker now, Colonel. Speed is three kilometers per second. Still no contact."

There was no inflection in Wright's voice; he simply recited the facts as he knew them. It was a trait that unnerved some of the crew, Hansen included. It sounded artificial, mechanical. Wrong.

"Do we have an ID yet?"

"Just got her registry from the transponder now, Mike," McKnight said. "It's the *Sovereign of the Stars*."

"The starliner?" Wright asked.

"One and the same," McKnight replied. He continued to play his recital on the keyboard in front of him. New telemetry scrolled up the main screen. "Looks like she left Earth four months ago. According to her scheduled flight plan, her course took her out to Pluto, then back to Earth. Your standard cruise around the block."

"Then what's she doing here?" It was a rhetorical question. Hansen was unaware he had spoken at all until Wright answered.

"She must be in trouble." Wright looked from Hansen to the monitor and back again.

"Maybe. Any sign of damage, Don?" Out of the corner of his eye, Hansen saw Wright wince at the way he addressed McKnight. It was a bit too informal for the executive officer of Armstrong Base. And hadn't McKnight addressed him by his first name? Hansen couldn't remember. He thought perhaps he had. That would probably be written up as insubordination in Wright's next report. Hansen could not wait to be rid of the man.

The small silver dot continued to grow in size on the screen. Hansen could see the sleek lines of the hull coming into focus. He could barely make out the light coming from what he assumed to be the windows high up on the ship's bridge. Even at a distance, the sunlight reflecting off the silver hull made the approaching object seem more like a star than a vessel built by human hands.

"No obvious damage, but her flight computer isn't talking to me," McKnight said. "I can tell you she is under her own power, but that's about all." He consulted his instruments. "Wait. She's reducing speed. Slight course correction, too." His fingers flew across the keyboard. "Looks like she's aiming for pad three."

"She's going to land," Wright said quite unnecessarily.

Hansen continued to study the image on the main monitor. It had tripled in size. He could make out, quite clearly, the full hull of the starliner. She was a beautiful ship, bigger than anything Hansen had ever seen. Her bow, shaped somewhat like that of an ocean liner from two centuries earlier, passed by the camera.   He could see the name printed on the hull in giant block letters as it passed: ***SOVEREIGN OF THE STARS***.

"Definitely slowing down." A pause. "Still nothing from her flight computer."

Hansen's eyes never left the monitor. "Don, can pad three handle something that size?"

McKnight's reply was immediate. "I've been crunching the numbers. If the pilot brings her in perfectly, and if there's no power spike from her ventral rockets, yes. But it's not a landing I'd want to attempt, even on a good day."

"Can the docking sleeve even reach any of her external hatches?" Wright's voice had regained its professional, clipped tone. 1

"Yes," McKnight said, this time without a look at the telemetry. "Assuming, of course, that the landing is perfect and she doesn't slide off the pad and wind up in the dust." He manipulated his keyboard. The view on the main monitor changed. Again, the *Sovereign of the Stars* was a small silver dot on the screen. In the foreground of the image was landing pad three.

"What's her ETA?" Hansen asked.

"Four minutes," McKnight replied.

Hansen spared a glance at Wright before his eyes returned to the monitor. Without looking, he reached down and pressed the intercom button for the infirmary. "Doc, it's Hansen."

Hasegawa's voice came through the speaker without delay. The doctor never left the infirmary unless it was to treat a sick or injured crewman at the scene. It was also rumored she slept there, and kept her quarters merely for appearance's sake. Hansen would swear the woman knew in advance whenever someone would need her services. "Here."

"I need you and Kehoe to meet me at airlock three in five minutes."

"On our way." Her reply came with no hesitation.

Hansen should have been used to it by now. Hasegawa never seemed surprised by anything. He knew she was methodical, professional, everything that could be asked of a chief medical officer on a frontier outpost. Still, he had expected her to at least question his sudden request.

Hansen closed the channel to the infirmary and hit the general intercom button. "Nix, where are you?"

This time, it took a moment for the reply to come through. When it came, the voice was rough, impatient. Clearly, Hansen had disturbed the man in charge of base security. He could guess why.

"Off-duty, Mike. What's up?"

"An unscheduled visitor," Hansen said. "I need you at airlock three in five minutes."

Another pause. "Roger that." The channel closed on the other end.

Hansen turned one last time to the main monitor. The starliner had grown in size again and approached landing pad three with her landing struts extended. Moon dust kicked up around the platform, flung in all directions by the mighty retrorockets that lined the vessel's belly. The dust billowed and obscured the image.

Hansen turned to Wright. "Contact the GSA. Tell them what's going on out here and tell them we're going to board her."

"Sir, is that wise?"

Hansen looked at Wright and saw genuine concern in the man's eyes. It did not reach his voice.

"We don't know anything about that ship. There could be a radiation leak or some other hazardous situation aboard. You could be endangering yourself and anyone who goes with you."

Hansen nodded. "That's a distinct possibility. But they came here for a reason. There might be people hurt there. I'd like to think they'd show me the same courtesy."

Wright nodded. "Understood."

Hansen was positive Wright did not understand, but he let it drop. There were more important matters at hand. He made for the hatch.

****

Nixon turned off the intercom and rolled off of Mikhailov. He rubbed his temples and stared at the ceiling. "I swear to bloody Christ that man knows exactly when not to call me, then he does it anyway." He slammed his fist down on the bed and looked at the naked woman next to him.

Mikhailov regarded him with a mixture of humor and sympathy. Her short pixie hair, usually strawberry-blonde, was dark with sweat and matted to her skull. Her breathing was heavy, as was Nixon's. She looked at him for another moment and then rolled onto her back and kicked the covers off her legs.

"Call of duty, love," she said.

Nixon sat up on the bed and grabbed for his trousers, which lay crumpled on the deck. "Yeah, yeah, yeah." He stood and pulled on his trousers on and began the search for his shirt. "All of eleven people on this base, and I still can't get some alone time."

"He wouldn't call you if it wasn't serious," Mikhailov said. She lit a cigarette. "He knows how much you value our…appointments."

Nixon located his shirt and draped it across his back. The fabric caught on the sweat that coated his back. He pulled on it impatiently. The sleeve ripped at the seam and he stopped and regarded the new tear. Mikhailov laughed loudly. He turned to her, fake outrage and not a little humor in his eyes. "You shut up! This is your fault!"

Mikhailov sent a couple smoke rings in Nixon's direction. "I'm sure you'll tell him that."

"Never you mind what I'm gonna tell him." Nixon grabbed his boots and pulled them on. He ran a hand through his short-cropped salt-and-pepper hair and looked at Mikhailov. "Well? How do I look?"

"Like you just had sex," Mikhailov replied and laughed.

"What a coincidence," he said wryly. He scowled at her, but he could not hold back a burst of laughter. He leaned across the bed and planted a kiss on Mikhailov's cheek. She responded by pressing her lips against his hard enough to make him squirm. "I'll be back as soon as I can."

Mikhailov smiled at him. "You'd better."

"Promise." Nixon kissed her again and made for the hatch; he buckled his belt as he went.

****

Hansen heard the footsteps approaching at a mild run and saw his security chief round the corner in the corridor. He finished pulling his gloves on and made sure the seals were tight. He regarded Hasegawa and Kehoe as they finished slipping into their isolation suits. It was the first time he saw Hasegawa in one of the large, bright white suits, and it made him laugh, if only to himself. Her five-foot one-inch frame was nearly lost inside the fabric. Only her head, with its unruly shock of jet-black hair, broke the color scheme. Kehoe, with his dark skin and eyes the color of the midnight sky, contrasted nicely with his surroundings. If not for Hansen's own pinkish skin and light brown hair, they would have made an excellent black and white photo.

Hansen allowed himself a moment of bemusement when Nixon saw the three of them suited up. If there was one thing Nix hated, it was outside work. Hansen held up a hand before his security chief could protest.

"Relax, Nix, we're not going outside. Not exactly."

"What, then?" Nixon asked, opening one of the lockers that held the isolation suits. He pulled the bulky white contraption off its hook and removed his boots.

"Our unannounced guest out there landed a couple minutes ago, but she's radio silent. We don't know why."

Nixon pulled the suit on over his clothes and zipped it up the front. He sat on the lone bench and reached for the matching boots. "They don't have atmosphere?"

"No, they do," Hasegawa said as he stepped away from the scanner console next to the airlock door. "In fact, environmental conditions are perfectly normal."

"Then why the suits?" Nixon asked as he finished with the boots.

"Because we haven't been able to talk to them," Hansen replied, and he pulled the helmet on. He heard the telltale *click* that told him the helmet was secured to the suit. "We don't know what to expect. It could be nothing, just a malfunctioning antenna array. Or, it could be a lot worse. So we're going aboard prepared."

"Let me help you with those, Nix," Kehoe said as he approached the big man. He took one glove, then the second, and slipped them onto Nix's hands. "We all know how much you *love* wearing these things."

"Wiseass," Nixon said. There was no anger in his voice; quite the opposite. If George Nixon could be said to have a friend among the personnel on Armstrong, it would be Kehoe. Their ever-escalating competition of practical jokes was the object of a lot of betting and whispered rumors on Armstrong. He looked at Kehoe with obviously mock concern. "Is that a tear in your suit?"

"Not as bad as the one you're sporting on your shirt. Had an appointment with Galina, did we?"

Nixon might have blushed had his frequent visits to Mikhailov's quarters been a secret. In truth, he had nothing to be embarrassed about. Most of the base personnel found their way to Mikhailov's door sooner or later, most for a purpose other than sex. A tour on Armstrong could take its toll on a person in a number of ways, which meant the base psychologist was almost never off-duty. It was also the reason most psychologists remained on Armstrong for only a single tour. Listening to the varied complaints took its toll on the doctor, as well. Had Hansen not been in charge, he may well have scheduled an appointment or two already. He hated the idea of being away from his family for so long. But the CO of a pseudo-military installation was not allowed to have weaknesses, psychological or otherwise. He felt the ring on his finger through the thick cloth of the glove. He pushed thoughts of Barbara and the girls from his mind. This wasn't the time.

"Docking sleeve is pressurized. We'll be entering through the D deck first-class reception area," Hasegawa said.

Hansen waited for Nix to put on his helmet. When he did so, Hansen reached for the intercom panel. "Wright, this is Hansen. Any word from the GSA?"

A momentary pause, then, "Negative, Colonel. They haven't responded yet. And still nothing from the *Sovereign,* either."

"Very well. We're opening the airlock momentarily. We'll stay in contact."

"Roger."

Hansen closed the channel and reached for the airlock control mechanism.

"Hang on," Nixon said, and Hansen stopped cold.

Nixon inputted a code on the small locker farthest from the airlock and opened it. He reached inside and pulled out a handgun. He pulled the slide back and checked the safety. He wrapped the belt around his waist and holstered the weapon.

"Is that really necessary?" Hasegawa asked. Her question was directed at Hansen, not Nixon.

Hansen glanced at the weapon before he nodded at Hasegawa. "It might be. Better to play it safe."

Hasegawa grumbled but said no more. Hansen looked over his team a final time, and then he pressed the red button on the airlock control panel. The hatch slid open. They were looking at the inside of the airlock. All four of them stepped inside, and Hansen closed the hatch behind them. He looked through the small window in the outer hatch at the umbilicus that would take them to the exterior hatch of the *Sovereign of the Stars*. He opened the hatch.

Chapter 2

Cruise to Nowhere

Thorpe entered the control room, Mason on his heels. Thorpe, who had the penchant for wearing clothes three sizes too large for his ample frame, noted the presence of McKnight and Wright near the front of the room. His eyes found the main monitor. The image should have been the starscape, or perhaps the screensaver he himself had installed – a live streaming image of the floor of the Pacific Ocean he had hacked into when nobody was looking. Instead, what he saw was the view from somebody's helmet camera inside the docking sleeve.

"What's happening?" he asked. His voice echoed in the large room. He noted, with some satisfaction, that the echo caused Wright to jump, just a little.

Armstrong's executive officer turned at the question and regarded the two geologists as they approached him. His eyes were cold, impatient — precisely the look Thorpe always received from Wright.

"We have a visitor," McKnight said without looking at them.

"I can see that," Thorpe said. "Who is it?"

Wright grimaced. "The *Sovereign of the Stars*." His annoyance announced itself as a long, slow sigh.

"No shit," Mason said. "Really? What is she doing here?"

"No idea," McKnight said and made an adjustment on his console.

"You know, I tried to get tickets on her maiden voyage," Mason said. "It sold out too fast." He sounded dejected, even though that voyage had taken place four years ago.

"It had nothing to do with the fact that you couldn't begin to afford a ticket on that beast, right?" Thorpe laughed, but only a little. Mason wasn't quite up to his level when it came to friendly ribbing. Mason was a fantastic geologist, brilliant even, but when it came to the back-

and-forth banter that occupied much of the downtime on Armstrong, he was a novice at best.

"Yeah, that too," he said, and lowered his head slightly.

On the screen, the owner of the helmet cam rounded a slight bend in the docking sleeve and came upon the gleaming silver hull of the starliner. The boarding hatch occupied the center of the screen.

"Okay, Wright, we've reached the outer hatch." It was Hansen's voice and it seemed to come from nowhere and everywhere around them.

"Audio and visual are both strong, Colonel," Wright said. "We're standing by."

Thorpe slid into an empty seat next to McKnight and ignored the look he was certain he was getting from Wright. Out of the corner of his eye he saw Mason take another unoccupied seat.

Wright sighed. "Okay, fine. If you two insist on being here, make yourselves useful. You," he pointed at Thorpe, "monitor their meds. And you, keep an eye on the integrity of the docking sleeve. Any changes in anything, let me know at once."

"You got it."

"Will do."

Wright sighed again, and Thorpe smiled to himself.

"Opening the hatch now," said the voice from the intercom.

****

Mikhailov stopped in front of the open hatch to the Gemini. She glanced up and saw the small slab of moon rock someone had mounted on the bulkhead long ago. **GEMINI CAFÉ** had been engraved upon the slab by some long-ago crewman. It had most likely been a joke, someone's attempt to give the room an added function besides the base mess hall. No one had bothered to remove the slab, and the name stuck. As did its role as the one place on Armstrong where one could procure alcohol. Sometime after that, someone had managed to install a bar, complete with stools that gave the room the appearance of an Old West saloon. Mikhailov appreciated the gesture. Certainly the GSA was aware of the Gemini's dual purpose. The appearance of *Machine Parts* on nearly every transport's cargo manifest was too obvious to fool anyone. GSA management might not be enamored with the idea of what occurred on Armstrong behind the scenes, but even they had to yield to the inevitable drinking that went on out of earshot of Earth.

She entered the Gemini and looked about. The small room that served as a mess hall, recreation center and alcohol dispensary was dark and nearly deserted. Most of the light inside the room spilled in from the corridor behind her, or was provided by the ancient pinball machine in the corner. The origin of the old gaming device was unknown. It was said that one of the original base staffers had brought it with him from Earth and left it behind when his tour was over. In the time she had been on Armstrong, Mikhailov had seen how the game was played by watching Kehoe and Nix compete against each other. Nearly everyone gave it a go when they first arrived, although Mikhailov herself had yet to try her skill. She simply did not see the appeal.

Only Duncan was present. The engineer sat at the bar with a glass half-full of what Mikhailov assumed was whiskey. Her head was down, she slumped on the stool, and it did not take Mikhailov's keen observation skills to see she was drunk. Mikhailov took the stool next to her, lit a cigarette and took the glass from Duncan's hand. She sniffed it; her guess had been correct. The engineer reacted slowly. She looked at her hand as if seeing it for the first time, and clearly wondered what had happened to her drink.

"How ya doin', Brenda?" Mikhailov sipped at the whiskey and puffed on her cigarette. "Tough shift?"

Duncan looked at her through half-lidded eyes. "Always. Where'd my drink go?"

Her normally accent-free voice found its Irish burr only when she had had too much to drink. It didn't happen often, as far as Mikhailov was aware, but when it did, it happened in spades.

"Bartender cut you off for the night, love." Mikhailov threw back the whiskey and put the glass back on the bar. "Come on, let's find your bunk."

She stood and placed one hand under Duncan's arm. The engineer did not resist, and she allowed herself to be guided toward the hatch. They had made it nearly out of the room when Duncan stopped and braced herself. She looked at Mikhailov with those half-lidded eyes as her black hair fell over her face for a moment. She blew at it, causing it to puff up before settling over her eyes again. "I like you, Galina," she said.

"I like you, too, honey," Mikhailov said, smiling to herself. "But you're gonna need some sleep. Something's going on and if the colonel calls for you, you can't be in this condition. Come on, let's get you to bed."

"Okay." Duncan smiled broadly. She draped an arm around Mikhailov's shoulder and allowed herself to be led down the corridor.

****

Hansen looked back at his team. They all nodded at him. He looked at the control panel next to the hatch on the *Sovereign*'s hull. He inputted the code he had downloaded from the GSA database, and a moment later, the hatch slid open. He looked into total darkness.

He got the impression the room was enormous, although he did not know why. He had never been aboard the ship, had never studied its schematics or pored over its brochure. Still, he was certain the room was bigger than anything they had on Armstrong, except perhaps the three hanger bays. And even then…

"Flashlights," he said over his shoulder, and then he activated his own.

Four beams of light stabbed into the darkness of the room, and Hansen saw immediately he had been correct. The reception area opened into what could only be the first class dining area. The room stretched into darkness in all directions, possibly the full width of the hull. Their suddenly-inadequate flashlight beams revealed tables that appeared to be made of real wood, draped with white cloths. Each table could seat a good dozen people. All the tables had plates and cutlery placed and ready for use. He moved his flashlight beam to the ceiling, and it reflected off cut-crystal chandeliers, which bent the light into every color of the spectrum and sent it all around the room. The effect would have been beautiful had it not been for the sinking feeling that crept into Hansen's gut. Particles of dust drifted lazily in the air. They pirouetted through and around the flashlight beams like a fine snow.

Portholes lined the bulkheads as far as the eye could see. Hansen looked back at his team again and then took his first step into the room. He could feel the rich, thick carpet give a little under his weight, even through the isolation boots. He took a few slow, cautious steps inside, enough for the people at his back to enter. He heard Kehoe whistle through his teeth.

"Earth-normal atmosphere," Hasegawa said after consulting the portable scanner she had brought. "No sign of any atmospheric contagions. All read-outs are green."

"Let's leave the helmets on, just in case," Hansen said.

"But Mike, what happens when I meet some fine, rich ladies? They might not be able to tell how handsome I am if I'm stuck inside this suit." Kehoe sounded only half-serious.

"Like you'd have a chance, anyway," Nixon said.

"Knock it off, both of you." Hansen did not turn to look at them. "Clearly something is very wrong here. Let's not take any chances."

"Roger," Hasegawa said.

Hansen knew without looking both Kehoe and Nixon acknowledged his order with a sheepish expression. He moved deeper into the room. His flashlight beam found an intercom panel on the bulkhead, and he pushed the button. "This is Colonel Michael Hansen of Armstrong Base. Does anybody read me?" He waited several moments before he tried again. As the first time, silence was the only reply. He closed the channel and turned to the three people at his back. "Sweep forward."

Nixon took the lead and drew his gun. He activated the small flashlight that sat atop the gun sight and moved it slowly back and forth in front of them. More dust floated through the light beam.

"Watch what you shoot, old man," Kehoe said.

"Be a shame if you walked in front of me, wouldn't it? God knows you're ugly enough to pass for an alien."

"Fuck you,' Kehoe said and laughed.

"Cool it," Hansen said. "Keep moving forward."

Kehoe approached the nearest table, which was set and ready to accommodate an even dozen people. A fine coating of dust covered everything. It dulled the silverware and the bright white of the plates. A laminated place card sat in the center of the table. He picked it up and shined his flashlight beam on it. Even through the dust, the print on the card was easily discernible. The card read: **SOLAR ENCHANTMENT CRUISE 2115**. "They actually named the cruise."

"What?" Hansen asked. He was nearly to the staircase that led to the next deck.

Kehoe held up the place card. "Do you feel enchanted?"

"Not today." Hansen motioned Kehoe to join them at the base of the staircase, and he started up the stairs. Kehoe replaced the card where he found it and hurried to catch up.

The stairs were carpeted as well. The details of the wooden railing were so intricate they could have been hand-carved by a master craftsman. Hansen kept his light trained ahead of them. The dust, which continued to drift lazily through his flashlight beam, was joined by smoke or steam. Not much, and if the staircase had been well-lit, he might not have noticed it at all. "Doc? What's this smoke?"

Hasegawa consulted her scanner. "Judging by its content, I'd say plastic, wood, numerous artificial compounds, and some kind of meat."

"Kitchen fire?" Kehoe asked.

Hasegawa nodded. "Possibly."

"Environmental systems must be offline," Nixon said.

"That would explain the smoke," Hasegawa added.

At the next landing, they saw a sign on the bulkhead that read: **C Deck**. The smoke became thicker. An intercom panel was mounted a few meters to the right of the sign. Hansen exchanged a look with Nixon and then he pressed the button. "Does anybody read me? This is Colonel Michael Hansen. Respond." He was not surprised when he received no reply.

C deck continued to his left and right, and it was as dark as the dining room below. A pair of ornate doors stood half-closed a few meters in front of them. Smoke drifted lazily from the other side of the doors. The gold plated sign above the doors was partially burned but still legible: **Main Ballroom**. "Nix," Hansen said, proceeding to the doors. Nixon joined him.

They did not see the body until they nearly stepped on it. Hansen ignored Kehoe's gasp and knelt beside the body. It might have been a man once, although Hansen was not convinced of the corpse's gender. It lay on its back, one arm outstretched toward the ceiling; its other arm was gone below the elbow. Its skin and what little remained of its clothing were the color of coal. Hansen heard the sound of Hasegawa's scanner behind him and moved out of her way. She took his place by the corpse and pressed buttons on the scanner.

"No surprises, Mike. Severe burns. If there was an explosion in there," — she indicated the partially-closed doors before them — "he caught the brunt of it."

Hansen took his eyes from the corpse and glanced at Nixon. The security chief returned the look but said nothing. Hansen inclined his head toward the ballroom doors. When Nixon nodded, they each placed a hand on the door handles and swung them open.

The room was nearly as large as the dining hall, and it was just as dark. Their flashlight beams revealed more dust and much thicker smoke in the air, swirling slowly this way and that. Their entry into the room had disturbed the air currents enough that the dust and smoke moved with greater speed and in various directions. It took a moment for Hansen's eyes to see through the cloud. When they did, he nearly dropped his flashlight.

Numerous bodies lay strewn about the room. Many were seated at tables that ringed the room. More lay or knelt about the polished wood of the dance floor. Some were coupled up, as if they had dropped in mid-embrace. Others were alone, but it was the formation of the corpses that struck Hansen as unusual. Something about their arrangement made him think of church. To complete the image, a single corpse lay in front of the stage, a dead preacher sermonizing to his dead flock. All were identical to the corpse outside the room.

Hansen was at once grateful for the isolation suit and its supply of oxygen. He had no desire to experience the scents of the ballroom.

"Christ Almighty," Nixon whispered.

"Doc," Hansen said.

Hasegawa moved to the nearest body. It was a man, but that was only evident by the scorched remains of his genitalia. He lay flat on his back a few meters inside the room. His mouth was stretched into a final, agonized scream. Hasegawa knelt down and held her portable scanner over him.

Nixon approached a small table that seated two more bodies. He held his gun in front of him and shined its light on two destroyed faces. They leaned across the table, their hands clasped. They appeared to stare into one another's eyes, although the eyes themselves were burned away. Nixon got the distinct impression they had been an elderly couple. What looked to be a gold cigarette holder had melted into the glass ashtray that remained on the tabletop. A small metallic place card on the side of the table was burned, but Nixon found the lettering was still readable. It contained the same message as the one Kehoe had discovered in the dining room. "Cruise to nowhere." Nixon gulped.

Kehoe had activated his own portable scanner and had moved to another table. This one was larger than the table that occupied Nixon's attention. Six people were seated there, as if in conversation only the dead could hear. Their heads were bowed and they held hands. He shined his light on the female body closest to him. An elegant string of pearls hung down from her blackened neck. He reached out a hand to touch those pearls, apparently thought better of it, and went to work with his scanner.

Hansen stood behind Hasegawa. His gaze alternated between her and the scene around them. The dust and smoke continued to swirl through his flashlight beam, slowly now, as if getting over their intrusion. The only sound he could hear was the soft *whirr* of the scanner in Hasegawa's hand. "Doc?"

"Same as the man outside," Hasegawa said. "Subjected to extreme heat, possibly a flash fire."

"Definitely a flash fire," Nixon said. "Over here, Mike."

Hansen stood and saw Nixon near the far bulkhead. He left Hasegawa to her investigation and joined his security chief. The first thing Hansen noticed was the missing panel on the bulkhead at waist-height. The area around the missing panel was a shade of black darker than Hansen had ever seen. The panel itself lay on the deck next to a blackened skeleton. A small amount of meat remained on its bones, but not enough to fill one of Thorpe's sample beakers. Its mouth hung open, and its hollow eye sockets stared at the ceiling. Something had melted across the skeleton's hand and pooled on the deck. Hansen could not begin to guess what the object had been. He looked from the skeleton to the open panel.

A thick length of what was probably once transparent piping ran horizontally through the panel. It was shattered in its center, and the jagged edges of the break were the same shade of black as the bulkhead around the missing panel.

"That's a plasma conduit," Hansen said.

Nixon nodded. "Yes, it is." He indicated the skeleton again. "I think our friend here shattered it."

"On purpose? That's suicide," Hansen said immediately. "Every school kid knows that. Why would…"

He looked again at the skeletal hand and the melted metal draped across it. It might once have been a hammer or some other tool strong enough to smash a plasma conduit. He looked about the room again. He took in the many corpses and the smoke and dust that continued to swirl about. "This guy decided to end it all, so he took a bunch of innocent people with him? Is that what you're saying?"

Nixon pursed his lips. "I'm not sure. Maybe. But look around you. Look at the posture of some of these people. That couple over there holding hands, the mother holding her child close. Look at the people on the dance floor, for Christ's sake. Looks to me like they knew the end was coming."

Hansen shook his head. "No. No, I can't believe that." He stepped in closer to Nixon. "You're talking about a suicide pact of some sort."

"I don't know what I'm talking about," Nixon admitted. "Just saying the evidence suggests this wasn't an accident." He inclined his head in the direction of the ballroom entrance. "Maybe that man out there was some sort of psychotic nutjob. If he was trying to get in here to kill these people…" His voice trailed off and he shook his head. "Forget it, stupid idea. He would have been outnumbered about a hundred fifty to one. I'd take those odds against any aggressor."

Hasegawa joined them. She had closed the scanner and clipped it to her belt. She regarded the open panel and the charred skeleton for only a moment. "This happened a few days ago, Mike. Three, maybe four. It's hard to be certain without a full examination."

"You want to take one of them to the infirmary?"

"Yes, I would." She brushed absently at the dust accumulating on her faceplate. "If Mr. Nixon is correct and this was a mass suicide, there might be something to be found in a toxicology analysis. And if there was something wrong with the man in the corridor, a brain scan might be helpful."

"If there's enough left of his brain to scan," Nixon said.

Hansen frowned. "Not my first choice, but I can't see any reason not to allow it." He regarded them for a moment. On the far side of the room, Kehoe approached the stage and orchestra pit. "You think they were drugged?"

Hasegawa shrugged. "Don't know. Won't know until I can get a closer look at what was going on internally."

Hansen's frown remained in place. "Very well. But not yet." He took in the three people around him. "We don't have enough oxygen in these suits to search the whole ship like this. Nix, take Kehoe and check the engine room. See if you can find out why internal power is down. The doc and I are heading to the bridge. Someone piloted this ship here, so somebody knows what happened."

"Roger that," Nixon said. He turned to Kehoe, who nodded at him.

"We meet back at the airlock on D deck in twenty, regardless. Understood?"

"Understood," Nixon and Kehoe said at the same time.

****

McKnight turned his eyes from the scene on the main monitor to the scrolling read-outs on his own console. He manipulated the controls and the lines of code on the screen were replaced by an image of the *Sovereign of the Stars*. The ship looked pristine on the landing pad, somewhat out of place with its backdrop of moon dust and star field.

His fingers flew across his keyboard as a thought occurred to him. After a moment, he found and accessed the controls for the camera mounted on the roof of B-ring. He transferred the display to his monitor and panned the camera around until it caught the *Sovereign*. "Whoa," he said, zooming in on the image.

"What is it?" Wright asked. He maintained his place, watching over the three men who worked the controls.

"Look at this," McKnight said, putting the image on the main monitor.

They had been watching Hansen and Hasegawa climb the ornate staircase to the next deck. Now they looked at the port side hull of the *Sovereign of the Stars*. The image began on the bridge and swept slowly along the hull.

"What are we looking at?" Thorpe asked.

"Nothing new," Wright said and turned to McKnight. "We've seen this already."

"No, we haven't," McKnight said. "Coming up on it now."

McKnight couldn't blame them for missing it; he himself had missed it the first time through. He worked his keyboard and zoomed in on a spot where a black mark marred the gleaming silver of the hull plates. It appeared to be no more than a half-meter long and wide. He stopped the camera and zoomed in as closely as the system would allow.

"What the hell is that?" Mason asked of no one in particular.

"Hull breach," McKnight said.

"What do you think did it?" Thorpe asked. "I mean, that hull was built to military specs. It's supposed to be impregnable."

"Minor damage," Wright said with a dismissive wave of his hand. "They have atmosphere so the isolation bulkhead obviously dropped when it was supposed to."

"Not really the point I was trying to make," McKnight said.

"Look at the damage to the surrounding area," Mason said. "Looks like shell splashing, like she was in combat."

"Almost any impact could have caused that kind of damage," Thorpe said. "Probably a micro-meteorite."

"You just said the hull was impregnable," Mason said, a hint of triumph in his voice. He smiled.

"'Impregnable' is not an absolute," Thorpe said.

"I'm pretty sure it is," Mason retorted. "Just admit I got you. Just this once. Admit it!"

"Pipe down, both of you!" Wright said, clearly irritated. "Christ, this is worse than kindergarten."

McKnight's attention was drawn to his console as a red light began to flash, followed by the chirping of the comm system. "Wright, we have an incoming transmission from the GSA." He paused a moment. "For the base commander."

"Very well," Wright said. "Put it through to the colonel's office. I'll take it in there."

"Roger."

****

Hansen and Hasegawa stopped when they discovered the dead body in the corridor on A deck. It was clearly a member of the ship's crew; the uniform said as much. It lay face down in the center of the corridor, arms splayed as if the man were trying to fly. Hansen knelt next to the body and turned it over gently. He recoiled, quite against his will, and managed to stifle a gasp.

The man appeared to have been dead a long time. His skin resembled old parchment and it clung to the body's shriveled frame. His eyes had receded into their sockets, but somehow they managed to appear much larger than normal. He mumbled for Hasegawa but she had already knelt beside him and was running her scanner over the body.

"Single gunshot wound to the head," she said.

Hansen looked more closely and found it difficult to believe he had overlooked the wound in the center of the man's forehead. Perhaps the man's hair had partially concealed the wound, or the lack of blood around it failed to grab his attention, but Hansen had indeed missed it.

"How long ago?"

Hasegawa continued to consult the scanner. "I don't know. This makes no sense to me at all."

"Not really what I want to hear, Doc." Hansen looked back the way they had come, then forward toward the dark, unexplored path to the bridge.

Hasegawa deactivated the scanner and looked at him. "I'm sorry, would you like me to make up something?" She stood and replaced the scanner on its hook at her belt. "He was shot in the head by a large caliber bullet, but that's not what killed him. According to the readings, he was dead already. Had been, in fact, for some time. The rate of cellular decay suggests he'd been dead for about two years."

"What?" Hanson shook his head. "That's impossible. This ship left Earth four months ago."

"I'm perfectly willing to accept this scanner is malfunctioning, even though I checked it myself before we left the infirmary. My professional medical advice is to bring this man back to Armstrong, Mike. It's the only way to find out for certain what killed him. And when."

"Bridge first," he said after a moment. He shined his light ahead of them. The corridor ended thirty meters away at a closed hatch. "That should be it. Let's see if we can find out what happened here before we start filling up your infirmary."

They approached the hatch and stopped in front of it. A gold placard on the bulkhead next to the hatch confirmed Hansen's guess. He moved to press the button labeled **Bridge Access**, and then stopped himself. The button hung from the wall by a single wire. Two other wires appeared to have been cut. He looked at Hasegawa and grimaced.

He knocked on the hatch. "Ahoy the bridge. Is there anybody there?" There was no reply, and he found himself unsurprised. "This is Colonel Michael Hansen of Armstrong Base. If you can hear me, you're safe. Please open the hatch." He paused, but heard nothing from the other side.

Hasegawa had opened her scanner, and she now lowered it. "Normal atmospheric readings from the other side."

"Yeah, just like the rest of the ship." He looked at the cut wires, turned them over in his hand. "Maybe I can splice these back together."

"With your gloves on?"

"I'm sure as hell not taking them off."

Hasegawa nodded her agreement. "Smart man."

Hansen's helmet comm chirped, followed by Nixon's voice. "Mike? It's Nix."

Hansen let go of the wires. "Go ahead."

"The engine room has been sealed off. We're staring at a blast door that's blocking the only access to that section of the ship. Without internal power there's no way to raise the thing."

"Okay, Nix. The Doc and I are right outside the bridge. The hatch is sealed and the lock has been disabled. We're going to try—"

A burst of static overcame the comm system, then came Wright's voice, much louder than it needed to be. "Colonel, this is Wright, sir."

Hansen winced at the sudden increase in volume but recovered his composure quickly. "Go ahead."

"Sir, we've received a message from President Cromwell. He's ordered all base personnel off the *Sovereign of the Stars* at once." His tone changed and Hansen was positive the man was reading directly from a communiqué. "Make no further attempts to search the vessel for survivors. Seal off all mooring and boarding umbilici. Quarantine the vessel immediately. A special response team is en route and should arrive tomorrow at or around 0945 hours. Acknowledge."

Hansen frowned and regarded the sealed hatch in front of him. "Acknowledged. Nix, you catch that?"

"Loud and clear." Nixon's reply was immediate and at a much more reasonable volume.

"Meet us back at the airlock. We're on our way." Hansen spared one more glance at the hatch and then he led Hasegawa back down the corridor.

A few moments later they reached the airlock. The first thing they noticed was the absence of Nixon and Kehoe. The second thing they noticed was the smeared blood on the deck and the bulkhead next to the open hatch.

"That wasn't there before," Hasegawa said.

They exchanged a glance and followed the blood trail with their eyes. It led down the docking sleeve.

"Nixon, report," Hansen said, a bit too loudly.

Nixon's reply was immediate. "Mike, we're at airlock three. You'd better get down here."

Hansen bolted through the open hatch, Hasegawa on his heels. He stopped, turned and inputted the code into the control panel on the hull. The hatch slid shut slowly. He did not wait to see it close completely. He caught up to Hasegawa as the two of them rounded the bend in the sleeve. The trail of smeared blood ran down the center. They were careful not to step into it.

Nixon and Kehoe both knelt on the deck in front of the airlock. It took Hansen a moment to realize there was a third person with them. A woman in a crewman's uniform lay just in front of the hatch. She lay on her back; her chest rose and fell slowly. Her short, dark hair was plastered to her skull with sweat. Hasegawa shouldered Nixon out of the way and knelt beside the body.

"Report," Hansen asked.

Hasegawa studied the scanner. "She's alive. But her pulse is weak and erratic. We need to get her to the infirmary immediately."

"What about contamination, Doc?" Nixon asked.

"We can try to save this woman's life or we can sit around and have a debate about it. What's your pleasure?" Hasegawa did not take her eyes from the woman as she spoke.

"We'll have to take her through decon with us," Hansen said.

"Hope that's enough," Nixon said.

"Doc? Is it?"

"The decon process eliminates one-hundred-percent of all known contagions," Hasegawa said, her patience clearly gone. "We'll be fine."

Nixon held a gun in his hand and showed it to Hansen. "She had this in her hand."

Hansen reached for the gun but thought better of it. "Analyze it when you get to the security office. See if it's been fired. We found a corpse upstairs with a gunshot wound to his forehead." He indicated the unconscious woman on the deck. "She may be the shooter."

"Roger that," Nixon replied with a nod.

"And Doc, keep her in restraints, just in case."

Hasegawa nodded wordlessly.

Hansen hit the button that opened the hatch. He stood back as Hasegawa and Kehoe slid the woman through and into the airlock. He stepped in after Nixon, closed the hatch and activated the decontamination sequence. He raised his arms, as did Kehoe and Nixon, as the sprinklers sprayed them with the powerful decontaminant. It washed over Hasegawa and her patient as well. After a few moments, the sprinklers went dry.

Hansen opened the inner hatch. "Okay, let's move."

Kehoe picked up the woman under her arms and Nixon grabbed her legs. They moved down the corridor quickly. Hasegawa hovered over the woman and took constant readings with her scanner. Hansen watched them go.

Chapter 3

Three Brainiacs and a Suit

Hague took his eyes from the forward windows just long enough to glance at the man seated next to him. When he thought about it, *man* was probably not the correct term to use in describing Sanchez. *The kid isn't even old enough to buy a beer*, he thought. As expected, Sanchez wore a grin from ear to ear. Since their launch from San Francisco the day before, the kid had slept perhaps fifteen minutes. He had spent nearly every waking moment in the cockpit, monitoring his controls and readouts. Hague had nearly had to force the kid to go in the back for a piss break or the occasional bite to eat. Had he been this way on his first space flight? He couldn't remember. He hoped so.

Outside the windows, the moon loomed large and gray. They were not in the correct orbit to see Armstrong, but that would change before long. He inputted the commands that would begin their de-orbit burn, then turned to Sanchez.

"First time in lunar orbit." It was not a question.

"Man, this is beautiful,' Sanchez said. "I can't believe I'm here." He took his eyes from the windows to consult his instruments. "Retrorockets firing. Beginning de-orbit burn. Velocity is five kilometers per second."

"Roger that," Hague said with a smile. Even in his obvious rapture, the kid was all business. Maybe there was hope for him yet. "After we break orbit, I'll call Armstrong and get landing coordinates. Want to go back and check on our passengers?"

"Hell no," Sanchez said.

Hague laughed, easily and honestly. "Don't blame you. Three brainiacs and a suit. I wouldn't want to, either." He laughed again.

The moon dropped down and under the windows. They were looking at the star field once more. The transport inverted momentarily as her retrorockets fired. Hague felt his stomach drop, and he swallowed hard. It was his least favorite part of the journey, and always had been. It was not something he had gotten used to with repetition. A quick glance at Sanchez told him the kid felt the same way. They swung back to their original position, the moon's surface much closer than it had been even a moment before.

Hague swallowed again and tried to settle his stomach. He hit the comm button and he adjusted his headset. "Armstrong Base, Armstrong Base, this is transport one-one-three-eight. Do you copy?"

"We read you, one-one-three-eight," said the female voice. "Go ahead."

Hague smiled. "Brenda, is that you?"

"The one and only," said the voice.

Hague broke out in a toothy smile. "How are you, darling?"

There was a short burst of static, then: "Hung over. You?"

Hague laughed and ignored the perplexed look he knew he was getting from Sanchez. "Not yet. The chessboard the way we left it?"

"Of course. With you two moves from checkmate." There was a short laugh followed by a cough, then silence.

"That sounds about right. Listen, honey, we'll be starting our approach in a few minutes. Where do you want us?"

There was a pause, and Hague could see the engineer checking her readouts, finding the optimal landing platform based on their course. "We'll take you on pad one, if you please."

Hague nodded. "We do, indeed. See you in about half an hour. One-one-three-eight over and out."

"Roger. Over and out."

Hague closed the channel and returned his full attention to the moonscape that filled the front windows. Impact craters made their way past the cockpit windows. A thought occurred to him, and he took the controls and altered course slightly to port.

Sanchez noticed immediately. "What are you doing? Our angle of approach has changed by three degrees."

Hague nodded with satisfaction. *Kid is sharp, no denying that.* "It's under control. Besides, I wanted to show you something. This being your first time here and all."

"And what's that?" Sanchez asked.

"You'll see."

Hague guided the transport on its new course. They passed over a mountain peak, then dropped altitude as the moonscape leveled off beneath them. He had memorized the coordinates of their destination, having been there multiple times himself. He never got tired of seeing her, and he was willing to bet Sanchez would inherit that particular love affair, as well. He hoped so, anyway.

Ahead, he saw the beginning of the slide scar, and the transport dropped a bit more altitude. He reduced speed, and his hand hovered over the controls for the retrorockets. "There," he said. "One-two-zero degrees."

Sanchez peered through the window, saw the slide scar and followed it to its conclusion. He gasped, his eyes growing wide. Hague could not help but smile again. *Love at first sight*, he thought.

"Is that what I think it is?" Sanchez's voice was full of awe, as if he had just been presented with a piece of Christ's cross.

"It is."

The wrecked ship below them lay half-buried in the lunar dust. The slide scar indicated its path once it made contact with the lunar surface. It had come to a stop when it collided with the base of a small mountain.

Pieces of debris littered the moonscape behind and around it. Its single engine port was clogged with moon dust. The portside hull bore scrapes and a few tears, telltale signs of the violence experienced in the ship's final moments. Its nose was buried inside the mountain face, and its forward-most hatch had sprung open, most likely on impact. Hague had seen the wreck many times. He was still in awe of it.

"The *Daedalus*," Sanchez whispered. His mouth hung open for only a moment, then his lips pulled back from his teeth and he smiled the widest smile Hague had ever seen. He nearly jumped out of his seat, but the harness restrained him. He clapped his hands together and looked at Hague. "That's the *Daedalus*, my God!"

"Yes, it is," Hague said, and he sat back and watched the young man's excitement.

"Oh man, I've known about her since I was a kid. I never thought I'd actually see her in person!" He clapped again and laughed. "Jesus, she's beautiful!"

Hague almost laughed himself, but caught it in time. They were, after all, hovering above a wrecked ship on the lunar surface. Wouldn't do to show too much excitement and be a bad example to the rookie. "I thought you'd like to see her."

"Like?" Sanchez turned to Hague and laughed again. "Man, I *love* this!" He craned his neck forward as far as it would go. He seemed to study every inch of the wreck, and his appreciation was evident in his expression. "Hague, I don't know how to thank you for this. This alone was worth the trip up here."

"Remember me in your will," Hague said, and he readied the controls.

"Did you know she was the first spacecraft to circumnavigate the solar system? I knew everything about her when I was a kid. I was just fascinated by her story the first time I heard it." He paused to take a breath. "Man, this is incredible." He turned to Hague so quickly the pilot thought the kid was going to give himself whiplash. "Can we go inside?"

Hague shook his head. "Doubt it. No one's been in there since the rescue team seventy years ago. Took them a couple days to recover all the bodies. But I guess you knew that already."

Some of the light disappeared from Sanchez's eyes. "Yeah." His voice was subdued, a startling shift from the excitement of the previous moment. "I do remember reading that." He regarded the wreck once again. "Sorry."

"Don't be."

The intercom chirped, and a woman's voice filled the cockpit. "Is there a problem, pilot? We're supposed to be landing right now. But it's funny. I don't even see Armstrong Base. All I see when I look out my window is empty moon and some derelict piece of shit."

The tone was of someone used to getting her own way. It carried authority the way Hague imaged Caesar's had. The voice held nothing but contempt and impatience. Hague knew immediately who had spoken, and would have even if there were more than one female aboard the transport.

He hit the intercom switch. "We're on our way, Ms. Dwyer. Just had to make some, um, adjustments to our engine controls." He pulled back on the yoke and the *Daedalus* disappeared from the windows. He shot a look at Sanchez, who looked both excited and disappointed. *Next time, kid. When we don't have the queen of all assholes in the back.*

"Don't give me excuses," said the icy voice on the speakers. "Just get me there. Now."

"Yes, ma'am," Hague said. He thumbed off the intercom.

He caught Sanchez looking at him out of the corner of his eye. The kid was trying hard not to laugh. Ultimately, he failed. He burst into laughter.

Despite himself, Hague joined him a moment later.

****

Sanchez got his first look at Armstrong Base ten minutes later. He had seen photos of her, of course, as had everyone. It didn't hold the same thrill as the *Daedalus*, but it was still a moment of excitement. The first thing he saw was C-ring, the outer-most wheel that housed the three landing platforms. Sanchez had expected the light gray skin of the base to blend in with the surrounding terrain, but it stood out quite nicely. Light spilled from nearly every window and porthole he could see. Unlike the *Daedalus*, which was dead and dark, this was a living, breathing facility. Barely visible on the far side of the base was the behemoth on pad three. He paid it little mind.

"C-ring is devoted to incoming and outgoing transports," Hague said in his best professor voice.

"I know," Sanchez replied. "B-ring is engineering and life-support, all the mechanical stuff. A-ring is living quarters and personnel spaces." He could see both inner rings and their connecting spokes as the transport moved closer to pad one. In the center, joined to A-ring by three spokes, was the command module. "And facility control in the center." He turned to Hague and smiled. "I studied up for this flight."

"Sounds like you did,' Hague said. "Care to take the controls?"

Sanchez went white. His smile vanished, and he gulped.

Hague laughed and slapped him on the shoulder. "I'm kidding. I'll take this one. Maybe you can land when we get back to Earth."

Sanchez relaxed visibly. He exhaled loudly and slowly. "Deal."

"Let them know we're here, will you?"

Sanchez reached for the comm switch. "You got it."

****

Wright entered the control room of Armstrong's underground hanger one. The room was small, cramped. Three workstations, each with its own monitor and control board, faced the enormous windows that looked out into hanger one. The hanger itself was large, with room enough for two transports. One of Armstrong's transports, seven-seven-zero, was stored here. It was old and beat-up in Wright's opinion, and had flown only once in the four months he had been stationed at Armstrong. He fell somewhat short of trusting it.

The transport coming down on the elevator from pad one above was newer and more advanced. He could see the two pilots through the cockpit windows. One of them waved to him. Wright did not wave back.

He turned to Narita, who worked the controls for pad one. The engineer's assistant was young, far younger than Wright would have liked. But the kid seemed to have a good head on his shoulders, and he had received nothing but glowing reports from Duncan. In truth, Wright liked Narita, as much as it could be said he liked anyone. His jet-black hair was a bit longer than Wright would have liked, but the kid was non-military, and not subject to its standards of personal grooming. He was young, true, and required seasoning, but he followed orders and addressed his superiors in the proper fashion. *Unlike McKnight and the geo twins.* They still required some work, as far as Wright was concerned. He hoped he would not see Narita give in to the informal atmosphere that reigned on Armstrong. He was, as far as Wright was concerned, the one bright spot on the personnel roster.

Under Narita's guidance, the elevator touched down and the hanger's landing pad slid into place above. "Pressurizing now, Major," Narita said, and he pressed a few buttons.

Wright watched the indicator lights on the hanger environmental systems go from red to green. He walked to the hatch that led directly into the hanger and opened it. He walked down the short flight of stairs and made for the transport.

He reached it just as the hatch opened. He stepped back and assumed his parade-rest stance. The first person through the hatch was a woman Wright had never met, but he knew her just the same. Late-forties with dark hair pulled back into a tight bun at the back of her head. She wore a gray business suit that looked as if it cost more than his annual salary. Her high-heeled shoes echoed when she stepped onto the hanger's concrete deck.

"Ma'am, I'm Major Wright, executive officer. Welcome to Armstrong."

"Executive officer?" Dwyer asked. The disdain in her voice was loud and clear. "Your commander sent a subordinate to meet me?" Her voice dripped with contempt and offense.

"Colonel Hansen had other duties to perform. He has requested you meet him in his office, ma'am. I am to escort you there."

Wright noticed the three men in the hatchway behind Dwyer. Unable to exit the transport until she moved, they looked sheepish and kept their silence. Wright regarded them for only a moment before he returned his attention to the woman in front of him.

"He thinks me someone who answers to his beck and call." It was not a question. She took a breath. "I am told you found a survivor from the *Sovereign of the Stars*. Is that information correct?"

Wright nodded. "Yes, ma'am. She is in the infirmary. Our medical staff is seeing to her."

"Take us there at once," Dwyer said, and she strode toward the stairs which led to the hatch that would allow her to enter the base. The sound of her footfalls remained in a steady rhythm. It sounded to Wright like inevitability. He did not bother to suppress his smile.

The three men who had been log jammed at the transport's hatch spilled into the hanger. They each carried equipment in duffel bags and steel boxes. They seemed to labor a bit under the weight. Each man nodded in Wright's direction and passed him as they rushed to catch up to Dwyer. Wright hustled after her, as well.

A moment later, Hague and Sanchez stepped from the transport. Hague looked at the control room and saw Narita wave to him. Hague waved back. He hoisted his rucksack onto his back and started for the hatch. Sanchez followed.

****

Hasegawa took her eyes from the medical monitor to spare a glance at her patient. The woman from the starliner lay on the nearest examination table. A simple sheet covered her naked body. Hasegawa watched her closely. She may have been asleep, had Hasegawa not known better. She returned her attention to the monitor in front of her.

Kehoe sat next to her at another medical console. Hasegawa did not watch him, but she knew he viewed the latest test results. She also knew what he would find even before he told her.

"Same as before, Doc."

"Naturally." Hasegawa sat back in the seat and rubbed her eyes. She looked again at the woman on the exam table. "I don't get this. I really don't. Aside from her brain activity, all her vitals are flat-lined. Zero respiration, no pupillary response. In fact, no response to any stimuli whatsoever. We're even seeing the beginning signs of *rigor*. She's dead. But her brain is still active." She stood and walked the few steps to the exam table. She looked over the body. "What the hell happened to her?"

"I thought we'd have heard from the GSA by now," Kehoe said. "I was sure the symptoms you described would have gotten *someone's* attention."

"Me too." She placed a hand on the woman's chest. No heartbeat, no rise-and-fall of respiration. The woman's eyes moved beneath their lids, as if she were in REM sleep. "Maybe I should try again. This time I'll send what we have to a friend of mine at the Piper Institute. He'll either think I'm insane, or he'll be on the first available transport up here. Or both."

The infirmary doors opened. A woman unfamiliar to Hasegawa entered. She took a single look about the room and strode to the occupied exam table. Hasegawa stepped back, momentarily surprised. The woman paid her no mind, seemed to not even notice Hasegawa standing two meters from her. The new arrival looked down on the woman who lay before her.

"Excuse me," Hasegawa said after she regained her composure. "I said, *excuse me*. Who are you and what are you doing here?"

The woman acted as if Hasegawa had not spoken. The doctor turned to Kehoe, who had vacated his seat and stood next to Hasegawa. The nurse looked the new woman up and down, and then he moved around the table.

"Ma'am, you're not authorized to be in here." He moved to place a hand on the woman's arm.

Dwyer's head snapped up. She regarded Kehoe with a look that was altogether unpleasant. Kehoe took a surprised step back. "If you even think about touching me, you'll be reassigned to combat duty along the Brazilian border. Do I make myself clear, medic?"

Kehoe looked at Hasegawa with as much surprise as he could muster. Hasegawa strode to the intercom panel. Before she could open the channel, the infirmary doors slid open again. Wright entered at a high rate of speed. He stopped short when he saw the look in Hasegawa's eyes.

"Wright, get this woman out of here," Hasegawa said. Her tone was even, neutral, but there was no mistaking the anger in her features.

Three more men unknown to Hasegawa entered the infirmary. They placed what they carried on the deck and walked to the exam table.

"What the hell is all this?" Hasegawa asked Wright.

"Doctor," Wright said, his tone calm if not condescending, "these people have every right to be here. They are from the GSA, sent here to assess the situation. We are to give them our full cooperation."

"Does Hansen know about this?"

The three men had opened the various boxes and bags they brought with them. Instruments were brought out and activated. Unfamiliar mechanical sounds filled the infirmary.

Wright walked around the four new arrivals and placed a hand on Hasegawa's arm. She allowed herself to be led away from the table. They stopped when they were on the other side of the infirmary. They were out of earshot of the GSA team, especially with the noise generated by their instruments.

"Doctor, that's Lindsay Dwyer. You know, the senior VP of the GSA, second only to President Cromwell himself. You've heard of her."

Hasegawa looked at the woman again and then returned her eyes to Wright. "So? That doesn't mean she can simply walk in here and—"

"Yes, it does."

There was an edge to Wright's voice Hasegawa had never heard before. It took her a moment to identify it. She almost smiled. Wright was nervous. For his job? No, she didn't think that was it. At least, not all of it. No, the major was nervous because, for the first time since she had met him, he had run into someone to whom he felt vastly inferior. His body language since he had entered the infirmary verified this fact, if only in her mind.

"She can do anything she wants here. Remember that, and don't get in her way. Am I making myself clear?"

Hasegawa's eyes flashed anger. She had never cared for Wright, but she cared for this woman even less. "We'll see about this." She strode from the infirmary.

Kehoe looked at Wright for a moment and he followed her out.

****

Hague stepped through the hatch and into the Gemini. Three people sat at the bar. The two men he did not know by name, although he had shuttled them both to Armstrong a few months before. They were geologists, to the best of his recollection. The woman, on the other hand, he knew quite well. Mikhailov sat on the stool with a drink in one hand and a cigarette in the other. She was engaged in conversation with the two men next to her. She glanced up when she saw Hague enter the room and she greeted him with a broad smile.

"Hague!"

Hague returned the smile as Mikhailov got up from the stool. "Hey, Galina. How's tricks?"

"Asshole," she said. She walked to him and hugged him. "That was back in grad school. I'm respectable now."

He gave her a peck on the cheek and returned the hug. She felt warm and soft in his embrace. He could easily have lost himself, but he heard Sanchez come in behind him. He nodded to his co-pilot. "This is Sanchez, my new trainee. Kid, this is Dr. Galina Mikhailov."

"Nice to meet you." Sanchez smiled and stuck out his hand. Mikhailov shook it, then she led Hague to the bar.

"What can I get you boys?"

"The usual for me," Hague said, taking an empty stool. "And the kid will have a lemonade."

Sanchez looked disappointed. Hague broke into a laugh and clapped him on the back. "Okay, okay, get him whatever he wants."

"Done," Mikhailov said. She raised an eyebrow at Sanchez.

"A beer will be fine," Sanchez said to her.

Mikhailov leaned across the bar. "Kid, Hague isn't known for his generosity. If he's buying, make it something expensive."

"That's not nice," Hague protested, but he was unable to suppress his smile.

"No, but it's accurate." Mikhailov returned the smile.

"Really, just a beer," Sanchez said.

While Mikhailov went to work, Hague regarded the two men next to him. "I'm sorry, I'm blanking on your names."

"Thorpe," said the older of the two. "And this is Mason."

Mason waved with a smile. "Hi."

Hague nodded. "Hello." A moment later, Mikhailov put a beer in front of Sanchez and a Long Island Iced Tea in front of Hague. He sipped it and put the glass down on the bar. He looked around the room, saw the chessboard exactly where it was the last time he had been here, on a table in the corner. "Hey, where's Brenda? She around?"

Mikhailov took her seat again and lit a fresh cigarette. "Think she's still on duty, champ. Might be a few more hours."

Hague sipped his drink again. "Good. That might give me enough time to study that goddamned board and find a way to beat her."

"Have you ever beaten her?" Mikhailov favored Hague with a sideways glance.

"Oh shut up," Hague said.

Mikhailov laughed and even Sanchez could not keep his smile from widening.

****

Hansen sat at the desk in his office. On the small monitor on the desk he watched the images of the hull breach on the *Sovereign*'s port side. It didn't look like much, and the emergency bulkhead must have come down instantly and sealed off the rest of the ship. They had certainly seen no signs of decompression during their time on the vessel. It bothered him nonetheless. The ship had been built with literally a thousand different ways it could avoid damage in-flight. The simple fact of the breach's existence did not sit well with him. If only he had been able to gain access to the bridge. If nothing else, the ship's flight recorder could have told them a great deal.

The knock on the hatch brought him out of his musings. He sat up straight in his chair and said, "Come in."

It was not Lindsay Dwyer who strode purposefully into his office, but Hasegawa, with Kehoe in tow. Hansen did not like the look on the doctor's face, nor the way her hands were curled into fists. She strode directly to his desk and stood in front of him. She shook with anger.

He stood. "What happened?"

"That bitch just showed up in my infirmary and took over, her and her goon squad. They went right to work on my patient."

"We were more or less kicked out of there," Kehoe added.

Hansen held up his hands. "Wait a minute. You mean Lindsay Dwyer? Wright was supposed to escort her here."

"He escorted her all right."

"Okay, settle down. I'm sure there's a perfectly good explanation."

"She threatened to have me transferred," Kehoe said. He looked sheepish and more than a little nervous.

Hansen sighed and ran a hand through his short brown hair. "Okay, I'll handle it. But you two stay outside in the corridor. You're both too agitated for this."

"Colonel, that's Lindsay fucking Dwyer," Kehoe said. "I don't think she cares much who's in command here."

Hansen pursed his lips and rubbed his chin. After a moment, he said, "We can't have someone just come in here and take over the infirmary, I don't care who they are. I'll have a talk with her. A *private* talk," he added when he saw Hasegawa about to respond. He walked around the desk. "Look, you two go to the Gemini and grab a bite to eat. Settle down. I'll call you when the situation has been resolved."

Hasegawa's shoulders slumped, but only a little. "I could use a drink," she mumbled.

"Good. Go get one. Both of you." He smiled. "It's an order."

"Yes, sir," Hasegawa said. She turned and left the room, Kehoe on her heels.

Hansen turned off the monitor and left for the infirmary. He arrived there a few moments later to find Wright standing outside the hatch. The windows that looked out on the corridor had been opaqued, something usually done only during surgery. He disliked it immediately.

"Colonel," Wright said, and he nodded at Hansen's approach.

"Open the hatch," Hansen said without breaking stride.

"Sir, Ms. Dwyer has ordered no one goes into the infirmary."

Hansen ignored him and hit the switch on the bulkhead. The hatch slid open and he stepped inside.

Dwyer and three men Hansen did not know leaned over the woman on the exam table. They wore protective masks and gloves. The infirmary had been rearranged, with instruments and devices scattered around and other exam tables pushed to the bulkheads. He halted his approach when Dwyer and her partners looked up.

"You must be Colonel Hansen," Dwyer said. "Lindsay Dwyer, GSA. Nice to meet you."

Hansen could not be certain, but he believed she smiled beneath the mask. Her tone was warm, friendly and completely unexpected. She stepped around the table and removed the glove from her right hand. She held her hand out to him. Hansen shook it absently. He looked over her shoulder at the woman on the table.

"Nice to meet you," Hansen replied. "Can I ask what you're doing with Dr. Hasegawa's patient?"

"She's the GSA's patient, actually," Dwyer said. Her tone was friendly, even conversational. There was no challenge in it; she simply stated a fact as she saw it. "And we're trying to save her life."

"I have every confidence in Dr. Hasegawa's skills. She should not have been removed from the infirmary."

"Colonel, may we speak in private? Your office, perhaps, in one hour?"

Hansen swallowed. "I thought you would have come to see me immediately after your arrival."

She placed a hand on his arm and walked slowly toward the hatch. Hansen allowed himself to be led. "I would have, but it was imperative we got to this woman as soon as possible. Her life is at stake, after all."

They reached the hatch. She pulled her mask down and looked up at him. A stray strand of hair found its way into her eyes. She brushed it aside absently. "One hour, then? Your office?"

Hansen frowned. "Very well. I'll be expecting you." He stepped through the hatch and back into the corridor. Wright moved out of his way.

"I won't be late," she said. The hatch closed on her smile.

Chapter 4

I Need You

This time, Hansen was expecting the knock on the office hatch. He counted to three, then said, "Enter."

The hatch opened. Wright poked his head inside. "Ms. Dwyer for you, Colonel."

"Send her…"

Dwyer stepped past Wright and entered Hansen's office. Her pace was leisurely. She took a moment to look about the office. A lithograph of Armstrong Base during construction hung on the bulkhead behind Hansen's desk. The painter had perhaps taken some artistic liberties with the accuracy of Armstrong's construction; Hansen knew the pay loaders would not have belched smoke from their imaginary exhaust pipes, and he was fairly certain there were not nearly as many transports and shuttles present at any one time. But it had hung there since the base became operational, and Hansen appreciated the sense of continuity the painting represented among Armstrong's commanders. A small table adorned with a coffee pot and a hot plate stood next to the bulkhead opposite the hatch. Two chairs faced the front of the commander's desk. Beyond those items and the desk itself, the office was barren. She completed her survey of the room and took one of the chairs in front of the desk. She folded her hands in her lap and favored Hansen with a smile.

Hansen nodded to Wright. "Thank you, Major. That will be all."

"Yes, sir," Wright said and closed the hatch.

Hansen looked again at Dwyer. She had taken the hard plastic case containing an ancient baseball card from his desk and examined it closely. After a moment, she held it up to him, the question evident in her eyes.

"Roger Maris," Hansen said. "From 1961, the year he captured the single-season home run record from Ruth." He smiled. "Been in my family for generations."

"I see," Dwyer said. She replaced the card to its original spot on the desk and smiled at Hansen. "It's nice to have something that connects us to our past."

"It is," Hansen said. He placed his arms on the desk and folded his fingers. "Ms. Dwyer, with all due respect, can you tell me why you're here? And what those men are doing in the infirmary? And why you kicked Dr. Hasegawa out of there?"

The smile never left her lips. "Colonel, we're here because a luxury starliner made an unscheduled stop at this facility. We're here because of the three thousand people aboard, there is a single survivor. The men who accompanied me are at the top of their field, and they represent, in my opinion, that woman's best chance for survival." The lips pulled back from her teeth in a smile that was probably intended to be reassuring. "Does that answer your questions?"

Hansen spun the small monitor screen around so Dwyer could see it. On the screen were the faces of three men. "Doyle, Millman and Sullivan, the three men who accompanied you here. Their personnel files say their field of study is xenobiology. Correct me if I'm wrong, but isn't that the study of extraterrestrial life-forms?"

Her smile faltered, but did not vanish completely. Her eyes flashed anger, perhaps even outrage, but her composure remained intact. She shifted in the chair. "Well done."

"Yeah, I have a chief engineer who works magic on computer databases." Hansen leaned across the desk. "Ms. Dwyer, what the hell is going on here? And please don't tell me you came all this way because of one woman's life. The GSA isn't in the habit of sending a senior vice-president to the moon just because there's a single life at risk. It doesn't make any sense."

Dwyer's expression did not change; she still favored Hansen with the same warm smile. It fell far short of reaching her eyes. "Colonel, I am not at liberty to discuss why I am here. This…mission, I suppose you could call it, is classified. All you need to know is I have the authority to take command of this facility and all within, if I so choose. So far, I have not seen the need for that." She leaned forward and placed her folded hands on the desk. "That may change, however, if you continue to interfere with me." Her smile widened. She allowed Hansen a moment to comprehend what she had said. "I'm not here to step on your toes, Colonel. The base is yours to command. I'll even keep you apprised of what we're doing, time permitting. But please do not make the mistake of challenging me or my authority on this matter. Am I making myself clear?"

Hansen's eyes hardened. "As crystal."

"Good!" She leaned back in the chair and folded her hands on her lap. Her smile seemed genuine. "I knew we would get along. In the interest of this spirit of cooperation we have now established, I can tell you that Doctors Millman and Sullivan are boarding the *Sovereign of the Stars* as we speak. Their findings will be made available to you, should I deem them to be of importance to you.

"Also, we've identified the survivor. Her name is Sofia Nelson. She's the third shift navigation officer. Just thought you'd want to know who you saved. Good enough?"

"It'll have to do," Hansen said. "You do know she most likely killed someone, right?"

Dwyer's smile remained fixed in place, but her self-control was not enough to keep one of her eyebrows from arching. "Excuse me?"

"Before we were pulled off the *Sovereign* we found a dead man just outside the bridge. He had been shot in the head. We don't have the body, but we have the weapon. Nelson was carrying it. My security chief told me it had been fired recently. Just thought you'd want to know"

"I'll keep that in mind," Dwyer said, a bit too casually.

Hansen's voice was neutral. "You do that. Can I ask what you expect Doctors Millman and Sullivan to find aboard that ship?"

"No, you may not. Now, if there is nothing else?" She stood. Her eyes traveled to the baseball card again, but only for a moment. She took a few strides to the hatch.

"I do have one question."

Dwyer did not turn to face him.

"Aside from what we saw in the ballroom, we came across only that one body. It's true we were not allowed to survey the entire ship, but the engine room was sealed off. There could be survivors in there. I assume Millman and Sullivan will investigate that possibility."

Dwyer said nothing but gave a short, terse nod.

"There is one other thing, Ms. Dwyer."

She held her position silently.

"Dr. Hasegawa is the chief medical officer of this facility. She is responsible for the health of everyone up here. That includes you and your men. Anything having to do with the medical department, she has the final say. That includes that woman we found from the *Sovereign*. Her access to her patient will be restored immediately. And that is not open for discussion."

Dwyer turned, her smile still in place. "As you wish." She opened the hatch and stepped through. She did not close it behind her.

****

Doyle sat at the workstation closest to the exam table in the infirmary. He studied the readings on the monitor in front of him. After a moment he shook his head. He sat back in the seat and rubbed his eyes. A moment later, he opened them again and folded his arms across his chest. "This makes no sense whatsoever," he said to the dead woman on the exam table. He glanced at her. The sheet, which covered all but her head, rustled a bit in the breeze coming from the ventilation duct above her.

He stood and walked to the table. He stared down into the face of the dead woman, watching her eyes dart back and forth beneath their lids. "I don't know. Maybe we're all imagining this."

Despite her lack of vitals and the onset of *rigor mortis*, the woman's body showed no sign of decay. She could easily have been asleep. Or, at least, killed within the past few hours. But he knew from the report made by Hansen the woman had died before they had been able to get her to the infirmary. The slope doctor, Hasegawa, had been prepared to perform an autopsy when she had discovered the brain activity. It was probably blind luck she hadn't started cutting into the woman before she noticed that.

"Yeah, you're one lucky babe, darling." He felt her neck. No pulse, same as before. And why was her skin so cold? No, not cold, not exactly. *Room temperature.*

He turned to go back to the monitor when he noticed her head turned slightly to the left. His eyes narrowed. Had he moved her inadvertently? He must have, although he didn't think he had touched her with enough force to move her. Certainly not with *rigor* making her all but a statue. Doyle took a deep breath and exhaled slowly. "I need some fucking downtime." Maybe he could discover the location of the facility's watering hole, if the super-bitch who accompanied him to Armstrong gave him the opportunity. It was common knowledge there was such a place, owing to the boredom that cropped up over the course of a tour. And he'd caught a glimpse of the base psychologist earlier. *Definitely doable,* he had thought at the time. And God knew he hadn't gotten laid in quite a while.

He returned to the workstation and started the scrolling readouts again. His eyes hurt from the data, his back hurt from the constant bending, not to mention lugging much of the equipment himself. He could use a stiff drink. "Fuck this."

He sat back in the seat again and reached for the monitor's power button. The screen gave him a *bleep*, as if in protest, and the image changed to an internal view of the woman's chest. Her lungs expanded then contracted. Doyle's jaw dropped.

He spun in the chair and looked at the body on the table. At first he saw nothing, just the dead woman whom he had studied since his arrival in the infirmary. He was about to write off what he had seen as a mirage, or perhaps a glitch in the monitor's software, when the woman took another deep breath.

His eyes widened. He sprang from the seat and dashed to the exam table, grabbing a portable scanner on the way. He stood over the body and held the scanner a few inches from the woman's chest. Again, there was a long pause, and then the woman took another breath.

It rattled in her throat, as if she were gasping after coming up from under water. "It's okay, you're okay. You're gonna be okay," Doyle said. The words flew from his mouth fast enough that they morphed together into a single sound.

He ran to the intercom panel and hit the switch. "Doctor Hasegawa, this is Doyle in the infirmary. I need you here right away!"

He didn't wait for a reply and didn't hear Hasegawa's response. He was back at the woman's side. He placed the scanner on the tray next to the table and bent down until his ear was only an inch or two from her mouth. He felt the breath on his ear, but something was wrong. The carbon dioxide she expelled from her lungs was not warm. Not in the least.

The woman's hand reached up, grabbed the back of Doyle's neck and pulled. Doyle shouted something that was not of any earthy language and tried to pull away. The woman opened her eyes and focused on him. Cataracts that had not afflicted Sofia Nelson in life gave her eyes a faded, milky hue. They drilled into Doyle.

Doyle struggled to break her grip on the back of his neck, but her hand may have been welded to his skin, her grip was so powerful. Each time he jerked back, he heard something creak. He realized it was the *rigor mortis* in her muscles, responding to his efforts. He gasped. His arms flailed. He knocked the portable scanner off the tray and sent it the length of the room. He did not notice. "Let go of me!" he shrieked, his voice cracking. The woman did not seem to hear him.

She sat up on the table and pulled him closer. He was absolutely convinced the last place he wanted to be in the whole solar system was any closer to her. He yanked back with everything he had. He put all of his two hundred pounds into the effort. He managed to pull perhaps three or four inches away from her. Her mouth opened. He looked into her eyes.

"I need you," she said.

Doyle screamed.

****

Hasegawa stopped so quickly outside the infirmary Kehoe nearly ran into her. His boots skidded on the deck. Hasegawa reached out and steadied the nurse. She let go of him and walked slowly toward the windows of the infirmary. They were still opaqued, but she could make out the flickering lights on the other side of the glass. Something that could have been a power cable dangled from the ceiling. She heard nothing from within the room.

"Get Nixon over here. Hansen, too."

"Right." Kehoe bolted for the nearest intercom.

Hasegawa approached the hatch. Her hand went to the control panel next to it. Her finger hovered over the door release button for perhaps ten seconds. She pulled it back. She looked at the windows again and swallowed. She could see no movement. She took a deep breath, held it for a moment and then exhaled loudly. *Wait for Hansen,* she thought. *No need to go in there alone when there'll be people here any minute.* She eyed the windows one last time and thought, *Then again, it* is *my infirmary....* She paused, took another breath and palmed open the hatch.

Surgical tools lay scattered about the deck. The room was filled with the scent of ozone. A thick power cable hung from the ceiling. Its severed end twitched and shot sparks into the air. The monitor to which it had been attached had been knocked over. It lay next to the closest exam table, its screen shattered. One of the ceiling lights had somehow been damaged. Glass from its protective panel had broken and lay sprinkled about the deck. The long glowing bulb itself flickered on and off rapidly.

The body of Sofia Nelson, formerly the third shift navigation officer of the *Sovereign of the Stars*, lay crumpled on its side on the deck next to the exam table. Hasegawa's first instinct was to check the status of her patient. She made it only a single step closer to the body before she stopped herself. Nelson had appeared normal the last time Hasegawa had seen her, only a few hours before. She no longer appeared that way. She looked like the ship's officer they had discovered outside the *Sovereign*'s bridge. Her skin had darkened and taken on the look of old parchment. Her eyes were bulged and slightly receded into their sockets. Her arms were held out in front of her body, as if she had died in an embrace with somebody. Both hands had curled into claws and then frozen with *rigor*.

Hasegawa heard a gasp at her back and knew Kehoe had entered the room. She spared him a quick glance and wondered if the look of shock and horror she saw on his face mirrored her own. She held a hand out to him. "Stay there. Don't touch anything."

Kehoe swallowed and nodded.

Hasegawa knelt beside the body. She reached out a hand, marveled at the absence of any trembling, and turned over the body. She was not at all surprised to see the woman's limbs retain their position, as if she were now trying to embrace Hasegawa. The doctor tried to imagine precisely how that embrace might feel. She shuddered.

****

Dwyer strode into the infirmary. She passed Nixon and Narita at the hatchway without a word. She walked purposefully to the exam table. For a moment she thought she might have to shoulder past Hasegawa and Kehoe, but they moved aside when they noted her approach. Hansen stood at the other side of the table. He continued to look over the body until Dwyer cleared her throat.

"Colonel, we discussed this," she said. Her tone was identical to a teacher's who had had to discipline a child for the same infraction over and over. "No non-essential personnel permitted inside the infirmary." She smiled but her irritation was visible to all. "That includes you." She turned and indicated the two men in the hatchway. "And you, as well."

"Hey, lady," Nixon began. He stopped himself when he saw the look from Hansen.

The colonel did not move from his position. "Ms. Dwyer, clearly this woman's status has changed significantly in the past few minutes. We've seen this effect before." His eyes encompassed everyone in the room and Nixon. "If whatever happened on that ship can happen here, we could all be in very serious trouble. As the base commander—"

"Colonel Hansen, I am content to allow you to continue to run the day-to-day operations of this facility." Her tone darkened considerably, and her voice dropped an octave. She leaned across the table. "But anything and anyone having to do with that starliner is under *my* jurisdiction. I cooperate with you and your personnel at *my* discretion. Are we absolutely, positively clear about this?" She tilted her head slightly. Her fingernails dug into the soft top of the exam table.

Hansen's lips became a thin line beneath his nose. "Yes, ma'am." He walked around the table. "But you should know, if Dr. Hasegawa believes there's even the slightest risk of contamination, she has the authority to order a quarantine of the infirmary. Or even the evacuation of Armstrong Base, if she believes lives are at risk."

Dwyer folder her arms across her chest and gave him a wry smile. "The only authority here is *mine*, Colonel. You would do well to remember that."

"You have a man missing," Nixon said from the hatchway. "Or does that not matter?"

She did not turn and look at Nixon; her eyes remained focused on Hansen. "Dr. Doyle?"

Hansen nodded. "The last time anyone saw him, he was in here. He won't answer the intercom. Judging by the state of this room—"

"Find him, Colonel. Find him immediately." Her voice remained calm and even.

Hansen seemed to regard her eyes, but only for a moment. Over his shoulder, he said, "Nix, get a search party started. Round up anyone you need. Find this man."

"On it, Mike," Nixon said. He tapped Narita on the shoulder, and the two men vanished down the corridor.

Dwyer began a slow orbit of the table. She dragged one finger along its edge. Her eyes took in the corpse on the tabletop. "Colonel, you are dismissed. And take the nurse with you. Dr. Hasegawa will remain here with me until Doctors Millman and Sullivan complete their assigned duties." She stopped on the far side of the table. She did not look up, nor did she notice when Hansen and Kehoe exited the room.

Without looking up, Dwyer said, "Doctor, we have work to do."

****

Only McKnight was present in the control room when Hansen entered. The image on the main monitor was of an empty corridor in C-ring. By the time Hansen reached McKnight, the image changed to the inside of an equipment room.

"Status report."

McKnight barely reacted at all. He did not turn, but kept his eyes on the monitor. "Looking for that missing doctor. No sign of him yet."

Hansen backtracked to his office. "Don, if you find this guy, don't keep it a secret. I have to make a phone call"

"Roger that," McKnight said.

Hansen entered the code for entry into his office. He looked back at the main monitor a final time, saw the image of another empty corridor. He entered his office.

61

He took the seat behind his desk and activated his monitor. The GSA logo appeared. Hansen got busy typing.

****

Duncan climbed down from atop the massive generator. She walked past it and its twin to the main control console and seated herself there. She hit buttons and flipped switches while her eyes scanned the main board in front of her. Several indicator lights changed from yellow to green and began to blink in sequence. She nodded and took a moment to bask in her satisfaction. She scribbled her findings onto the maintenance log's clipboard and returned it to its place on the bulkhead.

She stood and stretched her muscles and glanced at the clock on the bulkhead above the hatch. Quitting time. She had offered to assist Nixon in his search for the missing doctor, but he had told her they had enough people for the job. *Just as well*, she thought. She was still slightly hung-over from her endeavors at the Gemini the night before. She knew it would not be a good idea to repeat those endeavors, certainly not with a missing man and a starliner full of corpses on pad three. She would have taken the opportunity to finish her chess match with Hague, but Nixon had enlisted him, as well as most of the crew. She found herself in the rarest of situations on Armstrong, a night to herself.

And no one to enjoy it with. She sighed into the empty room.

She reached for the intercom switch on the board and hit the button. "McKnight, you there?"

"I'm here, Duncan," came the immediate reply.

"All generators are online. Maintenance complete. Generator room secure. I'm calling it a night."

"Roger," he said.

She moved to close the channel, stopped herself. "Did you find that missing technician yet?"

A pause. "Negative. I'm still in C-ring, though. Looks like those other two techs are at the airlock. They must have finished whatever it is they were doing on the *Sovereign*."

"I'm sure it's top secret, too," Duncan said. "Okay, I'm out. If you need me for anything, let me know."

"Will do. Have a good night."

With who? "Roger that." She killed the connection and stretched again. She removed her tool belt and slung it over the back of the seat. She thought about her nice, warm bunk. It was not her fault the Gemini was on the way to her quarters. Duncan took that as a positive sign, as if the gods intended for her to down a few drinks, missing technician or not. She exited the generator room and closed the hatch behind her.

Six minutes later she was inside the Gemini. She had come across no one since leaving the generator room. In the connecting corridor between B- and A-rings she had heard distant voices calling out for the missing man. She paid them little mind.

She found the whiskey bottle nearly empty. She upended its contents into a glass and sat at the bar. The lighting was subdued, as usual when there was no one making use of the facility. The ancient pinball machine flashcd its lights; every few moments, one of its sound effects would fill the room. She caught sight of the ceiling camera; its indicator light was dark. *McKnight hasn't gotten around to looking here yet*, she thought. Good. Hansen was a good CO but she didn't need another lecture from him about her frequent visits to the Gemini. She would be long gone by the time McKnight got around to A-ring.

Besides, one of the search teams had probably already found the missing tech, anyway. Perhaps she would not have long to wait before Hague returned. Then she could finish him off. This would necessitate feigned outrage on his part and an insistence she had cheated. And they would reset the board and start over, as they had many times in the past.

She tossed back the whiskey, felt its familiar burn as it worked its way down her throat. *Better already*, she thought, savoring the taste. She placed the empty glass on the bar, slid off the stool and turned toward the open hatch at her back.

The hand clamped itself around her throat with so much force she was unable even to gasp in surprise. Instinctively, she raised her hands and wrapped them around the arm of the man who lifted her feet from the deck.

She had no reason to recognize Doyle, having never met the man. Her feet kicked empty air, her hands worked against his arm with all her strength. Blood began to seep from his nostrils and his ears. It pooled at the corners of his mouth before it finally spilled out.

Duncan tried to scream, but no sound made it past the hand clamped on her throat.

He pulled her in closer until their noses nearly touched.

"I need you," he said.

Chapter 5

The Way Things Were Done

Millman and Sullivan entered the infirmary and immediately stopped just inside the hatch. Hasegawa leaned over the desiccated body and did nothing to note their arrival. Dwyer regarded them neutrally, saw the canvas bags they held and gave them a questioning glance. Millman nodded slowly. Sullivan was too busy looking about the room in obvious surprise. Hasegawa had managed to restore some order to the infirmary, but much of it was still a chaotic mess. The ceiling light had been deactivated at Dwyer's insistence; the constant flashing had given her a headache and put her in an even fouler mood than was usual. Their half of the room was darker than it should have been. Hasegawa was making due with a small light affixed to her headband.

Dwyer instantly disliked the look she saw from the two techs. They were visibly shaken, though they attempted to hide the fact. She should have known they'd be trouble. Of the three men Cromwell had assigned to her, the only one of the bunch worth a shit had been Doyle. And he was missing. She would have cursed her luck had she believed in it. She resigned herself to having to work with the two morons in front of her. In retrospect, it had been foolish of her to assign Doyle to examine the body. Had it been Millman or Sullivan who had gone missing, she'd still have Doyle and a reasonable chance of completing her mission successfully. She had thought the greater danger had been aboard the starliner. It had been a mistake, and she disliked mistakes. Especially her own.

Dwyer turned her attention to Hasegawa. The doctor hovered over the exposed chest cavity of the naked body on the table. She prodded the woman's insides with a device that was foreign to Dwyer. She tapped Hasegawa on the shoulder once, then twice. The doctor looked at her, found the woman's cold eyes drilling into her.

"You can go now, Doctor. Thank you. I'll summon you when we're ready for you to return."

Hasegawa started to protest, but apparently saw the folly of it. She removed the headband, placed it on the counter and exited the room.

"Shut the door," Dwyer said.

Millman waited until Hasegawa had cleared the hatch and then sealed it behind her. Sullivan continued to look about the room. Millman placed his canvas bag on the tray next to the exam table and opened it.

"We have a lot of data, ma'am," he said.

Dwyer stood with her arms folded across her chest. "Show me."

****

Nixon poked his head into the Gemini. The room was dark. It smelled of old alcohol, coffee and cigarette smoke. The pinball machine continued to light up and ring its mechanical bells at odd intervals. He noted the empty glass on the bar. He stepped through the hatch and into the room.

"Doyle, you in here?"

There was no reply. He took another few steps into the room. Hague and Mikhailov entered behind him. They stood in the middle of the room and looked about. The few tables with the customary three chairs apiece stood undisturbed. Peanut shells crunched under their boots, a sure sign Narita had been there recently (and had failed to clean up after himself, as usual, Nixon noted with some irritation).

"I'll check the storeroom," Nixon said. He made his way toward the hatch at the far side of the room.

"We'll check the bar," Mikhailov said. She shared a silent laugh with Hague.

Nixon frowned but showed no other outward reaction. He knew Mikhailov did not seriously intend to start drinking. She simply had to keep up appearances as Armstrong's resident bad girl. Nixon had more pressing matters. He reached the hatch to the storeroom. He spun the wheel and opened the hatch. He felt along the bulkhead until he found the light switch. The room was larger than it needed to be, and he reminded himself the base's original projected number of personnel had been much larger as well.

Cases of beer and other alcoholic beverages were stacked everywhere. Most were empty, but some still held contents ready for use. The transparent door to the walk-in freezer showed the base remained well-stocked with foodstuffs. It was always the alcohol that went first. At the beginning of the next tour, the stock would be full again. The GSA would see to it, even if the cargo manifest listed certain items as *generator parts* or *LST replacement modules*.

No Doyle.

He took a step back toward the hatch when he heard the scream. He was through the hatch in an instant. The first thing he saw was Mikhailov. She had thrown herself into Hague's arms and recoiled from the back of the bar. She buried her face in Hague's chest. Hague had gone ashen. He looked at Nixon and inclined his head toward the back of the bar.

Nixon walked around them and saw what had prompted Mikhailov to scream. There was a pool of blood in front of the bar. Nixon had missed it in his initial sweep because it sat entirely in the shadows. Two streaks emerged from the pool. Nixon followed them behind the bar with his flashlight, wishing he was armed with a suitable weapon.

The body on the deck belonged to Doyle. It lay crumpled in a heap behind the bar. Nixon approached it slowly. He shined his light on the corpse and found it to be in an identical state to the man Hansen had described aboard the *Sovereign*. He reached for the dead man's wrist, thought better of it. There would be no pulse. And despite what Hasegawa and Dwyer had said, he wasn't taking chances on this…*thing* being communicable.

"Jesus," Mikhailov said. Her face remained buried in Hague's embrace; her voice was muffled.

Nixon walked to the intercom unit on the wall and hit the button. "This is Nixon in the Gemini. We found Doyle." He swallowed. "He's dead."

****

Hansen watched the main monitor, as did everyone in the control room. It displayed an image of the infirmary. Nelson's body had been moved to an exam table on the far side of the room. It lay there, uncovered and chest opened. The dead woman's eyes stared at the ceiling. In the foreground of the image, Millman and Sullivan placed Doyle's body on the exam table formerly occupied by Nelson. Both men were dressed in isolation suits, as was Dwyer, who stood a few steps away from the table. Her arms were folded across her chest, and she looked impatient, even through her faceplate.

Hansen pulled his eyes from the monitor and surveyed the men and woman gathered around him. McKnight worked the main control board and Thorpe and Mason had taken what he came to think of as their regular stations on either side of McKnight. Wright stood next to him, in his familiar parade-rest stance. Hasegawa and Kehoe had taken the medical stations in the second row of control consoles. On Hansen's order, and against Wright's protests, Narita had connected the medical consoles inside the infirmary to Hasegawa's station in the control room. The doctor and her nurse watched their monitors closely.

Hague, Sanchez and Mikhailov stood near the back of the room. Hansen got the impression none of them particularly wanted to be there, or to watch what happened on the monitor. Mikhailov stood with her hand perpetually over her mouth. Her eyes were wide. He caught her attention, gave her a nod he hoped was reassuring. She took the hand from her mouth long enough to give him a half-hearted salute. She managed a weak smile.

Nixon and Narita stood to his left and watched the screen. They did so without comment.

He had debated sending someone to fetch Duncan. He decided against it when informed by McKnight the engineer had gone to bed. She had worked a full shift in the generator room and was undoubtedly tired. It was also possible she had had a drink or two before retiring. Best to leave her be for now.

Millman and Sullivan had gone into their bag of tricks and come out with more devices Hansen was unable to identify. They removed the dead man's clothing and tossed it to the deck. It was a difficult process with Doyle's limbs stiff as they were.

Hansen had initially asked why they had video from the infirmary but no sound. McKnight informed him the infirmary speakers had been deactivated at the source. It was a simple matter to conclude Dwyer knew they would monitor the events inside the infirmary, but she drew the line at letting anyone eavesdrop. He was at once grateful she had taken that course of action. He had no desire to listen to the dead man's limbs creak in protest, and he was willing to bet no one else did, either.

"Does someone want to tell me how a body can look like that?" Narita asked. "I mean, this guy was fine a few hours ago. What the hell happened?"

"We don't know yet," Kehoe said from the medical station.

"Doc, keep an eye on them," Hansen said, quite unnecessarily. "Let us know what's going on in there."

"No unusual readings so far, Mike," Hasegawa said.

"No unusual readings," Thorpe repeated. "Everything about this is pretty fucking unusual, if you ask me."

"Got that right," Mason added.

The men on the monitor continued to work on the corpse. One of them (Millman? Sullivan? It was impossible to tell with their backs to the monitors.) had attached another chest spreader to the body. There was a short but graphic burst of what appeared to be dust from the corpse. It appeared black as tar, but that could have been the poor lighting within the infirmary. Both men backed away from the table. Dwyer stood unmoved a few meters away and did not react at all. Mikhailov gasped at the image and looked away. Even Nixon grimaced.

"Fuck me," McKnight whispered.

"Same as the woman's," Hasegawa said after a moment. "Looks like a bomb went off in there. Major structural damage to all internal organs."

"Yeah, we can see that from here," Hansen said.

One of the techs reached into the chest cavity with a small glass beaker in this hand. He pulled back a moment later, capped the beaker and held it out to Dwyer. She said something that was probably insulting, based on her body language. The tech, who turned out to be Sullivan, held the beaker out to Millman. Millman went into his bag again and placed a device on the counter. He accepted the beaker from Sullivan and placed it inside the device.

"That's a portable scanner," McKnight said. "Looks like it has its own transmitter attached."

"They're going to send whatever that says directly to Earth for analysis," Nixon said, looking at Hansen.

Hansen grimaced. "Since she knew we were going to monitor this, she's keeping everything close to the vest. She wants to ensure we don't know what the hell's going on in there."

"Colonel, may I speak to you in private, please?"

It was Wright. Naturally.

Hansen peeled his eyes from the main monitor and nodded. "In my office." He led the way.

A moment later Wright sealed the hatch behind him. Hansen sat at his desk. He considered patching his personal monitor into the main in the control room, but decided they wouldn't be in there long enough to warrant it. Besides, he felt he knew what Wright was going to say, just as he knew what his response would be. He was not incorrect.

"Sir, I have to file a formal protest with what you're doing out there," Wright said. He stood before Hansen's desk at attention. "You're violating a direct order from Ms. Dwyer. She represents the GSA, and she has deemed what happens in the infirmary to be classified."

"Yes, she has," Hansen said. He kept his voice even.

"Then why are you keeping tabs on her? Section one-oh-five paragraph A of GSA operating guideline clearly states an executive of the GSA has final authority in all classified matters. Violating that order could be considered rank insubordination, *at best*. At worst, well, it's a court-marshal offense. Sir."

Hansen leaned forward a bit and placed his elbows on his desk. "Major, everything you just said is completely correct. But you're here, too. What happens down in that infirmary may well affect all of us." His voice took on an edge, despite his best efforts to keep his tone neutral. *Lack of sleep*, he thought. And why not? Not much sleep had been had by anyone since the arrival of the starliner. "If you want to trust the GSA, represented here by your Ms. Dwyer, be my guest. You may consider yourself dismissed from the con. But I and everyone else out there want to know what's happening."

He softened his tone. "Adam, the man on that exam table was perfectly healthy a few hours ago. Now look at him. That could be any one of us, including *you*. I'm trying to stop that from happening. You want to quote the rulebook, go right ahead. The men who wrote that rulebook are hundreds of thousands of kilometers away. We're not." He leaned back in his chair, and he kept his tone level. "We have to know what's happening here."

Wright stared straight ahead, above Hansen's eye level. "Will that be all, *sir*?"

Hansen looked at his XO closely. The man fairly trembled. Hansen guessed it was rage. Again, he was not incorrect. Hansen nodded. "That's all."

Wright turned on his heel and marched to the hatch. He was through it quickly. By the time Hansen returned to the control room, Wright was gone.

****

Wright paused at the hatch that led from the con and spared a final glance at the front of the room. The rest of the base personnel were still there, still eavesdropping when they shouldn't be. He grimaced, although no one took notice of him, and stepped through the hatch.

He remembered how aghast he had been (and that was the appropriate term, *aghast*) when he had first arrived at Armstrong and witnessed the utter lack of discipline evidenced by its personnel. Worse, that same lack of discipline had radiated from its commanding officer like heat off old blacktop in the Florida panhandle. At first, he had thought it some type of hazing of the new executive officer. Certainly no facility could be run in such a manner. He did not agree with the practice of hazing, and he had even considered bringing charges against all his subordinates who joined in the fun. He had been absolutely flabbergasted (again, the appropriate term) to learn it was how things were done on Armstrong. He had spent the first two weeks of his tour in a state of utter astonishment.

It had taken all his self-discipline and control not to request an immediate transfer off base. Not that such a request would have done him any good. The GSA was not in the habit of scheduling a shuttle flight simply to bring a disillusioned officer back to Earth. And any such attempt on his part would have simply alerted Hansen to his new executive officer's contempt (the *perfect* term) for him. So he had kept his mouth shut and resigned himself to the Way Things Were Done.

But this, this was too much. The Global Space Agency, represented in good standing by Ms. Dwyer, had established a set of rules since her arrival. And now his commanding officer was disobeying those rules. Blatantly. There was only so much Wright could take. Dwyer would have to be told, of course. And heads, he was positive, would roll. Perhaps all the way back to Earth and a general court-marshal. Hansen would be among them, and it was very likely Wright would be named commanding officer of Armstrong. Things would change them. You'd better goddamned believe it.

Wright set off for the infirmary.

****

Hansen yawned and rubbed his eyes. When he opened them again, he saw Thorpe look away, back to the main monitor. *Caught me,* Hansen thought. He was exhausted. He had gotten very little sleep since the arrival of the starliner. He knew the others were becoming sleep-deprived as well. He glanced at the chronometer on the bulkhead beneath the main monitor. It read 0235. He did not know how long he had been awake, but it was starting to show.

A quick glance at the men and women around him told him he was not alone. Aside from McKnight, who did not seem to require sleep, and Hasegawa, who was probably going purely on professional curiosity at this point, they all appeared as tired as he was. He didn't blame them one bit.

On the monitor, Sullivan pulled a sheet over the corpse of the man who had shuttled to Armstrong with him. In the background of the image, Hansen saw a sheet had likewise been draped over the corpse of the woman from the *Sovereign.* Dwyer was issuing orders, but even she appeared tired. Hansen had seen enough.

"Okay, let's get some rest, people. Don, you keep watch here. I'll relieve you at 0600."

McKnight nodded. It seemed not to matter to him at all. "Roger, skipper."

"The rest of you, get some rack time. We can reconvene at 0800. Doc, we'll go over the data, then."

"Affirmative," Hasegawa said. She sounded exhausted even if she did not look the part.

There were signs of relief and a few grumbled acknowledgments, and eleven people stood slowly and stretched their muscles. Hansen watched them file out of the control room. When they were gone from sight, he put a reassuring hand on McKnight's shoulder and then headed for his office. There was a sofa in there that was much closer than his bunk. All he wanted to do was shut his eyes.

****

Dwyer exited the infirmary and saw Wright leaning against the bulkhead next to the hatch. The executive officer snapped to attention when he saw her. She took a moment to savor his reaction, tired as she was. The man was clearly terrified of her and the authority she represented. *As it should be*, she thought. *At least one person here knows how to behave in front of his betters.* It was a quality she saw in abundance back on Earth; here, it was sorely lacking.

"What can I do for you, Mr. Wright?" She took one step toward the man, mostly to give Sullivan and Millman enough room to slip out the hatch and past her. Wright took his eyes from her only long enough to watch the two doctors depart the corridor.

"Ma'am, I need to speak with you." He remained at attention.

"Mr. Wright, I am tired. It was a lousy trip here, and I've gotten very little sleep the past two days." She regarded him for a moment. "This can wait." She started down the corridor.

To her surprise, Wright fell into step with her. He remained slightly behind her and to her right, but he kept pace with her.

"I'm afraid it can't, ma'am. Something serious is happening here, and you should be made aware of it."

Dwyer stopped, noting with some amusement that the executive officer nearly tripped over his own boots to avoid walking into her. She gave him no time to regain his composure. "If Hansen sent you here."

"He did not," Wright said at once.

Dwyer raised an eyebrow. Had he just interrupted her? He had. From a flea like him, that was tantamount to mutiny. Her flash of anger at his impertinence was replaced by genuine curiosity. She smiled at him. "Very well. What is it you wish to discuss?"

Wright began talking.

****

Mikhailov reached the hatch to her quarters. She turned to Nixon. The security chief looked as tired as she felt. She knew she looked no better. She had told Nixon he did not need to escort her, but he had insisted. As his quarters were on the opposite side of A-ring, he had assured himself of a long walk to his bunk. After Hague had left them, she thought perhaps Nixon was hoping to make up for his last appointment with her, which would explain his insistence in escorting her to her bunk. He had told her that was not the case, and she believed him. Neither of them, it seemed, had the strength for anything resembling physical exertion.

"Thank you, brave sir," she said and managed a weak smile. "Your company has been greatly appreciated."

Nixon seemed not to hear her. He looked down, his brow furrowed. *Exhaustion,* she thought. *I know the feeling.*

"Nix?"

He looked up so quickly she nearly took a step back. His eyes focused on her as if for the first time. He shook his head. "Sorry. I was thinking."

"Oh shit. Now we're screwed." She giggled despite the fatigue.

He either had not heard her or chose to ignore her attempt at brevity. "Did anything in the Gemini seem, I don't know, off to you?"

Her weak smile vanished. The last thing she wanted to think about before she climbed into her bunk was what they had found in the Gemini. She certainly did not need that running through her head. "Aside from the mummified dead guy?"

"Yes, aside from the mummified dead guy." He sounded tired, irritated, although not because of her.

She knew right away he had been dwelling on this for some time, perhaps since they had started their trek to her quarters. She had mistaken his silence for exhaustion.

"Nix, we're both tired. Get some sleep. It'll come to you in the morning." She leaned into him, stood on her toes and planted a kiss on his cheek. "Thanks for the company."

He nodded absently. She opened the hatch to her quarters. For the first time since her arrival on Armstrong, she thought perhaps she would lock it behind her. She stepped into the darkened room and turned to him again. "I'll see you in a bit. Good night, honey." Nixon nodded again as Mikhailov closed the hatch.

She slumped against the bulkhead on weak knees. Christ, she was wiped out. She could think about nothing but the comfort of her bunk. She hit the light switch on the wall and looked at the hatch control panel on the bulkhead. "I'll sleep better," she said to no one and inputted her code to lock the hatch. She took two steps into the room and stopped dead.

Duncan lay on the sofa. She was flat on her back, but she rolled onto her stomach and rested her chin on her laced fingers. She favored Mikhailov with a smile that was not altogether pleasant. Had

Mikhailov not been so tired, she would have known there was something wrong with that smile.

Mikhailov exhaled loudly. "Brenda, I'm really, really tired. Unless it's an emergency, the doctor's office is closed. Can we do this another time?"

"I need you," the engineer said. She continued to smile at her.

****

Nixon had made it only a few meters from Mikhailov's quarters. He moved slowly, and not simply because he was physically and mentally exhausted. Something nagged at him and it wouldn't go away. He looked along the bulkheads, the ceiling, every hatchway he passed. He hoped for a memory trigger, but none came. Perhaps Mikhailov had been correct. Perhaps he'd remember after a few hours bunk time.

It was about the scene in the Gemini, of that he was certain. It was something about the body. He knew that, too. It had bothered him for some time, like an itch that was just beyond his reach. He clawed at it, nearly got it, but ultimately he fell short. He ran a hand through his dark hair in frustration and rubbed his eyes.

He started down the corridor again. His head was lowered, his eyes closed. He heard the soft hum of the power conduits within the bulkheads. It was not something he would notice normally, for it was not an oppressive sound. In his exhausted state, those conduits thrummed. He was also aware of his footfalls. The slow, steady *click-clack* seemed to be in rhythm with his heartbeat. His eyes opened slowly, and he looked at his boots. They appeared blacker than usual against the white linoleum of the deck. They appeared—

"Jesus!"

He stopped in the corridor and stood ruler-straight. The boots. The dead man's boots. He had noticed it before he'd even seen the body, but the sight of the man had driven it from his mind. No, not driven it, just tucked it away in a quiet corner to be found later. There had been a small pool of blood in front of the bar. The body had been dragged around and dumped behind it. It had been dragged through the blood, and left two continuous smears of gore in its wake. It had been *dragged…*

Quickly, his mind completely alert and focused, he played back the scene in the control room. They had all been there, all except… "Duncan." And only a few moments before, he thought he had heard Mikhailov say something about her from the other side of the closed hatch to her quarters. Her quarters, which should have been empty.

Nixon turned and sprinted back the way he had come.

He reached the hatch to Mikhailov's quarters and pounded on it. "Galina, it's Nix. You okay in there?"

He put his ear to the cold metal, heard a sound from the other side he could not identify. It was muffled, barely audible. The hairs on the back of his neck stood at attention. He grabbed the hatch handle and found it locked. He fumbled at the access panel on the bulkhead. He tried to input his override code, but his fingers were slow and clumsy and he hit the wrong buttons. More muffled sounds from inside the room. He tried again, got it right, and the hatch opened.

Mikhailov and Duncan wrestled in the center of the room. The engineer had the upper hand, straddling Mikhailov and pinning her hands to the deck. Mikhailov looked from Duncan to Nixon. She seemed unable to speak, and Nixon could see the fresh bruises on her neck. Her eyes pleaded.

Nixon leaped at Duncan and grabbed her shoulders. He pulled her up and away from Mikhailov. Mikhailov rolled onto her side, coughing and rubbing her throat. Nixon backpedaled into the bulkhead. A framed photograph of a young girl riding a tricycle and smiling into the camera fell from its hook. It bounced on the deck and the glass broke.

Nixon struggled to maintain his grip on Duncan's arms. The woman twisted and turned in his grip. She snarled and produced sounds Nixon did not think were possible by human vocal cords. She was unexpectedly strong, and more than once he was certain she was about to break free. Somehow he managed to hold onto her.

Mikhailov pushed herself up onto all fours. She stayed that way for a moment, coughed blood and phlegm onto the deck. She got to her feet, almost went down again. She steadied herself on the coffee table, wiped the blood from her mouth.

"Duncan, stop this!" Nixon shouted. "What are you doing?"

She snaked one hand free and turned on Nixon. She grabbed his free hand and pinned it to the bulkhead. She leaned in close to him, eyes wide. Pinkish drool oozed from the sides of her mouth. "I need you!" she screamed. It barely rated as human language. Later, Nixon could not be certain what she had said.

Mikhailov stood behind Duncan and raised a lamp above her head with both hands. She brought it down with as much force as she could muster. The ceramic antique shattered like glass. Tiny bits of porcelain pelted Nixon's face and drew small beads of blood.

Duncan went limp. Nixon had to rush to catch her and stop her from collapsing to the deck. He held the unconscious woman in his arms, barely able to support them both on shaking legs. He leaned back against the bulkhead. His breath came quickly and in short gulps. He looked at Mikhailov.

She dropped to her knees on the deck and breathed heavy. She continued to rub her throat and gasp for air. "Jesus Christ," she said, weakly.

Nixon nodded. "Fuckin' A."

Chapter 6

The Dust Cloud

Hansen reached the holding area at a dead run. He stopped short when he saw Nixon. The security chief had been leaning against the bulkhead, hands on his knees. He was clearly exhausted. He stood up straight at Hansen's approach and tried to hide his physical state. Hansen ignored him and instead looked inside the holding cell.

Duncan sat quietly and motionless on the bench. She noted his arrival with a quick movement of her eyes. Otherwise, she might have been a wax sculpture of his chief engineer. She was naked and seemed either oblivious or uncaring of the fact. Her clothes lay scattered about the cell. Dried blood had caked on the sides of her mouth.

"Brenda, what happened?" He looked at her, although she once again looked straight ahead. She might have been looking at her own ghost-reflection in the transparent screen that separated the cell from the alcove that made up the holding area. She did not reply.

"She's been like that since I got her in there, Mike," Nixon said. "Well, aside from being naked. She tore off her clothes a few minutes ago, like they were suffocating her or something." He rubbed his wrist. "Believe me, I prefer this to how she was when I found her."

"How's Mikhailov?"

Nixon took a deep breath, exhaled slowly. "Kehoe is looking after her. She got roughed up a bit, but nothing serious. I checked on her a few minutes ago."

Hansen nodded. He looked again at his chief engineer. "Brenda, it's Mike. Are you okay? Can I get you anything?"

Duncan continued to stare straight ahead.

"What happened to her neck?"

Nixon inclined his head slightly. "Those bruises were there when I got to her. Galina says she never got close to her neck." Nixon swallowed. "We have to acknowledge the possibility she did that to herself."

Hansen shook his head. "I'm going to have a talk with Mikhailov, see if she can tell us anything else." He placed a hand on Nixon's shoulder. "How long since you slept, Nix? You look terrible."

"I'm fine, Mike," was the reply. "And thanks."

"Be that as it may, I want you to get some rack time." Nixon looked as if he was about to protest but stopped when Hansen raised a hand. "That's an order."

Nixon rubbed his eyes. "We can't just leave her in there unguarded."

"Oh, yes we can." He thumped his fist against the transparency. "She's not going anywhere."

"All right." Nixon looked inside the cell at the woman he thought he knew. He shook his head and left the alcove.

Hansen lingered a moment. He looked into the cell, into the eyes of Brenda Duncan. They remained blank. Hansen closed his eyes for a moment, took a breath. Duncan was certainly one to enjoy her whiskey, he knew. But he also knew she was not a violent drunk. He had hoisted a few with her himself. If anything, alcohol had the opposite effect on her. She became quite happy and pleased with everyone around her. *This has nothing to do with alcohol*, he thought. He'd feel much better if it had. No, this was something different. Against his will, his mind returned to the interior of the *Sovereign of the Stars*. He suppressed a chill.

Hansen opened his eyes. Duncan remained in place. Her eyes did not move. "We're gonna get you out of this, Brenda." There was no reply, nor did Hansen expect one.

He left the alcove.

****

Duncan watched him go, although her eyes did not follow him. She wanted to talk to him, to scream his name and ask him to help her. Instead, she remained motionless. Her hands remained folded on her naked lap. She could feel the cold faux-leather of the bench on her ass and legs. She could feel the slight breeze that came through the air vent high on the bulkhead. It tickled the hair on her arms. She could even hear the soft hum of the lights and the base's internal power grid. She would have usually taken pride in that hum, which meant the base's systems were running strong and normal. She did not. Such things no longer mattered to her.

She was unaware of the drop of blood that ran like a teardrop down her leg. It had originated in her vagina, and it would end its journey on the deck at her feet. More blood would follow. She sniffled and tasted blood at the back of her throat. A small bead of it found its way out of her nostril and began to drip onto her lip. She wiped it away without realizing she had moved.

She sat. And waited.

****

"Are we through here, Kehoe? I'm dying for a cigarette."

Mikhailov shifted a bit on the exam table in the emergency triage center in C-ring. The room was nearly as large as the main infirmary and well-stocked with medical devices and supplies. It was positioned halfway between landing pads one and two. The original base manual described its intended use as an emergency medical station for critically injured personnel arriving via shuttle. No one could remember if the room had ever fulfilled its purpose. Had Armstrong been built at the time of the crash of the *Daedalus*, the survivors might have been brought there. But construction of Armstrong had not begun until nine years after the *Daedalus*. And there had been no survivors in any case.

"Just about," Kehoe said. "Hang on." He tilted her head up gently, looked again at the dark bruises that adorned Mikhailov's neck. Normally, had he been this close to Mikhailov while she wore only her bra and panties, he would have become quite aroused. As it was, thoughts of sex did not enter his mind. "Still can't believe Duncan did this." He rubbed more salve onto the skin.

"Well, she did," Mikhailov said.

"So I understand. Okay, you're good to go."

Mikhailov slid off the table and gingerly pulled on her shirt. "Clean bill of health?" She grunted a bit at the pain in her neck and right shoulder.

Kehoe laughed a bit. "Not remotely. Try to keep your head as level as you can. No strenuous physical exertions for a few days. And the last thing you should do is rub your throat. I know it's sore and all, but you need to resist that particular urge. Also, quit smoking and start eating your greens."

Mikhailov finished pulling on her shirt. "Yes, mom." She scooped up her trousers and slipped into them when Hansen entered the room. She noted his look of concern and waved to him.

"How are you, Galina?"

"Considering my friend just tried to kill me, I'm okay, Mike." She buttoned her trousers and looked at Kehoe. She started to rub her throat but stopped when Kehoe shot her a look. Her hand continued its ascent until she ran it through her pixie hair. The move appeared casual, but

Mikhailov did not believe she had fooled Kehoe. "Dr. Hasegawa's little boy fixed me up pretty good."

"Hey!" Kehoe said in mock anger.

She flashed him her prettiest, innocent-girl smile, which had melted a few hearts and produced more than a few erections over the years. She knew immediately she had succeeded with the former, and guessed she'd succeeded with the latter, as well.

She turned to Hansen again. "Is Duncan okay?"

Hansen bit his lip. "Your guess is as good as mine. I just saw her. She's completely unresponsive, although she appears to be awake."

"I can take a look at her if you want, Mike," Kehoe said. "I like Duncan. Hell, everyone does. If there's something wrong with her, I'd like to help."

"Duly noted," Hansen said. "We'll wait for the doc first, though." He looked at Kehoe. "Nothing personal."

"We'll need the resources of the infirmary, Mike." Kehoe replaced some of the devices he'd used on Mikhailov. "This place isn't gonna cut it."

Hansen frowned. "I talked with the GSA. Even got through to President Cromwell. No dice. Dwyer is calling the shots."

"She can't just take over the infirmary. We need that for Duncan."

"I know." He took a breath. "Let's all calm down. Go get some rest, Kehoe. I want to talk with Galina alone, anyway."

"Yes, sir," Kehoe said, clearly disappointed. He made his way across the room and disappeared through the hatch.

Hansen turned to Mikhailov. They talked at length.

****

Hansen lay in his bunk a short time later. He tried to sleep, knew he needed it, but was just as certain it would not come. Not after what Mikhailov had told him. He tried to play the scene in his head, tried to see Duncan waiting for Mikhailov in her quarters. He tried to envision the fight which ensued. Mikhailov told him she feared for her life, and he believed her. She remarked more than once about the look in Duncan's eyes. Nixon had made the same comment. Now that same woman was seated in a holding cell and staring into space, apparently catatonic. He rubbed his eyes again.

In a few hours people would begin to wake up. Dwyer would continue her secret experiments on the two bodies in the infirmary. But not before Hansen had a chance to speak with her. He had a feeling she would not like what he had to say. He could live with that.

A moment later, he was fast asleep.

He awoke three hours later to chaotic sounds. It took a moment for the fog to lift and for him to realize the voices came from the intercom next to his bunk. He fumbled for the switch, cursed his clumsiness. There were too many voices shouting too many things for Hansen to make out anything. He found the correct switch and shouted, "Hansen!"

The tumult continued for another few moments. Hansen was already out of his bunk and reaching for a shirt. One male voice in particular began to outshout the others, and after another few moments of indecipherable chaos, he heard Nixon's voice cut through the background noise.

"Colonel, it's Nixon. We have a situation in the holding area. We need you down here right away."

"Be right there," Hansen said. He was out the hatch and down the corridor at a dead run. He knew it was something serious, not simply because of all the raised voices, but because Nixon had addressed him by rank. He knew what he would find before he got there, knew it would be Dwyer. He was correct.

Nixon, Hasegawa and Kehoe were there, standing to one side of the only occupied holding cell. Across from them, shouting with equal fervor, were the two technicians, Sullivan and Millman. A pair of steel manacles dangled from Sullivan's fist. They cut swathes through the air as the man gesticulated wildly.

The shouting continued as Hansen ran into the room. He spared a single glance at Duncan and was alarmed at the woman's appearance. Blood had run apparently from her vaginal area and pooled on the deck between and around her feet. Blood likewise flowed, slowly but steadily, from her nose and the corners of her mouth. Her chest was covered with it. It collected on her nipples and in her bellybutton. She continued to stare straight ahead.

Hansen held up both hands, shouted for everyone to shut up. The arguing continued for another few moments, until Hansen's shouts overpowered the last few voices. He surveyed the two opposing sides. Sweat had sprung up on nearly everyone's brow, faces were red with anger, hands shook.

"Colonel," Hasegawa said, her voice much louder than necessary, "these men are here to take Duncan to the infirmary. And they've informed me I am not permitted to accompany her. She is *my* patient and she will *not* leave my sight. Tell them!" She addressed Hansen, but her eyes never left the two men in front of her.

Hansen placed a hand on Hasegawa's shoulder. If the gesture was meant to calm the doctor, it failed miserably. Her dark eyes blazed with anger.

Hansen nodded at Sullivan and Millman. "Your turn."

Sullivan cleared his throat. "Colonel, with all due respect, we are under direct orders to escort this patient to the infirmary immediately.

Your…*people* are standing in our way." He regarded Nixon, Hasegawa and Kehoe with naked anger. He wiped his sleeve across his forehead. "As you can see, this woman is in need of immediate medical attention. If we don't move now, she could die."

Hansen spared another glance into the holding cell. Duncan remained motionless.

"I'm going to spell it out for you boys," Hansen said slowly. "This woman is the chief medical officer of this facility." He indicated Hasegawa with a nod of his head. "She has the final say in anything having to do with the health of every man and woman here. If she says she goes with her patient, she goes. And if she wants to examine and treat her inside the infirmary, that's what she'll do. Understood?" He noted with some satisfaction the look of anger and even fury he received from Sullivan. Millman looked at the deck, the bulkheads, anywhere but at Hansen.

"Ms. Dwyer isn't going to like this, Colonel," Millman said.

"If she has a problem with this, she can come see me."

"I'll see you right now, Colonel."

Six heads turned in the direction of the corridor. Dwyer approached. She had changed into yet another business suit. Her hair was once more neatly and tightly pulled back into a bun. Her high-heeled shoes clicked and clacked along the deck. Behind her and a bit to her left walked Wright. He regarded Hansen and the others with open contempt.

The pair stopped inside the room, beside Sullivan and Millman. Hansen looked into Dwyer's eyes. All traces of civility had vanished. The woman was in full-on command mode. He spared a glance at Wright. The major did not quite sneer at Hansen, but it was close. Hansen noted, with not a small amount of surprise and nervousness,

Wright wore a sidearm and holster on his belt. The major took his customary parade-rest stance next to Dwyer.

"I tried to cooperate with you," Dwyer began. "I briefed you in the spirit of that cooperation. I even allowed you to look into the infirmary when we were examining Dr. Doyle. None of that was good enough for you."

"Ms. Dwyer," Hansen said, trying to keep his voice level. "I don't think you realize the gravity—"

"*Don't interrupt me!*" Dwyer's voice jumped an octave as well as several decibels. She visibly steadied herself. "Listen to me, Colonel. *All* of you listen. This facility is under *my* command from this point forward. *I* will decide who does what and with whom." She pointed emphatically into the holding cell. "Starting with your engineer. She's coming with us to the infirmary so we can try to save her life. If any of you attempt to interfere…" She allowed her voice to trail off. She tilted her head slightly in Wright's direction.

The major stood with his hand on the butt of the gun. It remained in its holster, but Hansen's nervousness moved up a notch. Wright looked straight ahead, at attention. *The perfect little soldier*, Hansen thought. And if she ordered him to draw that weapon, he would. Of that, Hansen had no doubt.

Nixon took an angry step forward. Hansen's arm shot out in front of the security chief and stopped him in his tracks. Wright unhooked the leather strap that held the weapon in its holster, but he did not draw it. He looked at Nixon, as if daring him to move another step forward. Nixon's eyes spat fire, but he said nothing.

Hansen swallowed. When he spoke, his voice was neutral. "I'll be on the line to GSA corporate in a few minutes. Ms. Dwyer."

The woman's smile returned. She seemed genuinely happy. "As you wish, Colonel." She redirected her attention to the woman and two men at Hansen's back. "Step back, all of you. You're interfering with an official GSA operation."

Hansen looked back, saw three pairs of eyes looking back at him. He nodded wordlessly. Hasegawa swore, but she and the others stepped back and away from the holding cell.

"A wise choice," Dwyer said. She nodded to Wright without looking at him. He replaced the leather restraint on the holster. She turned her attention to Sullivan and Millman. "Bring her out here."

Millman placed his palm on the scanner screen on the bulkhead. The transparency rolled left into the bulkhead with a pronounced hum.

Duncan smiled and more blood dripped from her mouth. It spattered on her chest like an obscene rain. Her eyes focused on Sullivan when he stepped into the cell.

That was when all hell broke loose.

****

The explosion was so sudden and so unexpected it took a review of the security camera footage to determine precisely what had happened. One moment Nixon watched Sullivan enter the cell. The next, the security chief was back on his heels and holding his hands in front of his face. The noise was not great, more like distant, but approaching, thunder. The large billowing cloud of dust which plumed from within the holding cell was another matter entirely.

It engulfed Sullivan and he was lost from sight. Nixon saw Hasegawa take a step toward the cell. He grabbed her by her shirt collar and hauled her back. Then the dust was in his eyes. He wiped his sleeve across his face, breathed in and got a lungful of dust for his trouble. He coughed violently. Hansen shouted something unintelligible. Nixon's vision was obscured, but he saw his commander bolt for the cell. He did the only thing he could think of doing and tackled Hansen to the deck. He shielded the colonel's body with his own.

The dust cloud swirled around the holding area, as if blown by a perpetual tornado. From somewhere within the dust cloud, Nixon could swear he heard Sullivan scream. He moved his hands to his ears to keep out the roar of the storm.

Hansen struggled beneath him, and he shouted something. Nixon maintained his hold on his commander. He lifted his head, opening his eyes just enough to see what was happening around them. Hasegawa remained on the deck next to them. She covered her head with both hands and had curled into the fetal position. He saw a pair of boots a few meters away and guessed they belonged to Kehoe. The nurse clearly staggered against the force of the gale raging around them. Kehoe took a step forward, then two more steps back. Nixon tried to reach for him, but the torrent had picked up and the flying dust stung the exposed flesh on his hand.

He raised his head just a few inches. Two silhouettes that might have been Dwyer and Wright were huddled on the deck against the far bulkhead. The other GSA tech, Millman, was nowhere in sight.

A scream that could only have come from Kehoe momentarily overpowered the roar of the storm. Nixon looked again in the nurse's direction. The same pair of boots levitated a few inches from the deck. *Was the wind actually that strong?* Nixon reached out his hand a second time and ignored the stinging dust. He wrapped his fingers around the boot's ankle and dug into the leather. Later, he would not be terribly surprised to discover he had gripped the boot with enough strength to break Kehoe's ankle.

A moment later the nurse landed hard and heavy on the deck. Nixon released his grip on the man's boot and again covered his head.

The roar of the wind had begun to weaken, he was sure of it. A few moments later it subsided altogether.

Tentatively, Nixon opened his eyes. Dust fell gently around them like snow. It coated the holding area to a depth of an inch or two. The white bulkheads were dark with the stuff. Even the lighting was muted, the ceiling panels covered with dust. It was in Nixon's hair and on his clothes. He took a few breaths and rolled off Hansen.

Nixon rose on hands and knees and breathed heavy. He reached up to the panel on the bulkhead and hit the blue button. Air vents near the ceiling opened; he could hear the fans activate. He watched the dust swirl more rapidly as it was caught by the fans. Most of it vanished into the air ducts. After no more than a moment, the air inside the holding area was clear.

He surveyed the room. Both Hasegawa and Hansen were already climbing to their feet. The two silhouettes against the far bulkhead revealed themselves to indeed be Dwyer and Wright. The woman's hair was no longer pulled back in its customary bun; she appeared as if she had stood in front of an engine thruster during a test firing. Her eyes were wide, and Nixon knew the woman was in shock. Wright was visibly shaken and confused. One hand remained on the butt of the gun, but it did not appear to be a conscious act. The executive officer's eyes were identical to Dwyer's. Nixon paid them no further mind.

A man to his left coughed. He turned and expected to see Kehoe. Instead, it was Millman. The doctor had been standing to the side of the holding cell's transparency when the explosion occurred, Nixon was sure of it. Had the wind been powerful enough to hurl the man across the room? He thought perhaps it had. It had been powerful enough to lift Kehoe completely off the deck. Kehoe…

Nixon located him a moment later, although at first he did not realize it. He mistook the nurse for some object that had perhaps been blown into the room from the corridor and then covered in dust. It appeared much too thin to be a human being, let alone Kehoe. Nixon crawled on hands and knees to the object and turned it over.

Dust slid off the corpse and formed little anthills on the deck. Kehoe's eyes had sunk into his skull, and he stared at the ceiling through a thin layer of dust. His skin had shriveled and wrapped itself tightly around his bones. His mouth was open in an eternal, silent scream.

"Kehoe!" Hasegawa screamed from behind Nixon. She was at the nurse's side in an instant and brushed Nixon's arm away.

"Sullivan's dead, too," Hansen said from the threshold of the holding cell.

Nixon glanced inside the cell and saw the doctor appeared identical to Kehoe. He lay flat on his back, his arms outstretched and frozen in an invisible embrace. The pair of manacles still dangled from his skeletal left hand.

Nixon's eyes searched the cell. The blood that had dripped down Duncan's legs and pooled at her feet remained. It was black with dust. There was no other indication anyone had ever been inside the cell.

Millman tried to stand, failed. He slid down the bulkhead and sat on the deck and remained there.

Nixon rose to one knee, looked about the room again. The remnants of the dust cloud floated lazily in the air. The holding area's resemblance to the main ballroom aboard the *Sovereign of the Stars* was not lost on him. "Mother of God," was all he could manage.

Chapter 7

Breadcrumbs

Hansen offered a hand to Wright and the man accepted it. He reached across his body with his left hand, and Hansen knew it was a deliberate gesture. Wright's other hand remained on the butt of the gun in its holster. He hauled his executive officer to his feet, patted him on the shoulder and then offered his hand to Dwyer. She accepted it absently. Her eyes remained wide. Dust drifted from her hair and clothes as Hansen pulled her to her feet.

He glanced inside the cell again, saw the body on the deck. It's similarity to the body they found aboard the *Sovereign* was obvious; the dust that now coated everything reinforced the image. He rubbed his eyes and swallowed. He tasted blood and dust. He coughed and spat on the deck. His tongue was swollen and sore.

Hasegawa knelt beside Kehoe's body. Tears spilled from her eyes and traced paths of clean flesh down her cheeks. Like Dwyer, her hair was a rat's nest and covered with dust. She rested a hand on the man's sunken chest and wept openly.

Hansen's lips pressed into a thin line. He returned his attention to Dwyer. She leaned against the bulkhead and stared blankly ahead. He approached her with a bit more anger than he'd intended. He leaned down so they would be eye to eye. "What the hell was that?" He pointed in the direction of the holding cell. "You know. I know you do."

Dwyer's lips trembled, but whatever she had to say died in her throat. She continued to stare ahead, as if Hansen were not directly in front of her.

"You listen to me, Dwyer. I want to know what the fuck just happened. You're going to tell me or so help me God you'll be in that cell next."

The glaze over her eyes did not vanish so much as it lessened. She blinked, and her eyes went to Hansen as if she noticed him for the first time. She stuttered something unintelligible.

Hansen grabbed her shoulders and shook her. More dust floated from her hair, her clothes. "Talk to me, goddamnit!"

She looked into his eyes directly, and for a moment, she was no longer the senior vice-president of the Global Space Agency. She mostly resembled a little girl, perhaps the person she had been early in life. She was hesitant, reluctant to speak, perhaps even shy. Her eyes were full of fear, yes, but there was something else there, as well. Confusion? Certainly that. But something more. Hansen thought perhaps it was sheer bewilderment.

"That wasn't supposed to happen," she said. Her words were staggered, uncertain. Her breathing was quick and shallow. "That wasn't supposed to happen."

"No shit," Nixon said from across the room. He knelt next to Hasegawa, his arms wrapped around the doctor. Hasegawa trembled within the embrace. Even at a distance, Hansen could hear her sobs.

"Dwyer, where is my chief engineer?" Hansen maintained his grip on the woman's shoulders.

"We should have had enough time," she said. Her eyes were still fixed on his. "It's burning through them faster now."

Hansen opened his mouth to speak, closed it again. He searched her eyes, but the woman who had arrived at Armstrong a few days before was still among the missing. The shy little girl remained in her place.

Hansen pulled his hands away and looked at Wright. The man had regained much of his composure, but his hand remained on the butt of the gun. "Look after her," he said, moving away. Wright nodded wordlessly.

Hansen took a few strides across the room and stood in front of Millman. The doctor had managed to regain his feet. He leaned against the bulkhead and absently brushed dust from his sleeves. "Well?" Hansen asked.

Millman looked up at Hansen. He was more stable than Dwyer. His eyes focused immediately on the man in front of him. He started to speak, stopped himself. He looked over Hansen's shoulder at Dwyer. He regarded her for a moment before returning his attention to Hansen.

"I don't know anything, Colonel." He lowered his eyes. "I'm sorry."

"Fuck you are," Hansen growled.

He strode across the room to the intercom panel. He wiped dust from it and hit the button. "Con, this is Hansen."

Thorpe's reply was immediate. "McKnight and Mason are on their way to you now, Mike."

Hansen nodded. "Contact GSA corporate in Geneva, Thorpe. Tell them I'll be on the line for President Cromwell. Tell them he'd damned well better talk to me. Is that clear?"

"As a bell, sir," Thorpe said.

Hansen turned to Nixon. "Wait for the others to get here. Then bring everyone to the infirmary to be checked out. I'll be in my office."

"Mike, is that a good idea?" Nixon parted from his embrace with Hasegawa and stood. "I mean, shouldn't you be checked out, too? We have no idea what happened just now."

"Some of us do." He glared at Dwyer, and then he gave Millman the same look. Millman did not meet his gaze. "Follow my orders, Nix."

He set off for the control room without another word.

****

Had Sanchez known he was about to die, he would have spent his last hours more productively. Hague was with Mikhailov. Apparently, she had been attacked by the facility's chief engineer. He didn't have all the details, but he understood the woman was injured. This meant she was out of action, at least for a few days. That was the first thing about it that sucked. He had hoped to schedule some Sanchez-time with her. She was hot, single, and Sanchez had a reputation as a ladies man. Alas, he would need to find his recreation elsewhere. Since Hague was with her, and he knew no one else on the base, he was alone. That was the second part that sucked.

He spent an hour or so in his assigned quarters. He lay in his bunk and called up the library file on the wreck of the *Daedalus*. It contained no information that was new to him, and indeed, held a few inaccuracies. He knew everything he felt could be known about the ship and her crew. His decision to go through the library files was merely an attempt to kill time.

He went to the Gemini and found it deserted. He poured himself a beer and drank alone. He took a moment to regard the chessboard set up on one of the tables. It was a game in-progress, and he knew it was Hague and Duncan's game. But Duncan had been the one who attacked Mikhailov. As far as he knew, she was in a holding cell. It did not appear she would get to finish the game, after all. He sat at the table and attempted to get Hague out of check. He kept running into

Duncan's second bishop. He decided she had been correct; Hague was about to be in checkmate. Not that the psychotic bitch could celebrate her victory.

He tried his hand at the old pinball machine, but he knew nothing about how to play it. Three straight balls went between the flippers. The damn thing made such a racket he decided not to try it a second time.

Ultimately and unfortunately, he decided he needed more practice on his landing technique. He made his way to hanger one in C-ring. His transport sat where they had left it. He took a moment to look about the hanger and to marvel at its size and simplicity. The crane, which was used to move transports onto and off the elevator pad, stood poised above one of the base's own transports. The number *770* was stenciled on the hull beneath the cockpit.

Beat up piece of shit, Sanchez thought. *The 7-series transports were garbage through and through.* He had, in fact, been surprised to find a transport as old as a 7-series was still in use. He thought they had all been scrapped a decade earlier. He was happy he had gotten to co-pilot a much newer craft for his first lunar flight.

The hanger itself seemed roomy to Sanchez, even with the addition of the second transport. He imagined it looked positively expansive when seven-seven-zero was its sole occupant. The dull gray of the deck seemed to stretch on forever. The tops of the bulkheads were illuminated with a light mounted every three meters or so. He could not guess at the square footage of the hanger, but it had to be pretty damned big. When he took into account the other two hangers, it seemed to him Armstrong had more hanger space than would ever be needed. *Must have been a government contract to build this thing*, he thought. *Only they could possibly overcompensate to such a degree.*

He reached the bottom of the stairs and listened to the echo produced by his footfalls on the concrete deck. He began to walk toward his transport. He would not make it.

****

Hansen stood behind his desk and slapped the monitor activation switch. The screen came to life and showed him the GSA logo. He was about to shout for Thorpe, when the image changed. An old man in an expensive suit sat behind a mahogany desk that might not have fit inside Hansen's office. His white hair was trimmed quite neatly. Behind him was a picture window larger than the main monitor screen in the control room. The view was of Lake Geneva. Hansen could even see small boats cutting through the water, their white sails gleaming in the sunlight. The man wore a lapel pin adorned with the GSA logo. He sat with his arms on the desk and his fingers laced together. The look he gave Hansen was not pleasant.

When he spoke, his voice was rough, as if he had just been awakened. "Explain to me, Colonel, why my secretary was under the impression you demanded I speak with you."

"Because that's exactly what I did." Hansen tried to keep his voice level, failed miserably. "Listen to me, Mr. Cromwell. We have four dead here, to say nothing of the men and women aboard that starliner. I want some goddamned answers, and I want them *now*." His fist struck the desk on his last word.

The man on the monitor remained calm, despite the sour look he gave Hansen. "What makes you think I have answers to give? I'm hardly in a position to know something you do not. After all, I'm not there with you. Am I?"

"You know something, I know you do. My people are dying up here because of your fucking secrets. If you're going to keep playing this game with me, I'll have no choice but to order an evacuation of this facility." He paused, studied the man on the monitor. He saw anger flash across his eyes, and Cromwell's shoulders squared as if the man were preparing for a fight. At the last moment, he regained his composure. He even smiled.

"Colonel, I am willing to forgive your outburst, based on what you've just told me." He leaned a bit closer to the monitor. "But there shall be no evacuation of Armstrong Base. Do I make myself clear?" He leaned back in his chair. "Michael, we have no more idea what happened to the *Sovereign of the Stars* than you do, I assure you. We sent a team to you to assist in the investigation. That's all we know."

Hansen placed both hands on his desk and loomed above the monitor. "Bullshit. Since when does the GSA send the senior vice-president to the moon to investigate anything? We both know the answer to that. I think you have a pretty damned good idea what happened to the passengers and crew of the *Sovereign*. Now that same thing is happening to us. *Talk* to me, sir."

Cromwell leaned toward the monitor again. His voice dropped, became quiet, but acquired an edge that had not been present before. "That will be *enough*, Colonel. Do not forget to whom you are speaking. You're punching far above your weight class, and you are going to lose. Do you understand me? I have tried to be polite with you, but I have my limits. I will not tolerate your insubordination for another minute. Are we clear?"

Hansen took a deep breath for the reply he was not able to make.

The hatch opened and Dwyer stepped into the room. She had collected herself in the time Hansen had left her. He gave her only a cursory glance, but it was enough. The frightened little girl he glimpsed in the holding area was gone. She was back in command mode. She had even taken the time to retie her hair into its customary bun. She had brushed most of the dust from her clothing, although some still remained in the folds of her sleeves. She strode across the office and did not stop until she stood beside Hansen. Wright stepped into the room a moment later. He remained by the hatch.

"Mr. President," Dwyer said.

Cromwell nodded. "Lindsay. Report."

"Sir, I apologize for Colonel Hansen's behavior. I have officially informed him that he is relieved of command. It appears he has something to say about that, despite GSA regs."

"Your apology is accepted, Lindsay." Cromwell turned to Hansen. "Colonel, you have been relieved of your command. If you persist in causing trouble for Ms. Dwyer or me, you will be arrested and placed within a holding cell. Do I make myself clear, Colonel?"

"Sir, you can't—"

"Do. I. Make. Myself. Clear. *Colonel.*"

Hansen glared at the screen. "Yes, *sir.*"

Cromwell's smile returned. "Good. Then we have an understanding. You are dismissed. Lindsay, your report, please."

Hansen was already at the hatch when he heard Dwyer say, "One moment, sir. Colonel Hansen?"

Hansen stopped at the threshold and turned. Dwyer held the baseball card in its protective case. She tossed it to him. He caught it without taking his eyes from her.

"Don't forget your family heirloom." She smiled at him and then returned her attention to the monitor.

Hansen turned, nearly collided with Wright. He looked into the man's eyes. Like Dwyer, he had recovered from what had occurred in the holding area. Unlike Dwyer, Hansen did not believe the executive officer had recovered completely. He looked at Hansen for only a moment before he dropped his eyes and stepped aside. Hansen was through the hatch a moment later. It closed and locked behind him.

Narita was alone in the main control room, apparently having replaced Thorpe on monitor duty. He sat at one of the control stations near the front of the room. Hansen walked purposefully to him. The engineer stood at his approach. *He looks tired*, Hansen thought. *Like everyone else*. He was also the man Hansen needed at the moment.

"Can you access the *Sovereign*'s flight computer?"

Narita looked taken aback at Hansen's tone, and the colonel chided himself. He swallowed and nearly apologized, but found he was too angry and too tired. The engineer stuttered before he resumed his seat and began pressing buttons. Hansen placed a hand on the man's shoulder. It was the most he could manage.

"Can't get in there, Colonel," Narita said after a few moments.

Hansen swore under his breath. He started to turn away, stopped himself. "Why not?"

Narita shook his head. "I can't know for sure, but at a guess, I'd say remote access has been disabled." He looked at Hansen over his shoulder. "If you want the flight computer, you're going to have to go aboard her and access it manually. Even then, I can't guarantee you'd be able to get past the security."

Hansen placed his hands on his hips. "Could you?"

Narita froze for a moment, but only for a moment. He turned in the seat and looked at Hansen. "I think so."

There was a sharp *bleep* from the intercom system. Hansen and Narita both looked up out of habit. The signal meant the person who had opened the channel did so throughout the base. Hansen knew whose voice would issue from the speakers. He was correct.

"Attention all hands, this is Lindsay Dwyer. Effective immediately, Colonel Hansen has been relieved of his duties and is no longer in command of Armstrong Base. Major Wright is now your commanding officer. That is all." The intercom *bleeped* again.

Short, sweet and not unexpected. Hansen turned to Narita again. The engineer smiled at him.

"I didn't catch that, Colonel."

Hansen nodded and managed a weak smile. "I'm going to stop off at the infirmary. I'll get McKnight or Mason to take over for you here. When you're relieved, meet me at airlock three. Understood?"

"Absolutely," Narita replied.

Hansen started for the hatch, stopped, turned. "Oh, and if anyone should ask..." He let his voice trail off.

Narita nodded. "I'll tell them I don't know shit." He paused and smiled. "Which is true."

Hansen smiled in spite of himself and made for the hatch.

****

Millman hopped onto the examination table in the infirmary and waited for Dr. Hasegawa to approach him. He himself had opened the infirmary when they'd arrived. He had broken the quarantine imposed by Dwyer, but he knew there was no chance of contamination from the corpses stored inside. And Dwyer had been in no condition to object. The last he had seen her, she was still inside the holding area, trying to gather herself and leaning on the weasel she had just declared the commanding officer of Armstrong Base. The other survivors from the incident in the holding area paid little mind to the state of the room and the condition of the two corpses left there. They had other concerns.

He had stood and watched Hasegawa examine everyone else, waiting his turn. He did not believe he had been infected when that bitch engineer had performed her impression of a pipe bomb. Had he been infected, he knew he would most likely be symptomatic already.

What caught his attention was Hansen's arrival in the infirmary a few moments later. The man was out of breath, and he immediately summoned the rest of his former crew to him. They stood in a circle and spoke in hushed tones Millman could not hear. There was some nodding from everyone, and much gesticulation from Nixon. More than once Hansen looked up and eyed Millman. After a moment, Hansen headed out again. A moment after that, Thorpe (or perhaps it was Mason, Millman could not remember who was who) exited the room as well and took off in the opposite direction.

Millman stroked his chin. A few moments later he was given a clean bill of health by Dr. Hasegawa. By then, most of Armstrong's personnel had exited the room. Only Nixon remained. Millman made eye contact with him. Nixon looked away.

****

Narita arrived at airlock three and saw Hansen zipping up his isolation suit. Hansen nodded to him, and Narita opened up one of the lockers. He took out the suit and sat on the bench.

"Mason's at the con, Colonel," Narita said. "Major Wright was there when he came to relieve me."

Hansen sat on the bench beside Narita and began to pull on the boots. "Did Wright say anything?"

Narita shook his head. "Not really, no. Just insisted that we inform him every time there was an unscheduled change in duty shift. We said 'yes, sir', and that was that."

Hansen nodded. "Any sign of Dwyer?"

"No. I think she was still inside your office."

"It's not my office anymore." He glanced at the closed airlock hatch to their right. "You sure you can access the flight computer?"

Narita zipped up the suit and paused. "Well, Duncan was better at this sort of thing than I am. But yeah, I'm pretty sure I can get us in." He took a deep breath and gave Hansen a sad smile.

Hansen placed a hand on his shoulder. "I miss her, too. We all do. If we want to know what happened to her, we need what's inside the *Sovereign*'s flight computer."

"I know." He pulled on his boots and stood up. "I'm ready, Colonel."

Hansen pulled his helmet on and sealed it. Narita did likewise, and both men faced the airlock hatch.

"Listen. We're going to see some things in there that aren't pretty. Just hold it together and remember why we're there."

Narita took a deep breath and squared his shoulders. "Let's do this."

Hansen nodded and palmed open the inner hatch.

The docking sleeve remained brightly lit. Hansen led the way until they reached the starliner's hatch. It was open, left that way by Millman and Sullivan, Hansen assumed. He stepped through and waited for Narita.

The first difference he noted was the ceiling lights had been activated inside the first class dining hall. The cut-crystal chandeliers must have added ambiance to the five-star meals served to first class passengers. Mini-rainbows surrounded each chandelier and appeared as multicolored halos. Under different circumstances, Hansen would have appreciated the effect. Absently, he deactivated his flashlight and hooked it back onto his belt. He was able to get a much better look at the room than he had his first time there. The tables remained set and awaited guests who would never arrive. Dust still floated through the air and settled on the tables and chairs. It billowed up from the carpet and created small dust devils with each step they took.

"Millman and Sullivan must have reactivated internal power," Hansen said.

"Well, it's nice to see where we're going." Narita looked about the room and whistled through his teeth. "So this is how the other one percent lives."

"And dies," Hansen said. He immediately regretted the comment and changed the subject. "On our first sweep through, Hasegawa and I couldn't get inside the bridge. The lock was disabled. If the power grid is online, that means Millman and Sullivan must have made it in there."

"Or the engine room," Narita said helpfully.

Hansen shook his head. "The engine room was sealed by a blast door. Nixon couldn't get in there. My money's on the bridge."

"Then let's hope they left the key," Narita said.

Hansen caught sight of a man's legs poking out from beneath a table. The expensive-looking black pants were tattered just enough for Hansen to see the owner's shriveled legs within. He did not need to see the corpse up close to know it matched the appearance of the body he and Hasegawa had discovered outside the bridge. He steered Narita away from the corpse as casually as he was able.

Hansen set off for the bridge. Narita took one last look around the dining hall and rushed to catch up.

They bypassed the main ballroom. Hansen had no desire to enter the room again, and he thought it best to keep Narita's mind on the job. The last thing he wanted was Narita's head filled with images of plasma-burned corpses. They crossed corridors and climbed staircases until they reached A deck. They came across the body in the corridor outside the bridge. It had been propped up next to the bulkhead and resembled nothing so much as a man asleep. Hansen kept them moving. Narita did not require much prodding; the young engineer's assistant did not seem eager to examine the corpse. Hansen could not blame him.

The bridge hatch was closed. A small electronic device that had not been present during Hanson's last visit sat on the deck to the side of the hatch. Wires from the device led up to the exposed innards of the wall panel. Two red indicator lights on the panel's facing blinked at them.

"Portable power terminal," Narita said. "Until they could access the power grid, they needed this for the hatch locks." He knelt next to the device, flipped the red switch to the ON position. He stood and studied the hatch panel. After a moment, he said, "Colonel, this was damaged with the hatch in the closed position. Looks like somebody locked somebody else inside the bridge."

Hansen could think of a few scenarios that could account for that. He ran them through his mind, but all he said was, "Can you get us in?"

In reply, Narita hit a button on the panel. The hatch slid open.

Hansen looked inside the bridge. The room was much larger than he had anticipated. There were workstations along the bulkheads and in front of the three large windows at the front of the room. He could see no bodies. He looked out the windows, saw the curve of C-ring and a small section of B-ring. He wondered, if only momentarily, what was happening within the base. Then it was back to work.

He turned away from the windows and found Narita seated at the main computer station. The engineer flipped switches and pushed buttons on the console. Hansen walked around the bridge, checked every workstation. He lingered at the captain's chair, thought about what it would be like to command a ship such as this. He pictured the spectacular view of space afforded anyone who sat in that chair. Quickly, he realized the last person to sit in the chair was now a corpse. He moved away and joined Narita at the computer station.

The screen on the bulkhead above Narita's station had come to life. It was filled with snow, broken only by flashes of light. "Someone accessed this station already, Colonel," Narita said. His fingers flew across the keyboard.

Hansen looked at the screen. "How can you tell?"

"They left breadcrumbs," Narita said, as if that were explanation enough. "I'm following their trail now. Should have something in a minute."

"Can you tell what they accessed specifically?"

"Sure can," Narita replied. He paused for effect, and he hit one last button.

The image on the screen coalesced into a chart of the solar system. Two lines — one blue, the other red — ran across the image. Both led to Earth. The screen flickered for a moment, then it returned to its normal appearance.

"The blue line is the flight plan they filed with the GSA," Narita said. "Their course was to take them out to Plutonian space, then back to Earth. But see the red line? How it diverges near Jupiter? They changed course for some reason."

Hansen studied the chart and stoked his chin. "Do we know why?"

"Well, the sensor logs have been erased. It's possible they detected something out there and changed course to investigate."

"But what? And why erase the sensor logs in the first place?"

Narita shook his head. "No idea. Not just the sensor logs, either. The entire communications, navigation and medical systems have been wiped clean, too. Someone covered their tracks very well."

Hansen swore. "Millman and Sullivan. Damnit." He turned from the workstation and folded his arms across his chest. He and Hasegawa had been right outside the hatch. All they had needed was enough time to get through it and he would have gotten to the information before it had been erased. He would have rubbed his eyes if not for his helmet.

"Wait a minute," Narita said. "Looks like they didn't get to everything."

Hansen turned back to the workstation so fast that he nearly lost his balance. "What is it?"

"The last log entry," Narita said. "Looks like they didn't bother with the short-term memory. Or they missed it entirely." His fingers continued their dance across the keyboard. "It's stored in a separate section of the mainframe. Accessing now."

The star chart vanished from the monitor. It was replaced with the GSA logo, but a moment later, a woman's face appeared. Hansen recognized Sofia Nelson immediately. She sat in the same seat occupied at present by Narita. Her eyes were large, frightened. Her face, shoulders and hair were covered with a light coating of dust. It mixed with sweat and appeared dark, as if she had spent time shoveling coal into the furnaces of one of the *Sovereign*'s ancestors. Her hair and uniform were disheveled. Her eyes were wet with tears. Her hand shook as she moved a stray lock of hair from her forehead. She looked over her shoulder quickly, at the closed hatch behind her, and then she returned her attention to the screen.

"I think I'm alone now. I haven't heard from anyone since the captain and the others died in the ballroom." Her breath hitched in her throat. "Part of me wishes I had been there, too. It would have been more merciful, I think. I won't last long enough to make it to Earth, I know that now. It spreads too fast. My only chance is Armstrong Base." She looked over her shoulder again, but only for a moment.

When she spoke again, her voice was little more than a whisper and Hansen had to strain to hear her. "He's right outside the hatch, I know he is. If he's trying to get through that hatch then there must not be anyone else left anywhere on the ship."

There was a dull thud from the hatch behind her. Nelson screamed and spun in the seat quickly. The hatch remained closed. After a moment, she turned back to the screen. Her body shook more visibly. Her eyes darted rapidly right and left.

"I've locked changes out of the nav computer, but I don't know how much he remembers. It's still possible he could alter course and turn us around back toward McEnerney. I can't let him do that. I just have to hold out long enough to get to Armstrong. They'll help me. I know they will."

Another loud thud from the hatch. She shrieked and closed her eyes as tightly as she could. When she realized the hatch held, she opened her eyes again. It took her a few moments to regain the power of speech. "I haven't heard from Chief Engineer Watkins since he slaved all main systems to the bridge. That was two days ago, and so far, I still have positive control. If he's still alive, somehow, on the other side of that blast door…I just need that hatch to hold together until I reach Armstrong."

Fresh tears spilled from her eyes. She glanced at the hatch again. "I should be there in just over three hours. I hope I make it." She reached forward with one arm and the monitor went dark. The GSA logo reappeared.

Narita's hand rested on his faceplate as if he were covering his mouth. He leaned back in the seat, closed his eyes for a moment. "McEnerney? The comet?"

Hansen took a few steps back from the monitor. "Has to be," he said. "It's in Jovian space, right? And where did you say the course diverged from the original flight plan?"

Narita gulped. "Near Jupiter."

Hansen began to pace about the bridge. "The GSA redirected the ship's course. Think about it. Why else would Sullivan and Millman have wiped the comm log? They're covering the GSA's tracks."

Narita pursed his lips. "Okay, so the GSA detects McEnerney-1970 and contacts the ship's captain to alter course. But wouldn't all these super-rich passengers have something to say about cutting their cruise short just so they could investigate a comet?"

"They'd probably see the comet as a bonus for the trip. Something they could brag about to their friends when they got back home."

"But why alter course in the first place? It's just a comet. It's not like we've never seen one before. Even this particular comet comes through once every seventy years or so."

"Then why erase the sensor logs?" Hansen thought quickly. "They found something, something of interest to the GSA. Why else would Dwyer be here?"

"But what did they find?"

"Who knows? But it was something important enough that the senior VP was shuttled to Armstrong to obtain it. That's why they didn't want us to investigate the ship when it first arrived. They were afraid we'd find whatever it is they're looking for."

Narita shook his head. "I'm having a hard time with this." He licked his lips. He looked at the monitor, at the GSA logo. "She said 'it spread too fast'. What do you think *it* is?"

Hansen continued to pace. "Whatever's running around on Armstrong. Whatever killed Duncan and Kehoe. Whatever Dwyer is protecting."

He pointed at the small screen so recently occupied by the face of a dead woman. "Now, she kept saying 'I'. She even said she thought the others were dead. Nobody locked someone else inside the bridge. She set the course for Armstrong and then sealed off the bridge so no one else could change that course." He swallowed and looked at the workstation. "She didn't want to go back to the comet. She evacuated the bridge when the ship was on final approach. She burned out the locking mechanism on her way out so no one else could get in here and abort the landing. And if that body in the corridor belonged to whoever was pounding on the hatch, then she took him out at the same time."

"Then shouldn't the threat have been eliminated? How did she catch this…whatever it is?"

Hansen stroked his chin and looked out the open hatch. He eyed the body sitting against the bulkhead in the corridor. "Maybe she knew him. She hesitated before she pulled the trigger. By the time she did, she was too late to save herself." He could not keep the sadness from his voice. "She must have taken a different route to the airlock. That's why we didn't see her when we were searching the ship." He paused. "Maybe we could have saved her if we'd come across her sooner."

"You don't know that, Mike." Narita eyed the computer station. His Adam's apple traveled up and then down his throat. "You can't blame yourself for what happened to her. Sir."

"Can you upload that file to the security station on Armstrong?"

"Sure," Narita said. He worked the controls for a few moments. "Done."

"Let's get out of here. We have work to do."

"Roger that," Narita said. He was out of the seat in an instant and through the hatch.

Hansen lingered a moment. He looked at the now-empty workstation and pictured a frightened woman who had held it together long enough to see her salvation. She had been alive when he and the others boarded the starliner, he was certain. Still, they had been too late. He wished she'd made it. To go through all that only to fall so close to her goal.

Hansen exited the bridge.

Chapter 8

In the Wrong Place at the Wrong Time

Hansen paced back and forth slowly in Nixon's office. The last log entry recorded by a dead woman played on the monitor. Hansen had no wish to watch it again, nor did Narita. The young man stood with his back to the bulkhead, arms folded across his chest, head down. Nixon, Hasegawa, McKnight and Mason stood or sat around the monitor. Hansen heard an occasional gasp from Hasegawa, heard McKnight and Mason shuffle their feet. And, of course, he could hear the last words of a frightened woman. He thought perhaps he would continue to hear those words for the rest of his life.

When the log entry ended, he stopped his pacing and regarded his crew. They bore identical expressions, most likely the same one he and Narita had worn on the *Sovereign*'s bridge. He gave them a moment to process what they had seen. Then, "Thoughts?"

"She made mention of something that spread too fast," Hasegawa said. The doctor half-sat on Nixon's desk. "It couldn't be viral. How did this whatever-it-is get aboard the ship in the first place? If one of the passengers or crew was already infected when they boarded the ship, wouldn't this same thing be happening on Earth?"

"For that matter, how did it get *here*? We went through decon before we stepped through the airlock." Nixon had retreated to the far bulkhead, next to Narita. He leaned against it, hands on his hips. "That's supposed to wipe out all bugs, right?"

"All *known* bugs," Hasegawa corrected him. "I've been practicing medicine for twenty-three years. I've never seen anything that can do what this thing does. This is unknown to medical science."

"Dwyer said something similar," Hansen said. "In the holding area, right after Duncan…" His voice trailed off.

"Right." Hasegawa nodded her head. "Something like, it happened sooner that she thought it would. Something like that. I can't remember her exact words."

"Neither can I," Nixon said. "We had other things to deal with."

"It's an alien life-form," Narita said matter-of-factly. "Isn't it?" Five pairs of eyes turned to him. He shrugged. "C'mon, guys, I can't be the only one thinking this."

"You're not," Hansen said.

"Mike?" Nixon sounded incredulous. "Alien life-form? You can't be serious."

"Those doctors who arrived with Dwyer are, or *were*, xenobiologists. They were expecting to find an alien life-form. It makes sense."

"But where did it come from?" Mason asked. "And how did it get aboard the *Sovereign*? It's not like the ship landed anywhere out there. There's nowhere to go. So was this thing just flying around the solar system until it happened upon the ship? Seems too convenient."

"You know, I think that's the most I've ever heard you say at one time," McKnight said. He patted Mason on the back. "Thorpe would be proud."

Mason shrugged the hand off his back. "I'm serious. How did it get aboard the ship?"

"The hull breach," McKnight offered.

Mason perked up immediately. "*Of course!* We saw it on the main monitor. A patch on the portside hull. We never did look into what might have caused it. We thought it might be a micro-meteorite impact."

"Maybe it was," McKnight agreed.

"No," Narita said. "It was the comet. It had to be. McEnerney-1970. The ship altered her course somewhere in Jovian space on GSA orders. They would have gotten in close, probably got some oohs and ahhs from the passengers. It's possible some part of it impacted the ship's hull and punched through."

"They'd have to get awful close to the comet for something like that to happen," McKnight said. "Way too close. No pilot in his right mind would do that. It would be suicide."

"I don't think they got close enough to bump the thing," Mason said. "That hull breach is small, and there's no sign of damage around it. If they scraped the comet, there'd be serious damage to her hull. And there isn't."

"It's possible something on the comet's surface, oh, I don't know, reached out for the *Sovereign*." Narita shook his head. "Man, that sounds really stupid, doesn't it?"

"No. It doesn't," Hansen said. "Keep going."

Narita shrugged. "Well, if we're going on the assumption it's an alien life-form, and it's sentient, maybe it recognized the *Sovereign* as something different from itself. Maybe it was curious."

"Or hungry," Hasegawa added.

Hansen suppressed the chill running down his spine; several of the others failed to do so. He thought the same thing at the same moment Hasegawa opened her mouth.

A pair of footfalls echoed in the outside corridor. All conversation ceased. Six pairs of eyes turned toward the open hatch to the security office. Hansen was positive it would be Dwyer and Wright. He was just as positive he would be called to explain the reason the balance of the station's personnel had congregated in one room. That was fine with him. He had an explanation. And he'd get one from Dwyer, as well. A moment later, Mikhailov and Hague stepped inside the room. There were sighs of relief from several of the crew.

Mikhailov shook her head. "We can't find Sanchez anywhere, Mike. It's like the kid disappeared."

Hague nodded in agreement. "We need more eyes out there. This place is too goddamned big for two people to search."

Hansen nodded. "Okay, we'll form into three groups and find him. There's only so many places he can be."

"Thanks, Colonel," Hague said. "With everything that's happened already, I don't like the idea of this kid wandering around by himself."

"I don't, either," Hansen said.

"Mike, what are we going to do about what we learned here?" Nixon looked angry, and Hansen could not blame him. He himself had been angry since the *Sovereign*'s bridge.

"We haven't *learned* anything," Hasegawa pointed out before Hansen could speak. In response to the look she received from Nixon, she continued, "We just have a theory that happens to fit the facts. We have no concrete evidence."

"Fuck the evidence," Nixon replied. "This isn't a courtroom. You saw what happened to Duncan."

"Easy, Nix," Hansen said. "After we find Sanchez, we'll get some answers. I promise you that."

Nixon said nothing. Hansen eyed each person in the room. He turned toward the hatch. "Let's get moving."

That was when Sanchez stepped into the room.

****

Right around the time Narita was putting forth his theory about an alien life-form, Dwyer stood behind Wright's desk and watched the proceedings on the small monitor. Wright and Millman stood in front of the desk, the former in his usual parade-rest stance, the latter shifting his feet. Dwyer stroked her chin. Her eyes scanned everyone on the monitor, but they returned time and again to Hansen. *Relieved of duty but still in command*, she thought. *Troubling, if the others continue to follow him*. She had been too lenient with him, she knew. It seemed time to address the situation.

"Major Wright," she said, and she smiled inwardly as the man snapped to attention. *Certainly no trouble there*, she thought. "Break up their little meeting. Colonel Hansen is to be placed under arrest. Feel free to make use of the holding area as you see fit. Understood?"

"Yes, ma'am." Wright allowed himself a slight smile.

"Dr. Millman, go with him. Just in case there's…trouble."

Millman nodded wordlessly.

Wright turned for the hatch, stopped. "Ma'am, what about Thorpe? He's on monitor duty, but surely he's in on this."

"We'll deal with him later, after order has been restored. Clear?"

"Ma'am," Wright said. He exited the room. Millman followed him out, but slowly. His reluctance was obvious.

She watched them leave and then returned her attention to the monitor. Her eyes focused on Hansen. "I underestimated you, Colonel," she said to the empty room. "It won't happen again."

By then, Mikhailov and Hague had joined them. A moment later, Hague's co-pilot entered the room. Dwyer would be seated at Wright's desk, with her eyes on the monitor, when the major and Millman got there at precisely the wrong moment.

****

Sanchez nearly collapsed after he cleared the hatch and entered the security office. He staggered, got one hand on the bulkhead and steadied himself. Mikhailov and Hague were closest to him and they rushed to his side. His legs buckled at the knees as he collapsed into their arms.

"Doc!" Mikhailov shouted. She and Hague lowered Sanchez to the deck slowly and gently.

Hasegawa was beside them in an instant. She reached for the portable scanner at her belt, realized she did not have it with her. She swore under her breath. "We need to get him to the infirmary *right now*," Hasegawa said. Hansen watched her check the young man's pulse. Then she bent over him and placed her ear to his chest. After a moment, she opened both his eyes. "He's breathing, but he's got a fever like I've never felt before. He's dead if we don't get him on an exam table in the next five minutes."

"Is he infected?" Nixon asked.

"You mean possessed," Narita said. His voice was flat.

"Duncan was feverish, too," Mikhailov added, her voice soft.

Nixon started to protest, but Hansen stopped him with one upheld hand. "Not now." He looked down at Hasegawa. "Doc, can you override the quarantine lockout on the infirmary?"

"No," Hasegawa said without taking her eyes from her patient.

"I can," Nixon said. "My security override should still work."

Hansen nodded. "Let's move." He knelt down and took the young man's legs. He tried to ignore the blood that began to stream from Sanchez's nose. Hasegawa moved out of the way and allowed Hague to grasp the co-pilot under his arms. They lifted the unconscious man from the deck and started for the hatch. They stopped short.

Wright stood in the hatchway. He held his gun in one hand and had it pointed at Hansen. Behind Wright, Millman filled the hatchway. He was likewise armed, although the look in his eyes made it clear he wished to be anywhere but his present location. Hansen liked the look in their eyes even less than he liked the sight of the gun leveled at him. He froze.

"Major, safety that weapon and holster it," Hansen said. "You too, Millman. We have a dying man here. Get out of our way."

"I don't think so, Colonel," Wright said. "You are hereby placed under arrest. You will accompany me to the holding area at once."

"Major—"

"I said, *at once*, Colonel." Wright thumbed back the hammer. The gun remained pointed at Hansen's chest. "There are plenty of other people here who can transport this man to the infirmary. You do not need to be one of them."

Hansen lowered his burden to the deck and stood straight.

Nixon took an angry step forward. "You little motherfucker."

Wright swung the weapon in the security chief's direction. Nixon halted in his tracks. "Don't force me to place you under arrest as well, *Captain*."

Hansen saw Nixon's look from the corner of his eye. He shook his head. "Stand down, Nix. That's an order."

Nixon clenched and unclenched his hands. He swallowed hard. "Yes, sir."

Wright reached for his belt and withdrew a pair of manacles. He held them out with his free hand. "Dr. Millman, if you would?"

Millman stepped through the hatch. He reached for the manacles, hesitated, looked at Hansen.

"What the fuck are you waiting for?" Wright thundered. The irritation in his voice was evident to all present. "Take this man into custody at once."

Millman frowned and took the manacles. He approached Hansen.

Sanchez reached out suddenly with a trembling hand and grasped Hasegawa's arm. She screamed in surprise and pulled away from him.

She backpedaled until she hit the bulkhead. Sanchez was pulled to his feet and all but collapsed into her arms. Hansen heard the young man whisper something just before he kissed Hasegawa.

The doctor's body went rigid, as if she were on the receiving end of a powerful electric shock. She tried to scream, but the sound was muffled by Sanchez's kiss. Her fingers drove themselves into her palms with enough force to draw blood; it first spurted and then dripped from the small crescent moons she had carved into her flesh.

Hansen shouted "Doc!" and surged forward. He took three steps and launched himself at Sanchez.

"No!" Millman screamed. He leaped and tackled Hansen around his knees. Both men went down in a tangle of arms and legs. The impact knocked the breath from Hansen.

Sanchez ended the embrace. He staggered back and away from Hasegawa. He went down to one knee and then he collapsed to the deck. He lay on his back, as still as a corpse.

Hasegawa's knees buckled. She grabbed at the bulkhead for support. One hand went up and cradled the back of her head. She shook it, slowly at first but then fast enough Hansen thought she would give herself whiplash.

Nixon and McKnight rushed to her, but they stopped in their tracks when Millman shouted, "No, stay back! *Stay back!*" They looked at him, at Hasegawa, at each other.

Millman shifted his position atop Hansen and pinned the colonel's body to the deck. He turned and looked over his shoulder, at Wright. Armstrong's new commanding officer had not moved an inch since Sanchez's move on Hasegawa. His eyes were wide and frightened. "Shoot her, Major! Shoot her right now!"

Wright snapped out of it enough to look at Hansen. His eyes pleaded for an order. Hansen tried to speak, but he had yet to recover his breath; Millman's weight on his back made the effort even more difficult. He was able to shake his head, quite vigorously, but that was all.

"Wright, shoot her now or we all die!" Millman's voice was pregnant with terror and outright panic. His eyes drilled into Wright's.

Hasegawa took a lurching step away from the bulkhead. Her hair hung in her eyes. She moved like someone who had had far too much to drink. Her arms pin wheeled through the air as if she were warding off a swarm of insects. Hansen saw Nixon and McKnight retreat an equal distance. Hasegawa raised her head and fixed her eyes on Wright.

"Do it!" Millman screamed.

Hasegawa moved a bit more steadily and with more speed toward Wright.

Wright raised the gun and pulled the trigger.

Hansen tried to shout "No!" Later he would not be sure he managed to get the word out.

The bullet struck Hasegawa center mass. Her shirt puffed as if caught by a gust of wind. Blood flew from the wound and pattered on the deck. She staggered back against the bulkhead and hunched there. Her hands did not move to the wound, but she did look at it for a moment. Blood blossomed and turned her white shirt crimson. She gasped and looked at Wright. Her eyes were wild and full of fire. Her lips pulled back from her teeth. Blood trickled from the sides of her mouth. Her teeth were covered with it. She took a step away from the bulkhead.

Wright fired again. The bullet exploded through Hasegawa's throat and painted the bulkhead behind her red. She stepped back with the impact, looked at Wright again, then slowly slid down the bulkhead.

She came to rest in a seated position, head down and shoulders slumped. She took one last ragged breath and was still.

Nixon launched himself at Wright and managed to land a solid blow to the man's jaw. Wright squealed and went down. The gun flew from his hand and skidded across the deck. It stopped at McKnight's feet. He picked it up, looked questioningly at Hansen and then tossed it to Nixon. The security chief released the clip, checked it and slid it back home. He pulled the slide back, saw Hansen's eyes were on him and nodded.

He brought up the gun and leveled it at Millman. The doctor's hands went up immediately. He slowly released his grip on Hansen and stood. He kept his hands raised and said, "I'm the least of your worries."

"Keep your fucking mouth shut," Nixon growled. He nodded in McKnight's direction. "Don?"

McKnight covered the few steps to Millman and took the gun from the man's waistband. He stuffed it into his own and glared at the scientist. "Shoot her?" he said, and Hansen did not believe he had ever seen the man as angry as he was now. "Shoot her right now?" He showed his teeth and leaned in closer to Millman. "Open your mouth again and I promise you won't like what happens."

"Don," Hansen said and held up his hand. McKnight turned from Millman without a word and took Hansen's hand and helped him off the deck. "You cool?"

McKnight glared at Millman. His hands balled into fists, but he nodded. "Yeah, I'm cool." He reached behind him and pulled the gun from his waistband and handed it to Hansen. "But you'd better take this. I don't trust myself."

Hansen nodded and took it. "Good idea."

Mason and Mikhailov stood to the side, behind Hague. The pilot knelt beside Sanchez. Hansen needed only to see the look in Hague's eyes to know the boy was dead. The pilot did not produce tears, but his face was fallen and his shoulders slumped. One hand rested on Sanchez's suddenly-emaciated chest. Hansen was so taken aback by the state of the young man he looked again, more closely. Sanchez hadn't been the most muscular man Hansen had ever met, but the kid had had some meat on his bones. Now he more closely resembled the corpse they had found outside the starliner's bridge…and the ones in the infirmary.

Wright spat blood on the deck and rose to one knee. Nixon pushed him down again. "Stay right there, Major."

Wright looked up and glared at Nixon. Hansen hoped the man would come to his senses and remain on the deck. He trusted Nixon to obey his orders, but under the circumstances, he was not certain the older man would be able to restrain himself. Not after what Wright had just done.

Hansen afforded Nixon a quick nod of his head before he returned his attention to Millman. "No more bullshit. What the fuck is this?"

Millman licked his lips and rubbed his chin. Hansen swatted his hand away.

"What do you want from me?" Millman asked. His voice held a hint of honest bewilderment, almost as if his confusion was genuine. Almost.

"You're going to tell me what I want to know, or I swear to Christ I won't get in Nixon's way."

Millman's eyes darted to the security chief. Nixon must have presented a convincing sight. Hansen noted, not without some satisfaction, Millman suddenly paled. His mouth worked but nothing came out. Hansen shoved him into the bulkhead. He became aware of someone sobbing behind him, and he guessed it was Mikhailov. He did not take his eyes from Millman.

"Okay, okay." Millman licked his lips. "Your engineer is right. It's an alien life-form. Like nothing we've ever seen before."

"You don't say," McKnight said.

"What we think we know is it punched through the *Sovereign*'s hull and invaded the ship that way. It's been feeding on us ever since."

"Feeding on us," Narita repeated. His voice sounded dead to Hansen.

"It's small. No bigger than a grain of sand," Millman continued. "In fact, we think it's silicon-based."

"That would explain how the decon filters missed it," Narita said. "They didn't recognize it as a life-form."

"Yes," Millman said. He nodded in Narita's direction. Narita did not look at him. "It travels on the air currents. It can invade our bodies through any opening. Eyes, ears, mouth, whatever. It doesn't seem to have a preference." He looked directly at Hansen. "It needs us. We're its food supply. When it burns out the host body, it has to find another one soon or it dies." He swallowed. "That's what we think, anyway."

His voice gained momentum, as if he could not get the words out fast enough. "It jumps from body to body. We think it prefers to be alone when it transfers to a new host. That's what happened to Doyle. He was alone with the woman from the starliner. Then it transferred itself to your engineer when Doyle's body was no longer enough for it."

"Wait a minute," Mason said. He had recovered enough, apparently, to speak. "No one went missing after the incident in the holding area. And Sanchez wasn't there. How'd it find him? Is there more than one of these things?"

Hansen released his grip on Millman and took a few steps back. The scientist coughed again, straightened his clothes.

"We don't think so," Millman said. "As for the pilot, like I said, it travels on the air currents. It found him. He was in the wrong place at the wrong time."

"Wrong place at the wrong time," Hague said.

He launched himself at Millman and landed a blow against the scientist's jaw before anyone could stop him. Millman crumpled and began to slide down the bulkhead. Hague's next blow missed. His fist struck the bulkhead above Millman's head. The pilot howled with pain and backed away. He cradled his injured hand and breathed heavily. Mikhailov wiped tears from her eyes and put an arm around his shoulder.

"I'm sorry," Millman said from his seated position on the deck. "None of this was supposed to happen. We were to secure the specimen and return to Earth to study it. No one expected anything like this. How could we?"

"I've seen someone I know explode in front of me," Nixon said. He stood his ground next to Wright. The major glared at him but remained silent. The gun remained pointed at him. "Now I just saw this piece of shit shoot someone else. How the fuck does that happen?"

"As far as your engineer goes, the closest analog to anything we understand would be a feeding frenzy." Millman ran his fingers through his thinning hair. "That's this thing's last resort. It happened aboard the *Sovereign*, in the engine room. In that event, it takes as many people as it can all at once. It's akin to an addict who has gone too long without a fix." He nodded in Mikhailov's direction. "You smoke, right? How do you feel after you've gone too long without a cigarette? Multiply that by a factor of a thousand. That's what this thing feels."

Hansen's brow furrowed. "You're saying it's addicted to us?"

Millman nodded. "It displays that type of behavior, yes."

"Wait a minute." Narita held up a hand. "You made it inside the engine room?"

Millman swallowed and rubbed his jaw. "Not exactly. We got the blast door open, but there were quite a few corpses in the corridor. We couldn't get past them. We deduced what had happened by all the dust in the air. Like in the holding area, but much more. Made it almost impossible to see anything."

"Hold the fucking phone," McKnight said. "Sanchez wasn't in the holding area when this thing exploded out of Duncan. Why did it take him and not someone who was there?"

"Someone activated the ventilation system," Millman said and rose slowly to his feet. He looked as if he expected Hague to lunge at him again, but the pilot was paying more attention to his wounded hand. "Sucked it right out of the room and probably saved someone's life." He grimaced and nodded at Sanchez. "But not his."

Hansen stepped toward Millman and grabbed the man's arm. Millman winced and shrunk back against the bulkhead. "Is it over now? Is that why you had Wright kill Hasegawa?"

"Based on everything we know about this life-form, it's possible the threat has been eliminated. The host was killed before it could infect anyone else. But as far as being certain about this…I, I don't know, Colonel." At the look from both Hansen and Nixon, he quickly added, "I'm not any happier about that than you are. I assure you."

Hansen took a few steps away from Millman.

"What are we gonna do, Mike?" McKnight asked after a moment.

Hansen turned and faced everyone. "We're getting the fuck out of here, that's what." He strode to the intercom and hit the button with much more force than was required. "All hands, this is Hansen. We are evacuating Armstrong. I repeat, we are evacuating Armstrong. Report to hanger two on the double." He closed the channel without awaiting a reply.

Millman had regained his feet. "Ms. Dwyer will have something to say about this, Colonel." There was no malice in his tone. He simply stated a fact as he saw it.

"She can say all she wants as soon as we're off this base."

Hansen started for the hatch but stopped when Nixon called after him.

"What about Wright?" Nixon asked.

Hansen regarded his former executive officer. "Bring him. No one gets left behind just in case Millman's wrong." Hansen disappeared through the hatch.

Nixon nudged Wright with his boot. The major looked up at him, eyes filled with contempt. "This is your lucky day," Nixon said with a smile. He kicked the manacles. They skidded across the deck with an unpleasant sound and stopped a meter in front of Wright. He lowered his voice. "You give me any excuse at all…" He watched Wright eye the dusty silver bracelets and smiled to himself.

****

Dwyer glared at the monitor. She watched Wright, properly cuffed, step through the hatch. Nixon followed him out and the security office was empty. Save for the two corpses on the deck. Dwyer's eyes lingered on the bodies for only a moment before she turned off the monitor with a disgusted grunt.

He thinks he's leaving, she thought. *And with Millman and Wright out of the picture, he will most likely succeed.* She thought perhaps she might still be able to stop some of the base personnel from evacuating Armstrong, but not all.

Hague was a company man, and not stupid. One word from her and he would never fly in space again. She was certain he was aware of that particular fact. The two geologists and the engineer's assistant were spineless, in her professional opinion. They would follow the orders of whoever was in charge. And that most certainly was not Hansen. The company shrink would not present a problem, either. Dwyer was willing to bet anyone who took this assignment was out of options on Earth. A bad report would effectively end her career. She would find herself back to listening to middle-aged men whine about their lack of sexual prowess or to housewives who cried about the lack of appreciation they received from their husbands. Dwyer was certain this was something of which she would be aware. So Mikhailov would not resist, either.

That left Nixon and McKnight. She knew she would have problems with them. They were clearly more loyal to Hansen than to the company which signed their checks. McKnight meant nothing. He was a pilot, and she already had one of those in Hague. But Nixon was the security chief, and could be an asset, *if* she could break him of his slavish devotion to Hansen. She was not sure it was possible.

Not that it mattered, because she could not allow them to leave. They were too important to her mission. All of them, if she allowed herself to be honest. The situation had deteriorated since her arrival, through no fault of her own, of course. But she was keenly aware it could get much worse. If (*when*) it did, she would need them. It was simple arithmetic.

No. They could not evacuate. She would have to see to that immediately.

She reactivated the monitor and made a call.

Chapter 9

Aim for Earth

Hansen, McKnight and Millman approached the hatch to hanger two. Hansen was not surprised to find Thorpe standing outside the hatch. The geologist noted their approach with a wave and a smile. He met them a few meters in front of the hatch.

The man's expression darkened immediately. "Colonel, Dwyer is in there waiting for you. She said we're not going anywhere."

Hansen nodded and looked back at Millman. He watched the scientist intently, but the man seemed beaten. His eyes never met Hansen's. His feet shuffled on the deck.

"I bet she did," Hansen said. He opened the hatch and stepped through.

Hanger two was of the same size and design as hanger one. Armstrong's second transport, four-two-one, sat on the elevator. Hansen could not remember the last time she had flown, but he guessed it had been a while. McKnight had assured him there would be no trouble launching the transport, and Hansen believed him. *Well, no* mechanical *trouble*, Hansen thought when he got his first look at Dwyer.

She stood next to the hatch which led to the hanger's control room. Her arms were folded across her chest. Her shoulders were squared, her chin, up. She greeted Hansen with a look that could come close to melting steel.

"We are not abandoning this facility, Mr. Hansen," she said. Ice formed on each word. "Now take these men back inside and consider yourself confined to quarters for the duration. Am I making myself clear?"

McKnight snorted but Hansen held up a hand and the pilot fell silent. "Ms. Dwyer, we are indeed evacuating this facility." His voice was level, neutral, perhaps even pleasant. "The order has been given. Please accompany us aboard the transport."

"I will do no such thing," Dwyer said. Her voice rose in volume. It echoed off the bulkheads and filled the hanger. "You do not give the orders here anymore, *Mr*. Hansen. Major Wright is the current commanding officer of this facility. Where is he?"

"On his way to hanger one," Millman said. He looked at Dwyer but only for a moment.

"Divide and conquer?" Dwyer asked. "Is that it? At least one of your groups gets away?" Her words dripped venom.

"No, necessity," Hansen said. His voice remained neutral. "There are too many of us for a single transport to carry."

"For now," McKnight added.

Hansen ignored him. "We're *all* leaving, Ms. Dwyer. If you'll please follow us to the transport, we can be on our way."

Dwyer looked past him, into the eyes of Millman and Thorpe. Millman looked away immediately. Thorpe held her gaze, but only for a moment. He, too, found something else to study while the scene played out between her and Hansen.

"You men are in direct violation of so many regulations, I don't know where to begin. But I promise you, if you return to your duties immediately, I shall do my best to forget this incident ever took place."

Millman shuffled his feet some more. Thorpe looked everywhere but in her direction. McKnight smiled. Hansen did not react at all.

Dwyer took a few steps forward until she stood nearly nose to nose with Hansen. "You have absolutely no idea who you're fucking with."

Hansen silently applauded her apparent self-control. She had lowered her voice, although not enough so the others could not hear her.

"Ms. Dwyer, we are leaving now. You are welcome to join us. But once we lift off, you'll be stuck here alone. I strongly advise you to come with us."

Dwyer stepped back to her original position. She moved a step to her left, out of their path.

Hansen nodded. "Very well." He held her gaze. "Don, set the controls for manual liftoff and disable remote access."

"Roger that," McKnight said. He disappeared into the control room.

"Let's go," Hansen said. His eyes remained fixed on Dwyer until he moved past her.

****

Hague slid into the pilot's seat of transport one-one-three-eight. He pressed buttons and flipped switches. The panel in front of him came to life. Indicator lights flashed and several small monitors activated. One of the monitors displayed an image of the interior of the passenger area. He saw Nixon strap Wright to his seat. Mikhailov and Mason likewise strapped themselves in. They did so quietly and without conversation. Narita walked past the monitor. After a moment, he entered the cockpit. He took the co-pilot's seat.

Hague thought for a moment about the previous resident of that seat. The kid who knew his way around a transport, despite being fresh out of training. The kid who had looked out the windows and marveled at the starscape and the details of the lunar surface. The kid who had blanched at the prospect of landing the transport on his first flight. The kid who would never see Earth again, or his family. Hague swallowed, returning his attention to the controls.

"All secured back there," Narita said. He inclined his head at the monitor that showed the passenger area. "Hanger one is depressurized. Landing pad controls set for manual liftoff."

"Roger," Hague said. "Diagnostic on all systems nearly complete. Standing by."

Hague watched the indicator lights intently. One after another winked out red and came back on green. He acknowledged each with a curt nod of his head.

"Online with landing pad controls. At your command," Narita said. His hand hovered above the switch that would activate the elevator and open the landing pad in the hanger's ceiling.

The last indicator light went green. Hague nodded. "Hit it."
Narita did so.

There was a slight jolt as the elevator activated. The floor of the hanger fell away from the windows. There was no sensation of movement, although the view told them the elevator ascended. The landing pad opened slowly, the sound of its electric motors inaudible in the near-vacuum. A few moments after that, they got their first look at the moonscape. C-ring continued its curve in either direction away from them. B-ring loomed in the distance, and it made Hague think of Duncan. He clenched his jaw.

The elevator stopped. The transport sat exposed on the moon's surface. Hague sat back in the seat for a moment. He hit the comm button. "McKnight, you there?"

After a moment, "Roger that, Hague."

"We're sitting on the pad and good to go. Standing by for you."

"Activating the elevator right now."

Hague looked again at the people in the passenger area behind the cockpit. "Is Dwyer with you?"

The reply was immediate. "Negative."

Hague frowned. She had decided to stay. He knew if anyone else had elected to remain on Armstrong, McKnight would have told him. That meant Dwyer would be alone. *Well, perhaps not* completely *alone…*

Hague took the controls in his hands as he had a hundred times before. "Stand by on ventral rockets," he said. "As soon as they're ready, we're out of here."

"On it," Narita said.

Out of the corner of his eye, Hague saw the young engineer fix his gaze on B-ring. Hague did not need to be psychic to know Narita was thinking of Duncan. How many hours had they spent in B-ring, ensuring the continued smooth operations of the facility? They had joked with each other as they worked, Hague was positive. Duncan had had a wonderful sense of humor, and he did not doubt for one moment she had shared that with her young assistant. *I miss her too, kid*, he thought. *More than you know.*

"We're green across the board here, Hague," McKnight said from the speakers. "Good to go."

"Input the return trajectory," Hague said.

Narita pulled himself away from the ghosts of B-ring and nodded his head. "Acknowledged."

Hague waited, perhaps impatiently, for Narita to complete the task. He wanted more than anything to lift off and put as much distance as possible between himself and Armstrong. His fingers tapped the control yoke, and his feet kept time with them.

"Having a problem here," Narita said.

"What kind of problem?" There was an edge to his voice, an edge he should have kept dulled. It wasn't Narita's fault he had gone into engineering instead of becoming a pilot. Hague chastised himself immediately. "What is it?"

"I don't know. I'm getting nothing from the nav computer." He flipped a couple switches again and again.

"Let me in there," Hague said. He reached across Narita as the young engineer sat back in his seat. Hague flipped the same two switches Narita had played with. He received the same result. "That's impossible," he said to no one in particular. He returned to his own controls. After a few futile moments of hitting buttons and flipping more switches, Hague sat back in the pilot's seat.

"It's dead, isn't it?" Narita asked.

Hague shook his head. His brow was furrowed. "No, it isn't. That's the problem." He reached for the comm button again. "McKnight, you there?"

There was a tense moment when only silence came from the speakers. Then, "Roger that. I was just going to call you."

"We have a problem here," Hague said. "We're getting *nada* from the nav computer. And I mean *nada*. All trajectories gone. Even the flight log is blank."

"We're having the same problem here," McKnight said.

"What does that mean?" Narita asked. There was a twinge of fear in his voice. Hague could not blame him.

"It means we can't liftoff. We can't go anywhere." Hague dropped his other hand from the control yoke and sat all the way back in his seat. He looked sideways at Narita. "We're stuck."

****

Nixon exploded into the main control room. He saw Dwyer seated at one of the main stations. The woman looked up at his arrival, and she treated him to a smile. Nixon walked quickly and purposefully toward her. Behind him, Mikhailov, Mason and Narita entered the room. By the time Nixon had reached her, Hague and Wright entered, the latter still manacled.

Dwyer swiveled her chair to face him. Nixon grabbed her by her suit vest and hauled her to her feet. Dwyer squealed. Her hands locked themselves on Nixon's wrists. "You *bitch!*" Nixon roared. He shook her, taking some subconscious satisfaction in the way her feet dangled inches above the deck. "What did you do, huh? What *the fuck* did you do?"

His eyes drilled into hers. The vein in his forehead bulged, and his face was red with rage. Sweat had begun to bead on his short salt-and-pepper hair. He might have noticed, with some pleasure, the fear he saw in her eyes, had he not been so enraged. In truth, he noticed no reaction from her at all. It made him angrier, if such a thing were possible. "Answer me, goddamn you."

"Let her go, Nix."

Nixon turned and saw Hansen enter the room. Thorpe and Millman followed him in. Hansen moved quickly to Nixon's side. "I said, let her go."

Nixon looked into Hansen's eyes. He saw his own anger reflected back at him. Hanson simply had greater self-control than Nixon. Nixon turned again to Dwyer and realized for the first time he had gotten through her armor. She was back to the scared little girl from the holding area. He let go of her.

Dwyer nearly did not get her feet under her in time. She stumbled, but did not fall. She steadied herself on the control console. Nixon backed away, but only a few steps. Dwyer straightened her vest and blouse, took a breath and looked at Hansen.

"Despite his anger, Mr. Nixon asked a valid question," Hansen said. "What the fuck did you do?"

She steeled herself, and Nixon saw the familiar arrogance return to Dwyer's eyes and posture. He took an angry step in her direction. Hansen must have anticipated that, because he extended an arm in front of Nixon. The security chief stopped in his tracks and stared daggers at the woman.

"I told you you wouldn't be leaving," Dwyer said. She took a few steps back, away from Nixon, as if she did not trust the former commanding officer to restrain his man. "Didn't I say that? You wouldn't believe me."

Nixon watched Hansen's back arch. His fists clenched and unclenched. The man was close to losing his cool. Nixon doubted the colonel would actually snap. But if it happened, Nixon hoped he was there to see it. He could think of nothing he'd rather see at that moment than for Dwyer to get her ass handed to her, with extreme prejudice. With a deep breath, Hansen seemed to regain his composure. Nixon did not know whether to be proud of the man or disappointed.

"The question stands, Ms. Dwyer," Hansen said. The sharp edge in his voice could not be missed. "And I won't ask it again."

Nixon spared a glance at the others in the control room. Most stood silent and unmoving. They watched the exchange with a kind of grim fascination. Mikhailov paced and smoked. She was the only one among them not rooted to the deck.

"I called GSA corporate and told them you were planning a facility-wide evacuation against orders," Dwyer said. Nixon detected a hint of smug satisfaction in her tone. It made him want to hit her. Repeatedly.

"I knew they would stop you from leaving, although I confess I did not know how. Navigation computers wiped. Nice touch."

"How'd they do it?" Hansen asked.

"The *Galileo* Space Station," Hague said. He sat at the medical monitoring station. "It's the only thing that could broadcast a database wipe from a distance." He shrugged. "The GSA could easily bounce a jamming signal off the station and direct it here. That has to be it."

Dwyer smiled at him, returned her gaze to Hansen. "Mr. Hague is correct."

"How do we fix it?" Nixon asked. "There has to be a way."

"We can download the database again," Narita said. "The software is resilient enough, that's not the problem." He stood next to Mason and Thorpe, arms crossed and appearing quite depressed. "The problem is the only way we can download the charts again is through the *Galileo* Station."

"He's right," Hague added.

Nixon gave a sharp bark that was intended as a laugh. It sounded far from it, even to his own ears. He put his hands on his hips and turned away from Hansen and Dwyer. "I don't believe this."

"What about the other transport? Seven-seven-zero?" Mason asked. "Have we checked that one?"

Hansen nodded. "McKnight is checking it as we speak."

"He won't like what he finds, Hansen," Dwyer said. Her tone was nearly malice-free. "The wipe signal enveloped the entire base. All transports were affected. And before you bother debating the idea, you can forget about the *Sovereign of the Stars*. Like I said, it affected the entire base."

"Like you could pay me to go aboard that death ship," Mason said under his breath.

"Why can't we just take off without it?" Mikhailov asked. She stamped out her cigarette on the deck, lit a fresh one. "We can aim for Earth once we're off the lunar surface. For Christ's sake, it's a *planet*. Kind of hard to miss. No?"

"It's not that simple," Hague said. He snatched the cigarette from Mikhailov's hand as she walked by. He puffed on it and thought. "Even if we could 'aim for Earth', as you put it, we would have no idea of our approach angle. Too shallow, we bounce off the atmosphere. Too steep, we burn up on reentry. We don't have the fuel to keep trying. We'd get two or maybe three attempts at most. Then we'd be dead in space. Without the nav computer, the odds of hitting just the right entry angle are about three thousand to one."

"They'd have to come pick us up," Mikhailov said. "They wouldn't just let us drift away."

Hague shot her a look that mirrored Nixon's. Mikhailov lowered her head.

Hansen turned back to Dwyer. "Call them. Call them and tell them to restore the nav computers in the transports."

"No," Dwyer said.

Nixon surged forward. This time, Hansen had to place his body between the security chief and the GSA executive. Nixon clawed at the empty air. Dwyer took a surprised step back. She looked at Nixon with genuine fear in her eyes. Nixon took no pleasure from her reaction. He was certain the only way he would feel pleasure now was with his hands wrapped around Dwyer's throat. Nothing less would do. He realized he had left the two handguns inside the transport, a fact for which he would eventually be grateful. He thought he might use them if they were still stuffed into his waistband.

"That's enough, Captain," Hansen shouted. He continued to struggle against Nixon's strength and momentum. "I said, *that's enough*."

The words cut through Nixon as he backed away. He glared at Dwyer, but his posture softened somewhat when he locked eyes with Hansen. "Sorry, Mike. I'm cool."

"I know you are," Hansen said. "Stay that way."

Nixon licked his lips. "Roger that."

"Watch your dog, Mr. Hansen," Dwyer said. She had not regained total control of herself, but she was close. Nixon could see her attempts to mask the fear she evidenced a moment before.

Hansen's lips compressed into a single, thin line. "Ms. Dwyer, perhaps you don't understand. This alien life-form, or whatever it is, may still be here and free to move about the base. It can invade any one of us at any time, including you. We're just trying to survive this."

"Of course you are."

Christ, could her tone be any more condescending? Nixon thought.

"If I were in your position, I might even be doing the same things. But I am not in your position, am I? I have my orders, Mr. Hansen. They supersede yours. It's that simple. We stay. We capture this alien life-form, and we study it. True, it'll be more difficult with only one xenobiologist instead of three, but we'll make do. When we've learned all we can from it, we will return to Earth."

She took a deep breath. "Now, release Major Wright immediately. He is the commanding officer of this facility. Mr. Hansen, I will allow you free roam of the base. But I warn you, if you attempt to interfere with this mission, you will be placed under arrest immediately." Her eyes swept the room. "That goes for all of you. Major Wright, join me in your office at your earliest convenience, please. You, as well, Dr. Millman."

Nixon watched her make her way toward Hansen's office. She disappeared through the hatch. Wright stopped in front of him and held his hands up. The manacles gleamed in the overhead lights. Nixon glared at him.

Chapter 10

Creative Engineering

Hansen sat at the forward control console. Save for Narita, everyone else had vacated the room. Most likely they had headed to the Gemini. Hansen could not blame them. He himself could use a drink or three. He was tired, as well. He saw the exhaustion he felt in the movements of his personnel. They were just as wiped out as he was. He hoped they wouldn't overdo it in the Gemini. He trusted Nix, if no one else, to keep it together. The security chief would see to it no one got too out of control.

McKnight had joined the others after his report to Hansen. As Dwyer had promised, the base's primary shuttle had been spiked, as well. He did not know if Dwyer spoke the truth about the *Sovereign of the Stars*, but he had already decided not to attempt that course of action. Not publicly, anyway. He thought he could slip away, perhaps after he got some rack time, and check the *Sovereign*'s nav computer. If it worked, proving Dwyer had bluffed, great. He'd get everyone aboard the starliner, whether they liked it or not. But he suspected Dwyer had not bluffed. The transmitter aboard the *Galileo* Station was certainly powerful enough to hit the nav computers of all three transports and the starliner. He agreed with Hague's assessment of their chances of returning to Earth without a working nav computer. It seemed they were stuck until Dwyer got her trophy. Assuming the fucking thing was still around. He held out hope the threat had ended when Hasegawa slid down the bulkhead.

Hansen yawned, despite his efforts to repress it. He saw Narita out of the corner of his eye, and he knew the young engineer had seen it. Hansen shrugged.

"I have this, Colonel. Why don't you get some sleep? I'll call you if anything happens."

Hansen nodded and yawned again. The kid was right; he was dog-tired. "Very well." Hansen stood, stretched his legs. "Thanks."

"You're welcome," Narita called after him.

But Hansen was already halfway to the hatch.

****

"To Sanchez!" Hague shouted.

The five others in the Gemini echoed the toast. Everyone emptied their glass in one gulp. Nixon coughed, felt the bile rise in his throat and forced it back down with nothing more than willpower. He slammed his glass on the bar. Everyone else mimicked him. Mikhailov upended the bottle of scotch over each glass until they were all filled again. She tossed the empty bottle into the refuse bin.

"Who's next?" Hague asked.

"To Kehoe!" Mikhailov shouted.

"To Kehoe!" the others replied. They emptied their glasses again and slammed them onto the bar.

Nixon felt good, better than he had since the arrival of the starliner. The alcohol felt warm in his belly. The warmth spread throughout his body, even finding its way into his fingers and toes. He knew he shouldn't have had so much to drink, knew Hansen would count on him to make sure the crew maintained at least a semblance of control. That went by the boards after the third shot (Duncan's). Nixon found he could not regret his inappropriateness too much. After everything they had gone through, the crew needed a drink. Or ten.

He watched Hague stumble to the table with the chessboard. He tried to sit, missed the seat and landed hard on the deck. After a moment of confusion, during which he surely wondered how he had come to be on the deck, he pulled himself onto the chair. He banged his empty glass on the tabletop. Some of the chess pieces skipped about, but surprisingly, none toppled. "You're checkmated in two moves, Hague," he said. He tried to adapt Duncan's Irish accent, failed. Mikhailov laughed and joined him. She had a bottle of clear liquid in her hands. She topped off his glass, then poured one for herself.

Mason's head rested on the bar. Nixon could not tell if the geologist was conscious or not. Thorpe and McKnight sat to either side of the man and carried on a conversation as if Mason was not there. In point of fact, they did not seem to notice the man at all.

Nixon took a step toward the hatch, stumbled a bit and braced himself on the bar. He had had enough. The last thing he wanted was for Hansen to enter the room and find him in his present state. He wasn't drunk, not exactly, but he was close enough. Better to retire for the night and sleep it off. He considered ordering everyone to their respective quarters. Ultimately, he decided against it. He was not entirely certain he could get the words out in a coherent manner.

Best to hit the bunk. Been up too damned long as it is.

Nixon made for the hatch. Fortunately, his quarters were not far. In surprisingly short time, he reached the hatch to his quarters and inputted the code. The hatch slid open. He had one foot inside when he heard footfalls from down the corridor. He hesitated long enough to see Hansen round the bend in the corridor. The man looked tired, as tired as Nixon felt. He nodded to Hansen, who nodded back. Nixon stepped through the hatch and closed it behind him. A few moments later he was in his bunk. A moment after that, he was sound asleep.

****

Hansen awoke a full seven hours later. He squinted at the chronometer next to the bunk. 1107 hours. He was thankful all the chronometers on the base were set to military time. Otherwise, he would have had no idea if it was late-morning or late at night. He had experienced that sort of time-disconnect only once before, on the day he arrived at Armstrong. He had no desire for a repeat of that confusion.

He kicked off the covers and swung his feet onto the deck. He felt better, he had to admit. More alert, more alive. He even took a moment to enjoy the cold deck beneath his bare feet. He took a deep breath, held it, released it. He had managed to make it through the night without the intercom calling for his attention. He was thankful for that. He hoped everyone else had likewise had an uneventful night.

He stood and stretched and eyed the door to the head. "Shower," he said to the empty room. He knew he'd have a full day of dealing with Dwyer and her new watchdog, Wright. A shower and a hot cup of joe would go a long way in assisting him through it.

A few moments later he was in the shower. The hot water felt good on his skin and served to bring him fully back to the land of the living. In his younger days, he would joke that he did all his best thinking in the bath. This once, it turned out to be true. His eyes flew open as the plan blossomed in his head, fully grown and begging to be implemented at once.

Hansen cut short his time in the shower. He needed Narita. He needed him *now*.

****

Hague stirred and tried to lift his head from the pillow. He instantly regretted the movement. His head felt as if it weighed a metric ton. He felt slightly nauseated, although, given the manner in which the night ended for him, he could not complain. He knew he had asked for a hangover, and it was no surprise to him he had received one. He'd deal with it in his usual manner. Said manner consisted of lots and lots of coffee and cigarettes.

He opened his eyes and saw the woman sleeping next to him. Mikhailov was still out like a light. Perfectly understandable. She might have had even more to drink at the Gemini than anyone else, Hague included. Add to that she hadn't bothered to eat anything before the festivities began. And she didn't weigh shit, either. He thought perhaps it would be a few hours yet before Mikhailov awoke. He did not envy her that moment.

Nothing had happened between them. He had been content to escort her to her quarters and call it a night. She had asked him to stay. It went unspoken that sex was not an option. They were both exhausted and quite drunk. And there was the matter of the severe bruising on her neck. (He still had a hard time believing Duncan had been responsible for that, even knowing she had not been herself when the assault occurred.) Had they both been stone-sober, he doubted anything would have happened anyway. Rumor was she had developed quite a thing for Nixon. He didn't understand her fascination with a man who was old enough to be her father, but then again, it was hardly his business. He would have liked her just as much had they never shared a bed. She was simply…his kind of people.

He tried to lift his head again, but he felt dizzy and did not want to chance crashing to the deck. He groaned. Mikhailov stirred but did not wake. Hague rubbed his eyes.

Without meaning to, he thought of Sanchez. He remembered how his first impression of the kid had been so off-base. At the mission briefing, Sanchez had sat there silently. He took notes and nodded in all the right places. He had appeared studious and very by-the-book. Hague had rolled his eyes and convinced himself the outbound flight would be tedious, at best. He could not have been more wrong. Once the transport had left Earth's atmosphere, the child inside Sanchez took over. He marveled at the brightness of the stars. Their flyby of the *Galileo* Space Station had produced a look of awe from the kid. He opened up to Hague quite quickly. Two hours after leaving Earth behind, they were laughing and joking. Hague knew he had misjudged the boy. The balance of the trip was perhaps the most enjoyable time Hague had spent in space.

And now the kid was dead. He would never marry, never have children of his own. Never get to do a lot of things. That included—

"Jesus!" He sat bolt upright in the bunk. He grimaced and clutched his head with both hands. He thought for a moment his head would explode. It did not. The inside of his eyelids put on a fireworks display that rivaled the one he had attended in New York City on New Year's Eve a few years back. He groaned loudly and forgot for a moment about the woman next to him. It took a few moments for the pain to relent and for the fireworks to subside. Once he felt stabilized, he threw off the covers and stood on the deck. His knees wobbled, but he kept his feet under him. His head still pounded, and the pain was intense, but it had begun to subside. He reached for his trousers and pulled them on.

He needed coffee. He needed a cigarette. But mostly he needed to find Hansen. He bolted from Mikhailov's quarters half-dressed and slightly off-balance. The woman in the bunk remained blissfully asleep.

Moon Dust

****

"Captain Nixon, this is Major Wright. Respond."

The voice penetrated through the fog. Nixon groaned loudly and rolled onto his side. Blindly, he reached out and fumbled for the intercom switch. It took him a moment, during which he knocked his chronometer off the nightstand. It clattered on the deck. The sound reverberated inside his head. "Fuck," he said. His hand traveled up the bulkhead until he found the intercom. He flipped the switch. "Nixon here."

Wright spoke immediately and in clipped tones. All business. The tone climbed up Nixon's spine and set up shop in his brainstem. He would have given anything to get it out of there.

"I need you to bring Dr. Hasegawa's body to the infirmary for analysis. Immediately, Captain. Dr. Millman will meet you there. Copy."

Emotionless prick, Nixon thought. It wasn't as if Hasegawa had been a stranger to Wright. He had known her for the past several months. They had even shared a drink or two at the Gemini. Nixon had witnessed the scene himself. It stuck with him specifically because it seemed so odd at the time. But the man's voice, monotone and matter-of-fact, grated on Nixon's nerves. The shop inside his brainstem flung open its doors for business.

"Copy," Nixon said. He closed the channel before Wright could say more.

He rolled onto his back and exhaled loudly. He was somewhat surprised to remember they had indeed left Hasegawa's body inside the security office. Everything had happened so quickly after that. He had had other things to deal with at the time, most notably Wright. But that

151

did not excuse him from simply forgetting about the dead woman they had left behind. She had been his friend, as well. Nixon chided himself for it.

He did not relish the idea of spending time alone with the corpse. It wasn't that he was squeamish or fearful. There was nothing to fear from a corpse, after all. He simply did not want to see what Wright's marksmanship had done to a woman he had known. He liked even less the idea of turning her over to Millman for dissection. But it seemed he had no choice in the matter.

Nixon climbed out of his bunk and entered the head.

****

Hansen controlled his pace through the corridors of A-ring. He wanted to run, but he did not want to draw attention to himself. The worst thing that could happen was for Dwyer or Wright to see him moving with obvious purpose. That would invite suspicion, perhaps questions he had no wish to answer. He was not nearly a good enough liar to assuage their suspicions. So he walked, calmly and nonchalantly.

He reached the hatch to Narita's quarters. He sounded the chime and waited. After a few moments, he hit it again. *He couldn't possibly still be on monitor duty*, he thought. *The kid has energy, but he's not superhuman. He has to sleep sometime.* He sounded the chime a third time. Still no reply. Hansen started for the main control room.

The hatch behind him opened and Narita poked his head into the corridor. His eyes were lidded, his hair a mess. He squinted against the bright lights of the corridor. "Colonel?" His voice was rough, the voice of a man who had just been woken against his wishes. Hansen felt pity for the engineer, but only for a moment. He walked back to the hatch, pushed Narita through and stepped into the room. He closed the hatch behind him.

The room was dark, and it took a moment for Hansen's eyes to adjust. Narita stood in front of him, unsteady and still half-asleep. The young man even yawned, adding a groan at the end for good measure.

"Narita, I need you to hack into the GSA mainframe. Think you can do that?"

Narita blinked away the sleep and focused on Hansen as if for the first time. "What?"

"The GSA mainframe," Hansen repeated. "Can you do it?"

Narita collapsed into the chair behind him and rubbed his eyes. "What's this all about?"

Still groggy, Hansen thought. He couldn't blame him. "Can you do it? I need to know."

Narita fell silent. He closed his eyes and swayed side to side. After a few moments, during which Hansen was certain he had fallen back asleep, Narita opened his eyes. He looked at Hansen. "I think so. Probably. Maybe. I might be able to get in through the *Galileo* Station. Piggyback the signal they're transmitting to us and get in that way. Why am I doing this?"

Hansen activated the ceiling lights. Narita winced at the bright light and shielded his eyes. "They uploaded all their information directly to the GSA, remember? When they were working on Doyle and that woman from the *Sovereign*. We need to know what they found."

"They already told us. Didn't they?"

Hansen shook his head. "They didn't tell us everything. We're on a need-to-know basis, and we *need* to know. So the question stands. Can you do it?"

Narita rubbed his eyes again. Then he looked at Hansen and smiled. "I think so. It won't be easy. And I assume you don't want Dwyer to know about this."

"You assume correctly," Hansen said. He nearly laughed. Nearly.

Narita nodded. "I'll use the uplink controls in the mainframe room. No one ever goes in there, and I'll need the privacy."

"Do what you can, and report to me immediately if you gain access. This is between us, so don't tell anyone else. And stay off the intercom. Understood?"

"Understood."

Hansen placed a reassuring hand on the man's shoulder, nodded his acknowledgment and left the room.

He made it all of five steps from the hatch when he saw Hague walking toward him. The pilot's eyes lit up when he saw Hansen. He wrestled his arm through his shirt sleeve, and still struggled with it when he came to a stop in front of Hansen.

It was clear the man was hung-over. His disheveled appearance was almost an artist's exaggerated drawing of a man after a night of drinking. His longer-than-regulation, more-salt-than-pepper hair was wild, his eyes more so. Hansen realized Hague was attempting to put on his shirt backwards. He decided not to correct him. He clearly had something important to say.

"Colonel," Hague began, "I might have a way out of this."

Hansen raised an eyebrow. Despite the pilot's appearance, his eyes were clear and focused. "Tell me."

Hague told him.

****

Nixon stood in the center of the security office and fumed. It was the first time he had seen his office since the deaths of Sanchez and Hasegawa. It surprised him how much he hated the room. He had never given it a second thought before now. It was his work area, and he had accepted it and performed his duties and that was that. Until he had watched a friend take two bullets and collapse.

It angered him, enraged him, that Wright had been so willing to pull the trigger. He did not know if the decision had been a difficult one for the major to make, but he doubted it. Wright was a creature of rules and regulations, and in the absence of Dwyer, his world was under the command of Millman. And Millman had given the order to kill Hasegawa. And now he had been ordered to deliver her body to the man who had ordered her killed. But it was not this knowledge that caused his hands to quiver with rage. It was Hasegawa's body. More specifically, its absence.

The spot on the floor that had previously been occupied by Hasegawa's body was bare. There was no question it was the correct spot; her blood stained the bulkhead and was smeared where she had slid down to the deck. More blood had congealed where her body came to rest in its sitting position where Nixon had last seen her. A single set of footprints tracked blood nearly to the hatch. Nixon stared at them and clenched his fist.

Sanchez remained where he fell. Nixon was aghast at the state of the young man's corpse. The hours had added years, perhaps decades, to the corpse's appearance. His clothing was wrapped tightly around the skeletal frame. His mouth remained opened, his lips pursed in the kiss he had given Hasegawa. His eyes had receded into his skull, and much of his hair had fallen out and littered the deck around his head. His skin looked as old as the Dead Sea Scrolls.

Nixon's eyes traveled back to the spot last occupied by Hasegawa.

Millman had not waited for him. He had probably come here himself, surely complaining about Nixon's lack of professionalism in disobeying a direct order from Wright. It wasn't that Nixon cared what Millman thought (or Wright, either, for that matter). He disliked the idea of the little bastard handling Hasegawa. He would not be gentle or respectful, Nixon was sure. He would treat her as a lab experiment. Had he simply dragged the corpse from the room and down the corridor to the infirmary? It was probably precisely what he had done. The skinny fuck wouldn't have the upper body strength to lift and carry her, Nixon was certain. That thought made him angry.

He moved to the intercom, but his hand stopped a few inches away. No. He wouldn't call Millman. This was something Nixon wanted to say in person.   Nixon left the security office and made for the infirmary.

It would not occur to him until much later that he had missed something obvious in the security office. By the time he realized his error, he was running for his life.

****

Hansen entered the mainframe room in B-ring. McKnight, Thorpe and Mason followed him inside. The room was darker than Hansen had anticipated, but not so dark he could not see. The giant computer that ran all the base's systems occupied the center of the room. It stretched from deck to ceiling. Most of its panels contained lights and small read-out screens. A single operator's chair stood at the main interface control panel. Ancillary banks of computers lined two more bulkheads. All flashed lights in various sequences; some added an occasional chirp. An old-fashioned clipboard hung from a stud on the bulkhead next to the entry hatch. The print-out on the clipboard was covered with Duncan's scrawl. They would be status reports and maintenance logs Hansen could not bring himself to read at the moment. Duncan's death was too fresh for him; the last thing he wanted to do was read her handwritten reports and think of the fate of the woman who wrote them. He looked away from the clipboard.

Narita manned the main control console. He worked the controls with practiced ease. He looked up when the hatch opened, then he returned to his work. The new arrivals joined him. "Report," Hansen said without preamble.

Narita did not look up from the controls. "I'm in. But this isn't easy. All files relating to the *Sovereign of the Stars* and Armstrong Base have been encrypted. I'm having a hell of a time trying to get through their security." He finally looked at Hansen. "I'm sorry, Colonel. I don't think I can do this."

"Why would they encrypt the files?" Mason asked. "That makes no sense."

"It makes all the sense in the world," McKnight said. "Think about it. They don't want anyone back home to know what's happening up here. If this thing goes south, they can make up any story they like."

"It's already gone south," Narita replied.

"Yeah, but wouldn't the news services have already picked up on the *Sovereign* landing here?" This from Thorpe. "All those super-wealthy passengers have super-wealthy friends back home. Super-wealthy *influential* friends, I might add. They can't cover this up."

"And what about us?" Mason asked. "We know what's happened, even if we don't have the whole story. How do they know someone from Armstrong won't go to the media with this once we're back home?"

Hansen sighed. "Because we're not going back home."

Four pairs of eyes turned to him.

"I thought maybe they'd restore the data to the nav computers after Dwyer signaled them. But if they're keeping everything about this under wraps, it stands to reason they'll want it to stay that way." He eyed each man in turn. "That means one way or the other, we're staying here."

"But that would include Dwyer and Millman," Thorpe protested. "It's not like they could leave and stop us from joining them on the transport. Is the GSA really going to write off their own senior vice-president?"

"Off-hand, I'd say yes," McKnight said.

Thorpe swore and turned away from the others.

"I don't believe it," Mason added.

"Believe it," McKnight replied.

The hatch opened and Hague and Mikhailov stepped into the room. Several sighs of relief told Hansen the men around him were relieved it hadn't been Dwyer and Wright instead. Mikhailov looked tired. Dark circles had blossomed beneath her eyes. She walked slowly. *Lack of sleep and a little too much drinking last night*, Hansen thought. He'd had a night or two like that in his time, and given the circumstances, he could hardly fault her. But he needed her alert, as he needed everyone else.

Hague closed the hatch behind him as they joined the others at the interface station. Hague settled Mikhailov against the bulkhead. She looked at the men in the room, then she placed her hand on the back of her neck and rubbed.

"You okay, Galina?" McKnight asked.

"I'll live," she said. Her voice was weak but she managed a smile.

"Glad to hear it," McKnight replied.

"Everybody listen up." Hansen nodded at Hague. "Okay. Tell them."

Hague cleared his throat. "We know we can't liftoff because the nav computer in each transport has been wiped. The cast-iron bitch said they also took out the nav computer on the *Sovereign*."

"They did," Narita confirmed. He worked the buttons on his console until an image appeared on the monitor. Armstrong Base was represented as a computer generated three-dimensional image. The image was accurate to the last detail; the *Sovereign of the Stars* sat atop landing pad three. As Narita worked the controls, what appeared to be blue snow fell from the stars and blanketed the base. "That's the signal that spiked the nav computers," Narita continued. "As you can see, it affects the starliner, as well. And gentleman…and lady,"—he nodded at Mikhailov—"it's still active. So even if we could somehow recover the data or download it again, we'd lose it again just as fast. They made sure we can't leave."

"They left us here to die," Mikhailov said. Her voice was marginally above a whisper.

"Yes, they did," Hague said, "but we may have a way around that." He took a deep breath. "Narita, you're sure this jamming signal of theirs is confined to Armstrong?"

"Positive."

"So what?" Mason asked. "It's not like there's another base around here."

Hague broke into a grin. "True enough. But there's something else. They forgot about the *Daedalus*."

"What?" McKnight's voice was even, but it was clear he believed he had misheard Hague.

"The *Daedalus*," Mason said. His tone was identical to McKnight's.

"Yes, the *Daedalus*. Think about it. It's sitting out there, what, thirty-five kilometers from here? That's outside the jamming signal."

"Who gives a shit?" McKnight asked. "What are you saying? We repair a wreck that's been sitting there for how long?"

"Seventy years," Narita said.

"Seventy years," McKnight repeated. He turned to Hague. "What the fuck are you smoking? And can I have some?"

Hague held up both hands. "I don't want to repair her. We couldn't anyway, even if we had an army of engineers. But we might be able to salvage their nav computer."

"What makes you think it's still there?" Thorpe asked. "That ship was salvaged, no?"

"No," Hansen said. "They never performed any salvage on the ship. They recovered the bodies of the crew, but they left everything else in place. And why not? Who was going to steal anything? It's not like just anyone could even reach the wreck, let alone help themselves to the equipment."

"Does that even matter?" Mason asked. "I mean, what are you suggesting? That we go out there, find the nav computer and download the flight data? That won't mean anything. As soon as we get close enough to Armstrong the jamming signal will simply wipe it away again. Then we're back to square one."

Hague nodded his agreement. "That's true. *If* we download the data. But what if we take the nav computer's core?"

"I'm sorry, I don't understand," Mikhailov said. "What difference does it make how the data is stored? This fucking wipe signal will still do its job, won't it?"

"It might not," Narita said. He stood and walked slowly about the room. His eyes darted about. "The *Daedalus* is an *Olympus*-class spacecraft. They still used magnetic memory cards back then. The signal from the *Galileo* Station isn't keyed to affect those."

McKnight's eyes widened and he nodded. "That technology is obsolete. It hasn't been used in decades."

"Precisely." Hague smiled broadly. "We can grab the nav computer's core and hook it into one of the transports."

"Wait, I'm confused." Mason scratched an itch on the top of his head. "He just said the technology is obsolete."

Hague nodded his agreement. "It's a dinosaur, yes."

"Then are the transport's systems compatible with that antique?" There was hope in Mason's tone, but it was guarded.

Narita continued to pace about the room. "It'll take some creative engineering, but I think we can do it. Our best bet is transport four-two-one. It's the oldest and most likely to be compatible with the old nav core." He stopped his pacing and looked at Hague. "That new transport won't cut it this time, sorry."

Hague waved off the apology and clapped his hands together. His smile widened even further. "As long as we can get out of here, who cares?"

Hansen nodded his agreement. "Okay, here's how it's going to go down. Narita, you and Hague take one of the LSTs and go out there. Don't do any sightseeing. Grab the computer core if you can and hightail it back here on the double."

"Roger that," Hague said.

Narita stopped his pacing and regarded Hansen. "We'll go as fast as we can, Colonel. Figure ninety minutes travel time, at least that long to salvage the core, and another ninety minutes back. Assuming, of course, the nav computer is still there and functional."

"Let's hope," Hansen said.

"Sounds like a plan. You ready?" Hague asked Narita.

The engineer nodded. "Let's go."

They exited the mainframe room.

Hansen turned to everyone. "Go about your duties. Try not to draw attention to yourselves. Act depressed."

"That won't be a stretch," Thorpe said.

"You got that right," Mikhailov said. She rubbed her neck and swallowed. The bruises had begun to fade, but she was still clearly in pain. She caught Hansen's eyes and managed a very weak smile.

"Get to it," Hansen said. As they reached the hatch, he added, "No one stays alone. We need to keep an eye on each other. Remember, this thing might still be out there." They nodded wordlessly and filed out of the room. McKnight got as far as the hatch before he turned and looked in Hansen's direction. "What is it, Don?"

"Hague's plan, Mike." McKnight licked his lips. "Let's assume for a minute it works and we get four-two-one ready for flight. We'll only be able to take six people, total. We might be able to push it to seven, but after that, the environmental systems won't be able to compensate. So even if this plan works, not everyone is going home."

"I know," Hansen said. "I've thought of that. We'll worry about that when the time comes."

"*If* the time comes."

Hansen found he had no reply.

Chapter 11

The Dead Behemoth

Nixon reached the infirmary. The windows were still opaque. He could barely make out the shadow he assumed to be Millman on the other side of the glass. He strode to the hatch control and inputted his code. The hatch did not open. Nixon swore and pounded his fist on the hatch once. The silhouette inside the infirmary looked up and made its way to the hatch. A moment later it swung open to reveal Millman.

Nixon caught a glimpse of the infirmary over the scientist's shoulder. He saw the desiccated bodies of Doyle and Kehoe laid out on exam tables. Another body too far away for him to identify had taken up residence on one of the last two tables. A fourth corpse lay on the deck, placed inside a black plastic body bag. Nixon wondered briefly who it was before he decided it did not matter. Not unless it was Hasegawa. He returned his attention to Millman.

"You couldn't wait for me," he said by way of preamble. "If I find you were rough with her, I won't be happy. Am I making myself absolutely fucking clear, Doctor? She was a friend, and I'll be damned if you're going to treat her like a lab experiment."

Millman cocked his head to one side and regarded Nixon with a puzzled expression. "What the hell are you talking about? And where's Hasegawa's body?"

"In there," Nixon replied. "On one of those tables."

Millman licked his lips. "Umm, no, it isn't. I've been here waiting for you to bring her to me for the last twenty minutes."

"What are you talking about?" Nixon muscled his way past Millman and his objections and entered the infirmary. He stopped just inside the room. The body on the other side of the infirmary belonged to Sullivan. Even from his position Nixon could see the corpse's chest had been spread open and held that way by some of Hasegawa's surgical instruments. Sullivan's arms remained outstretched, as if he were about to hug someone who floated invisible above the table.

Nixon turned his eyes to the body bag. "Finished with her already?" He treated Millman to a furious glare before he knelt beside the body bag and zipped it open. Sofia Nelson stared blankly at him. The top of her head had been removed and then reset. He caught a clear glimpse of the thin red line that traced a path around the skull and just beneath her hairline. Nixon grimaced and resealed the bag.

He looked at Millman and regained his feet. "Where is she?"

"I've been trying to tell you, Captain. She's not here. I didn't do anything with her." He swallowed. "Yet."

Nixon glared at him. He seemed to be telling the truth. *Or he's an accomplished liar*, he thought. He got to his feet and regarded Millman. "She's not in the security office, and she's not here. You didn't take her and neither did I. So what happened to her body? She sure as shit didn't get up and walk away herself."

Millman swallowed nervously and looked away. Nixon's eyes narrowed and he looked closely at the scientist. He had been present when Duncan died. He had also been there when Sanchez purchased the plantation. Both times, Nixon had seen him and his reaction. He had been surprised, perhaps even fascinated, but he had always kept his scientist's cool. If nothing else, the man conducted himself professionally, Nixon had to admit. Those *were* two of his buddies spread out behind him, after all. But this was different. Millman appeared frightened.

"What is it?" Nixon's brow furrowed. He was genuinely curious.

Millman recovered quickly. His professional demeanor reared back up quickly enough that Nixon thought perhaps the quick expression of fear had been in his imagination. The man stuttered once or twice before he was able to speak. "Thank you, Captain. I must return to my work. If you'll excuse me, please." He extended an arm in the direction of the hatch.

"What was that?"

"Nothing," Millman said. This time, the lie was transparent. "Nothing at all."

Nixon allowed himself to be led toward the hatch. He stepped through and turned again toward Millman. The scientist closed the hatch. Nixon heard the lock engage from the other side. *What the hell just happened?* Whatever it had been caught Nixon completely off-guard. It was even enough to make him temporarily forget about Hasegawa. He had been too surprised by Millman's reaction.

He needed to find Hansen. He needed to find him *now*.

****

He watched through the glass as Nixon's silhouette disappeared down the corridor. Once he was certain the security chief had departed the area, Millman let out a deep breath and leaned against the bulkhead. He regarded the corpses that shared the room with him. He licked his lips. Could they have been so wrong? The answer seemed to be a resounding *YES*. If that was true, they were all in much deeper trouble than anyone believed.

She sure as shit didn't get up and walk away by herself.

In point of fact, Millman believed that was *precisely* what had happened. He looked again at the body bag on the deck. He watched it intently for some moments. Then he turned his eyes to the other three corpses in the room. Before Nixon had blundered onto what could be the truth, Millman had seen them simply as dead animal matter. Now they looked different, *quite* different, in fact.

He pulled his eyes away from them and hit the intercom switch.

****

Dwyer awoke with a start. She sat bolt-upright in her bunk with a startled grunt. Her hand went to her chest. Her heart pounded. The sound of the blood in her ears was deafening. It took a few moments for her to steady her breathing, during which she looked about her quarters. Dark and empty. She was alone.

She did not remember the dream, could not recall even the vaguest detail. She knew, however, it had been a nightmare. A *bad* one. She felt tightness in her chest and reached for the inhaler on her nightstand. She took two pulls from it, replaced it.

She had kept its presence from everyone. It was a needless effort on her part, and she knew it. The knowledge that she had asthma would hardly damage her authority, but she disliked any sign of weakness. She tolerated it in her underlings, for such was their nature. She could not tolerate it in herself, however. No one, not even Cromwell, knew about it. Only her doctor, whom she had threatened most effectively, knew of her condition. Her *weakness*. Dwyer gulped in more air and got out of her bunk.

She was almost to the head when the intercom chirped. She swore into the empty room. It would either be Millman or Wright, she knew. *Christ on a crutch, can't anyone do anything on their own on this fucking base?* She retraced her steps and hit the intercom switch. "What is it?"

"It's Millman, ma'am. We might have a serious problem."

Dwyer shook her head in disgust. "Is that so, Doctor?" She did not bother to hide her contempt. "What is it?"

Moon Dust

****

Narita pulled on his helmet and watched Hague do the same. They stood inside the garage in C-ring. Four Lunar Surface Transports sat parked and ready near the rear bulkhead. They resembled the dune buggies Narita had seen in action in the Nevada desert when he went there with some classmates during Spring Break. They consisted mainly of a chassis and two seats, with some storage space added behind the seats and a roll cage, which surrounded the passengers.

The garage itself was large, nearly half the size of the three transport hangers. It had been built to accommodate a dozen LSTs, but since no need had been evidenced for more than four such vehicles, the GSA had decided against transporting more to Armstrong. That decision gave the garage the appearance of wasted space. The thick bulkheads were solid concrete and nearly a half-meter thick. Three large tool chests occupied the room. He had spent some time inside the garage, mostly when the maintenance schedule told him it was time to check the LSTs.

Duncan had hated working there. She complained of the cold, and she insisted the atmospheric pressure was off. Narita felt she simply did not like spending time in the room. He suspected he even knew the reason. It was somewhat unnerving to think that on the other side of the massive door was the vacuum of the moon's surface. The deck, bulkheads and ceiling were concrete; the door was titanium alloy and thin. Despite the environmental controls, Narita always felt colder near the door. He suspected Duncan noticed it as well and had made up her mind to avoid the garage as much as possible. She had placed him in charge of vehicle maintenance simply so she could avoid it. He paused a moment and pushed thoughts of Duncan from his head. This wasn't the time.

"We good to go?"

Narita saw Hague take the driver's seat of LST I. He secured his helmet, nodded and scooped his toolkit from the deck. "Yeah, let's do this." He climbed into the passenger seat and secured himself. He placed the toolkit at his feet.

Hague activated the controls. The LST hummed to life as the instrument panel lit up. The lights on the top of the vehicle began to flash and spin. They painted yellow beams on the bulkheads and the garage door. "Decompressing garage now," Hague said. They could hear the rush of escaping air. A moment later, they were in vacuum.

The garage door shuddered and began its slow disappearing act into the bulkhead. Light spilled into the room, bright enough to cause the men to drop the shields on their faceplates. The lunar surface spread out before them. It appeared white in the sunlight, as if a blizzard had recently come through the area.

A hundred meters from the garage, the hills began. Beyond them, mountains. At the base of the closest mountain was a wrecked ship that had lain in the lunar dust for nearly three-quarters of a century. It was the excursion of a lifetime, something everyone on Armstrong thought about at one time or another. Narita was no exception. He had even discussed with Duncan what they would be likely to discover if they ever made it to the wreck. Even people who had never been to the moon dreamed of what it would be like to walk the corridors of the *Daedalus*. Now all Narita wanted was the goddamned nav computer. To hell with the rest of the ship.

"Here we go," Hague said. He leaned forward on the controls, jolting the LST to life. In moments they were outside Armstrong. Narita hit the switch that closed the garage door.

Ninety-three minutes later, they would reach the *Daedalus*.

****

The light on the security station in the main control room began to flash. Hansen deactivated it immediately and sat back in the seat. No need for Dwyer and Wright to know someone had gone outside. He resisted the urge to put Narita and Hague on the main monitor, as much as he wanted to keep an eye on their progress. It wouldn't do for Dwyer and Wright to enter the con and see that. No, that would not do at all.

Hansen turned at the sound of approaching footsteps, saw Nixon enter the main control room. One look at the security chief told Hansen the man had something important on his mind. He stood from the chair and waited for Nixon.

"They lost Hasegawa's body, Mike," Nixon said while still halfway across the room. His arms gesticulated, a clear sign of his frustration. "Millman claims he doesn't have her. She isn't in the security office. So what did they do with her?" He stopped in front of Hansen and stood with his hands on his hips.

"Calm down, Nix," Hansen said, raising his hands. "What are you talking about?"

Nixon took a deep breath. "I was supposed to bring Hasegawa's body to the infirmary, but I was late. When I got there, she was gone. I checked with Millman, and he didn't have her, either. Or, at least, he says he doesn't have her."

"You think he's lying." It was not a question.

"I'm not sure," Nixon said. He looked away. "That was my first thought, but now I don't know. I have a pretty good ear for bullshit, Mike, you know that. I don't think he was lying. But if he's telling the truth, then where is she?"

Hansen's eyes went briefly to the hatch to Wright's office. Just as quickly he turned them away. It was too late. Nixon saw him.

He turned and pointed at the hatch. "You think that little weasel had something to do with it?"

There was unmistakable anger in his voice. Nixon had never cared much for Wright, Hansen knew. The man was too beholden to rules and regulations for Nixon's taste. For Hansen's, too, but he would never let on about it. Nixon had confided in him once or twice before about the major's insistence on proper procedure and how it irritated most everyone on Armstrong. Given the events of the past few days, Nixon's aggravation with Wright had reached an all-time high. And Hansen had just added to it. He cursed himself for being so obvious.

"No. No, I'm sure he didn't. And Nix, he's in charge here now, like it or not. So don't call him a weasel. At least, not out loud. Clear?"

Nixon clenched and unclenched his jaw. His eyes remained hard, unforgiving. "Yes, sir. But Mike, we have to find her."

Hansen nodded. "Agreed. But I can't help you. Major Wright put me on monitor duty. I'm stuck here until Mason relieves me at 1600 hours."

"Then I'll do it alone," Nixon said.

"Nix, wait," Hansen said. He knew Nixon had not been informed of their plan. It might help calm him if he thought they had a chance to evacuate Armstrong, despite Dwyer and the GSA's attempts to stop them.

Nixon turned but made it only a few steps toward the hatch before Wright stepped out of his office. Wright seemed surprised to see him. He stopped and regarded Nixon with a cold eye.

"Captain Nixon, please accompany me to the infirmary."

"I'm a little busy," Nixon said.

"It wasn't a request."

Nixon started to protest, remembered the man at his back. "I just came from—" He swallowed hard and squared his shoulders. "Yes, sir."

Nixon crossed the room and disappeared through the hatch. Wright remained for a moment. He treated Hansen to a cold stare and then followed the security chief out of the room.

Hansen was once again alone in the main control room. He cursed Wright's ability to arrive at just the wrong moment. He had been this close to letting Nix in on their plan. He'd need to get word to the security chief, and soon. He did not know how much longer the man would allow himself to be led around by Wright. An act of open mutiny would help no one, least of all Nixon, who would likely find accommodations in the holding area. Hansen hoped he would not have to see his friend in a cell.

He cursed silently and hoped Nixon's common sense would hold back his temper, if only for a little longer.

****

Nixon did not wait for Wright. His stride was quick and steady. He did not look back, but heard Wright rushing to catch up to him. He took some small satisfaction in making the overbearing little prick move just a bit faster. It took a few moments for Wright to match Nixon's stride, during which they had nearly reached the infirmary. Finally, Nixon said, "What's this about?"

"Ms. Dwyer has requested our presence in the infirmary, Captain. Now you know as much as I do."

Don't insult me, Nixon thought. He nearly said it, but in the end, Hansen was correct. Wright was in charge, like it or not. And Nixon most assuredly did *not* like it. But he would be no good to anyone sitting in a holding cell on a charge of insubordination. He did not doubt for a moment Wright would place him under arrest, even given the present circumstances. They walked the rest of the way in silence.

They reached the infirmary. Nixon could make out two silhouettes through the opaque glass. Wright inputted his code into the security panel and the hatch opened. Nixon could see the second person in the room was Dwyer. She was speaking to Millman in hushed tones. She looked up briefly when the hatch opened. Millman looked, as well. In the split-second they made eye contact, Nixon saw that same look of fear he had seen in the scientist's eyes during their earlier conversation.

Wright stepped through, stopped and turned. His hand went up. "Remain on guard out here," he said.

Nixon started to protest, but Wright closed the hatch before he could get a word out. Nixon put his back to the hatch and kicked it. "Damnit," he said to the empty corridor. He ran his hands through his short hair and resisted the urge to pull some out.

****

Narita had seen the wreck of the *Daedalus* only once before. When he first arrived at Armstrong and Hague had flown over the crash site to afford his passengers a look at the legendary wreck. It was the closest he had ever been to the vessel. Through the shield on his faceplate, he could see her much more closely now, and in greater detail. Their LST plodded through the moon dust at a steady pace. Hague negotiated around boulders and avoided ditches until the old wreck loomed ahead of them. A fortuitous outcropping of rock blocked them from the sunlight. Narita immediately raised the shield on his faceplate and took in the sleek lines of the ship.

Her steel hull had gleamed silver once, he was certain. In her prime, she had probably appeared much like the *Sovereign of the Stars*. Her single engine port was enormous, large enough that Hague could have driven the LST straight inside and parked it there. It was pitted and scarred, and a three meter section of the cone was torn away and missing. The aft hull was heavily damaged, as if punched by a giant. The main fuselage was likewise pitted, and Narita counted no fewer than five small breaches in the hull.

Hague steered around pieces of debris. They drove through a patch of the lunar surface that was smooth and recessed to a depth of perhaps sixty centimeters. "The rescue craft landed here," Hague said. "We're in their footprint." He took one hand away from the controls and pointed. "Ten-man rescue team. You can see some of their footprints in the dust."

In point of fact, Narita could see those footprints. He wondered what sights had greeted the men when they entered the wreck. They must have known their chance of finding survivors was almost nil. If the interior of the ship had been exposed to vacuum, and it appeared very likely it had, it would not have been a pretty sight.

The LST moved slowly along the starboard hull. Nearly scraped away by the rough landing and partially covered by moon dust, Narita could just make out the letters along the hull: *DAEDALUS*.

A chill worked its way up his spine. He was mere meters away from the most famous wreck in human history. Despite the reason for his being there, he took a moment to allow the little kid inside him to marvel at the wreck. How many people had dreamed of being in this precise spot, about to enter the ship that had become the subject of so many books and documentaries? *They can have it*, he thought. *The price of coming out here is too fucking high.* The moment passed quickly and he was back to business.

Hague stopped the LST twenty meters from the boarding hatch. The ship had come to rest against the side of the mountain. Its nose had penetrated perhaps fifteen meters into the ancient rock. The hatch had nearly been buried in the avalanche. Perhaps it had been, and the rescue team cleared the way. Loose rocks and a few boulders the size of the LST littered the lunar surface around the hatch. It was wide open, left that way for seventy years.

Narita unhooked his seat restraint and stepped out of the LST. His feet hit the surface and sent little clouds of dust swirling about. He reached into the back of the LST and removed his tool kit. He noticed the shaking in his hand, and clenched it into a fist. The shaking obediently stopped. He slung the tool kit over his shoulder and took another look at the dead behemoth in front of him.

"You ready, Narita?" Hague stood on the opposite side of the LST and looked at him.

Narita nodded. "Ready."

They set off in tandem for the *Daedalus*.

****

Nixon leaned against the hatch to the infirmary and listened. He could hear the voices from within the room. Unfortunately, due to the thickness of the hatch and the sound-deadening qualities of the alloys used in the construction of the bulkheads, he could not understand what was being said. He found he could not even recognize the speaker. At times someone would raise their voice slightly (he guessed that was Dwyer), but he was unable to understand anything. The discussion, which at times sounded more like an argument, continued for some time.

The discussion ceased suddenly. Nixon smartly pulled away from the hatch. He resumed his position against the bulkhead as the hatch opened. Dwyer stepped into the corridor. Nixon studied her expression. Her face was red, her breathing noticeably elevated. She glanced in his direction but said nothing. She stepped away from the hatch, and Wright exited the room. He looked squarely at Nixon.

"Captain Nixon, you will remain on station here. That will be all." He started down the corridor after Dwyer.

"What? Wait a minute. What the hell am I standing around here for?"

Wright stopped, turned. "You have your orders, Captain. Carry them out." He disappeared around a bend in the corridor without another word.

Nixon stared down the corridor for several moments. He wanted nothing more than to find Hasegawa's body. To stand around outside the infirmary, with no explanation as to why, increased his frustration and made his vision swim.

"Fuck!" he shouted into the corridor. He pounded his fist against the hatch. On the other side of the opaque glass, Millman looked up, but only for a moment. The scientist resumed his work. Nixon began to pace.

****

Mason looked at the chronometer on the bulkhead in the geology lab. The red LEDs read 1307. He knew he had to relieve Hansen in a few hours. That gave him plenty of time. He sat at his workstation and watched the scanner readings on the small monitor in front of him. Across the room, Thorpe was likewise engaged in their first bit of honest geological study since the arrival of the starliner.

Mason was occupied with a core sample he had taken from a spot on the north ridge, several kilometers from Armstrong. The sample had sat in the stasis bank for several days, as had everything else he and Thorpe had carted back to the base. When his partner had suggested they return to their work, Mason had laughed. They would be leaving Armstrong soon enough, he had argued. What was the point of continuing their studies? But Thorpe had been insistent, and Mason had long ago learned the futility of arguing with him. So he followed his partner to their lab and got to work.

"Think they'll let us take these samples back to Earth?" He knew the answer before he asked. He simply wanted some conversation, anything to break up the monotony of the readings on the monitor.

"No," Thorpe replied. "I mean, if there wasn't a weight limit on the transport, maybe. But we're gonna be jammed in there pretty good, I would think. We won't have the room to bring anything with us."

"Guess you're right," Mason replied. Of course he was right. He suspected Thorpe knew he had asked a question to which he knew the answer. Thorpe had replied anyway. He was just that kind of guy. Not for the first time (but, as it turned out, for the last) Mason was happy to be able to work with someone like Thorpe. He'd been paired up with some winners in his time, but Thorpe was the real deal. He had never gone out of his way to poke fun at Mason. He had, in fact, done quite the opposite, time and again. He had stuck up for Mason a few times after Wright's arrival on Armstrong, when the new executive officer had singled out Mason as the weak link in the science department. Thorpe had even seen to it that Mikhailov scheduled a session or two with Mason just so the man could vent to someone other than his fellow geologist. Sometimes all it took was someone new to listen to one's problems to make a person feel better. The sessions had done Mason some good, he had to admit. It had also given him a crush on

Mikhailov, which he was willing to bet was not an isolated event in the psychologist's career.

He smiled to himself and returned his attention to the monitor.

"I need a short break," Thorpe said. "Think I'll go to the Gemini and see what's left to steal. Want me to bring anything back for you?"

"I'll go," Mason said. "You've done enough. What do you want?"

Thorpe considered for a moment. "Coffee. And see if there are any sandwiches left."

Mason smiled. "Absolutely. Be right back." Thorpe nodded as Mason exited the lab.

A few steps outside the room, Mason decided he could use something a little stronger than coffee. The activities of the previous night had put a serious dent in the Gemini's supply of alcohol, but he thought he'd be able to find something acceptable. He didn't consider until he had already crossed into A-ring that Wright would not take kindly to alcohol being removed from the Gemini. It was well-known the executive officer (*commanding* officer, Mason corrected himself) was no fan of alcohol being available on the base. He had accepted its presence grudgingly. Without Hansen to overrule him, it was not outside the realm of possibility Wright would lock all the alcohol in the storage room. And if he happened to look at his monitor at the wrong moment and see Mason roaming the corridors with a bottle or two in his hands…

Mason quickened his pace.

He found the hatch to the Gemini closed. He tried it anyway and was relieved when it opened easily. He stepped inside the room and activated the ceiling lights.

The room always looked different in full light. It appeared dirty, the kind of place you would expect to find along the wharves of a nineteenth century harbor. If he could tune out the soft hum of the generators and the base's power grid, he could almost see the men who would populate such a place three centuries past.

He found no sandwiches in the refrigerated cabinet. Two empty plates were adorned with incriminating crumbs, but the food itself was not in evidence. He settled on a box of doughnuts. Thorpe would just have to deal with it.

A coffee pot sat on the small stove at the far end of the bar. Mason leaned over it and inhaled through his nose. Armstrong's coffee was not the greatest by any stretch of the imagination, and the current pot smelled even less so. He poured two cups anyway and placed them on the bar.

A few bottles lay on the deck, empty and forgotten. He strode behind the bar. There was still a large enough selection of bottles to choose from. The first few he picked up were cognac and some type of malt liquor with which he was unfamiliar. The third bottle was bourbon, as was the fourth. Good. It was nice to have choices.

He placed both bottles on a tray and rounded up the two coffee cups and the doughnuts. He walked out from behind the bar and stopped at the threshold. He took one last look at the Gemini and then deactivated the ceiling lights. The room once again resumed its familiar darkness. In the corner, the pinball machine continued to flash its lights. Mason had never been able to beat Narita's high score, and he had a good idea he would not have another chance to try again. Not if their plan worked.

He turned from the room and managed one step down the corridor and back toward B-ring when he ran, quite literally, into Hasegawa.

Chapter 12

The Final Voyage of the Daedalus

Narita took his first step aboard the *Daedalus*. Under any other circumstances, it would have felt like a momentous event, the kind of thing one would brag about to friends and family. It did not. It was dark, too dark to see even his hand in front of his faceplate. He activated his flashlight and got his first look at the ship he had first heard of when he was seven years-old. The bulkheads were slate-gray and covered with a thin layer of dust. A dark strip of dead lights ran through the center of both bulkheads. Narita knew when they had last been lit seven decades previous, they had flashed red. The flashes would have told the crew that the ship was in serious trouble. Narita had the feeling they had not need the flashing red lights to know that particular bit of information.

Dust was piled high on either side of the hatch. Handprints were visible where the rescue team had pushed it away from the hatchway. It made perfect sense; if the hatch had sprung open on impact, the opening would likely have been blocked. A strip of ancient carpet ran along the center of the grated deck. It appeared to have been yellow-gold at one time. Footprints of dust led away from the hatch in both directions. He saw a sign on the bulkhead a few meters away. He approached it and shined his flashlight beam on it. **C-3**, it read. Beneath the letters was an image of an elevator with □ next to it. Narita shined his light in the indicated direction. The corridor ended fifty meters away at a set of double doors. On the port bulkhead to the side of the elevator doors was an open hatchway.

"We'll be taking the ladders," Hague said from behind him.

Narita jumped a bit.

Hague laughed. "Sorry."

"Forget it," Narita said.

Hague led the way toward the open hatchway. "We're on C-deck. Two decks down from the bridge. That's where we're going."

"Right behind you," Narita replied.

Moon dust jumped up a few inches from the carpet with each footfall. It reminded him of the interiors of the *Sovereign.* He put that thought out of his head and concentrated on the sound of his suit's respirator. His breathing was slow and steady. It was a reminder of why they had come out to the wreck. Had he been allowed to see the *Daedalus* in a less-than-drastic situation, his breathing would have been fast and excited.

They reached the ladder. It ran through both the deck and the ceiling. He flashed his light beam down. The ladder descended into darkness. He caught a glimpse of what he assumed to be D-deck, the lowest level of the ship. The engine room would be down there, as well as various machine shops; nothing with which they needed to be concerned. Hague started up the ladder. Narita allowed the pilot to get a few rungs up before he began his own ascent.

Hague stopped at the entry point to B-deck. He said something too softly for Narita's helmet speakers to make out. "What is it?"

Hague did not respond at first. He maintained his position on the ladder. After another moment, he resumed his ascent. "Two bodies. Guess the recovery team didn't find all the remains, after all."

Narita swallowed and followed Hague. When he reached the landing, he shined his light into the corridor. Ancient power cables hung down from the ceiling. A pipe had broken, most likely during the crash, and lay on the deck in two sections. Frozen water had welded the broken ends to the deck. Two bodies lay no more than five meters away. The man had apparently attempted to shield the woman from the collapsed pipe and he had paid for his protective act with his life.

Ice clung to his hair and his uniform shirt. The woman's face was burned. Her mouth was open in a perpetual, silent scream. Narita's light beam found the exploded panel on the bulkhead that had claimed her. If not for their injuries, they might have been asleep. The bodies showed no signs of decay; the vacuum had preserved them for all time.

"How did they miss these two?" Narita asked. "The rescue team had to have come this way."

"Never mind," Hague said. "Let's just get what we came here for and get the fuck off this ship."

Narita nodded silently. He let his flashlight beam linger on the corpses a moment longer and then he continued his ascent up the ladder.

He was nearly to A-deck when he heard Hague whistle through his teeth. Narita did not ask the question this time. He knew why the man had whistled. When he pulled himself onto A-deck, he saw he had guessed correctly.

Three more bodies lay sprawled on the deck. They appeared much the same as the two below, minus the trauma. One of them, a man in an officer's uniform, had died with his hands on his throat. His mouth was open, his eyes bulged.

"The vacuum got them," Hague said without emotion.

"This doesn't make sense. I remember reading that the rescue team successfully recovered all the bodies from the wreck. It was in my seventh grade history book, for Christ's sake."

"That would mean the GSA lied. And they wouldn't do *that* now, would they?"

"But what about the families? They would know."

Hague nodded. "They would also probably be paid to keep their mouths shut. Or threatened. Does it really matter?"

"I guess not. But then why send a rescue team at all? It's too expensive a mission to do just for publicity. And we know they were here." He indicated the footprints of dust that led in both directions of the corridor.

"They must have been after something else." Hague shined his flashlight on the sign on the bulkhead in front of the ladder. It read:

Bridge

Authorized Personnel Only

Another sign next to this one indicated the crew's quarters were in the opposite direction. "Come on, let's get this over with." Hague started in the direction of the bridge.

Narita followed.

****

Thorpe pulled his eyes away from his monitor and rubbed them. He glanced at the chronometer next to his workstation. 1345. He had lost track of time. He had allowed himself to temporarily forget what was happening on Armstrong and had instead concentrated on the rock samples he had collected during his last trip outside the base. It was not that he had made an important discovery. He found he relished the idea of simply getting back to his job. But he had indulged himself for too long.

And where the hell was Mason? It wasn't as if the Gemini was on the other side of the base. Had he run into someone there and forgotten about his partner? That was possible, but unlikely. Mason might appear absent-minded to some, but Thorpe knew better. Perhaps he had run afoul of Wright? The man's disdain for the crew's alcohol consumption was well-known. It was easy to imagine Mason walking out of the Gemini with a bottle or two, only to see Wright standing in front of him, arms crossed and a scowl on his face. What would happen then? Thorpe did not know, but he could not discount the possibility Mason had been confined to his quarters. Or, even worse, the holding area. It was certainly not beyond a bastard like Wright to do something like that.

Thorpe left the lab. A few meters into the corridor his walk became a jog. He could not rid himself of the image of Mason sitting inside a holding cell. Not that there was much he could do if that was indeed Mason's location. He couldn't go to Hansen; the colonel no longer had the authority. Wright would not listen. Dwyer was out of the question. Could he release Mason on his own? Not without the code to release the locks. Normally, that was Nixon's area. But Thorpe did not delude himself into thinking the security chief had that authority any longer. He knew who was running the show. And even if he could somehow get Mason out of the cell, doing so would only earn him a place next to his partner when Wright found out what he had done.

He made his way across the connecting corridor between B- and A-rings. He slowed his pace when he heard voices in the corridor ahead of him. He rounded the turn and saw the voices belonged to McKnight and Mikhailov. They turned at the sound of his approach. McKnight was back to his normal self but Mikhailov looked as if she were still recovering from the night before.

"Hey," Thorpe said.

"Thorpe," McKnight nodded.

"What's up?" Mikhailov asked.

"Have you two seen Mason? He was supposed to go to the Gemini, but that was a while ago."

"No, we haven't," Mikhailov said. McKnight nodded his agreement.

"Shit. I have to find him." He resumed his jog.

"We'll join you," McKnight said. He took Mikhailov by the hand and led her after Thorpe. "No one should be wandering alone, anyway."

Thorpe could not argue with the pilot's reasoning. It had been Hansen's order, anyway. He nearly stopped when he considered the possibility that Mason had been taken by whatever had killed Duncan and Hasegawa. It hadn't occurred to him until that moment. He prayed he was wrong. He'd rather see the man in a holding cell, if it came down to it.

Thorpe quickened his pace. McKnight and Mikhailov needed to run to keep up with him.

****

The bridge of the *Daedalus* had taken heavy damage, presumably when the ship impacted the lunar surface. Power cables hung from the ceiling. Two of the control consoles had exploded. Charred pieces of their once-state-of-the-art technology lay scattered about the blackened deck plates. The front windows were cracked, but appeared to have remained in one piece. They told Narita the interior pressure had equalized rapidly enough that the thick, tempered glass hadn't had time to shatter.

Three bodies occupied the bridge. A man lay on the deck next to one of the destroyed consoles. He had landed on his side, and he remained that way. Narita was fine with that. He could see signs the front of the man's body had been burned badly. Narita had no desire to get a better look at him.

A woman's body sat strapped into her seat at one of the intact consoles. Her head was thrown back, her arms hung at her side. An emergency respirator hung from the overhead compartment above her. It would have made no difference even had she survived long enough to use it. The shifting pressure inside the ship would have killed her in seconds.

The man's body in the center seat belonged to the captain. Narita knew not just from the stripes on the man's uniform, but from his appearance. He was familiar with Captain Matsui, as was anyone who had studied the *Daedalus*. The man appeared almost as he had in the many books Narita had read about the disaster. The vacuum had preserved him, as well. Narita reached out a hand to touch him, but pulled it back at the last moment.

"Narita, over here."

He turned and saw Hague standing over an undamaged workstation. Narita made his way to him. He sat down in the seat last occupied by Lieutenant Mark Shields seven decades prior. He opened his toolkit, pulled out the portable power generator and began to hook it into the nav computer. It took some moments, during which Hague stood over him. Narita got the distinct impression the pilot was protecting him. From what, he could not imagine. None of these people had moved since before either of them was born. After a few moments, the connections were made. Narita flipped the main toggle on the generator.

The nav computer came to life. Several lights began to blink. The monitor, dark for seven decades, lit up with the old GSA logo. The image wavered, went out, then came back. Both men shielded their eyes to the new, unexpected brightness. "Nav computer is online," Narita said.

Hague clapped his hands together and laughed. He patted Narita on the back. "Good job."

Narita made adjustments on the small generator. Some of the blinking lights stopped their blinking and remained lit. The monitor glowed in the gloom of the darkened bridge.

"Okay, let's see if the database is still intact." Narita began to operate the workstation. The old GSA logo disappeared from the screen. Lines of code scrolled up too quickly to be read. Narita and Hague kept their eyes glued to the monitor. After a few more moments of code lines, the screen went black. A moment after that, the menu appeared.

"Star charts," Hague said, pointing to the menu item. "That's what we need."

"I know," Narita replied. He selected the appropriate option and hit the button.

The monitor flashed a few times. Snow appeared on the screen. Narita could not hear the static from the workstation speakers due to the vacuum inside the ship, but he knew it was there just the same. His face fell.

Hague saw Narita's reaction. "What's the matter? Is the monitor shot? We don't need it, right? Just disconnect the nav computer and we'll be on our way."

Narita shook his head and swallowed. "No, it's not the monitor." He turned and looked over his shoulder at Hague. "The nav computer has been wiped."

****

Thorpe reached the open hatch to the Gemini. He stopped and looked inside. Aside from the pinball machine, the room was dark.

"Mason?" There was no reply, and Thorpe's heart sank. He took a single step into the room, and his foot nearly went out from under him. He lost his balance, and it was blind luck he fell backward, directly into McKnight's arms.

"What the hell was that?" McKnight asked.

Thorpe recovered, dropped to one knee and reached his hand through the hatchway. He placed it on the deck. It came away wet. He held his fingers to his nose. "Coffee and bourbon," he said to McKnight and Mikhailov. He reached in again and picked up a small piece of glass. He stood and held it in front of them, as if it were the missing clue needed to solve a crime.

"Someone broke a bottle?" Mikhailov asked.

"He was here," Thorpe said. "Something happened to him."

McKnight held up his hands. "Slow down, Thorpe. We don't know that."

Thorpe tossed the broken glass over his shoulder. It landed somewhere within the Gemini with a *chink*. "How else do you explain that?"

McKnight tilted his head and furrowed his brow. He shrugged. "Could be any number of explanations."

"Name one," Mikhailov said. She sounded as if she was on Thorpe's page.

Thorpe strode to the intercom without another word. He hit the button. "Mason, respond." His voice echoed from down the corridor, and from every other intercom station within Armstrong. He stood by the intercom panel and waited. The seconds stretched into a full minute. Thorpe looked at McKnight as if to say, *See? Told ya!* "Mason, this is Thorpe. Respond, please."

The intercom remained silent. Thorpe reached for the button that would close the channel when the small speaker came to life. At the first crackle, Thorpe thought perhaps he had been mistaken and Mason was about to admonish him for leaving the geology lab. Instead, it was Hansen's voice.

"Thorpe, this is Hansen. Report."

Thorpe could not hide his disappointment, did not even try. "Mike, I can't find Mason. He won't answer the intercom."

A pause. Then: "Report to the con."

"Roger." Thorpe closed the channel. He looked at McKnight and Mikhailov.

"We're coming with you," Mikhailov said.

"Thanks," Thorpe replied. And he meant it. He offered them a weak smile.

They made their way to the main control room.

****

Hansen closed the channel and activated the main monitor. The GSA logo appeared, bigger and brighter than ever. Or it might just have been his imagination. He frowned and stabbed at the control that would activate the internal cameras. In truth, he simply wanted to change the image.

Nothing happened.

His eyes narrowed as he hit the button again. The GSA logo continued to stare down at him. "What the hell?" He took the seat and tried again. He swore. He stood and strode up the stairs that led to the loft where the engineering stations were located. All four consoles were inactive. He activated the first console and took the seat. He eyed the main monitor. The GSA logo continued its mocking stare.

Hansen pushed buttons and flipped switches. He gave all his attention to the small monitor on the workstation. He knew what he would find, if anything. It would depend on how well Dwyer had covered her tracks. He felt her arrogance would not allow her to do a thorough enough job. He was correct.

"Bitch," he said.

He stood and took the stairs two at a time. He reached the hatch that led to Wright's office and pounded on it. He could have used the chime, or opened the intercom to the office. He did neither. He was beyond that.

"It's Hansen," he said, and he pounded some more.

He heard the lock disengage from the other side. The hatch swung open. Wright stood partially behind the hatch, as if it were a shield. He poked his head out from behind it. "Yes, Colonel?"

Hansen had had enough. He shoved his way past Wright and walked purposefully to what used to be his desk. Dwyer sat at one of the chairs in front of the desk. Her legs were crossed and she sipped coffee from a rather large mug. Her head was only half-turned in his direction. He saw the smile on her face and used most of his self-control to stop from strangling her.

"Restore access to the main monitor, please, Ms. Dwyer. We might have a man missing and we need to find him."

Dwyer sipped her coffee and offered him another smile.

"Who's missing?" Wright asked. He maintained his position next to the hatch.

"Mason." Hansen did not take his eyes from Dwyer.

"Mr. Hansen, access to the main monitor has been restricted, I am afraid," Dwyer said. "Authorized personnel only." She placed the mug on Wright's desk, in the precise spot once occupied by Roger Maris. She turned to Hansen. "At the moment, that means Dr. Millman, Major Wright and myself."

Hansen's eyes flashed anger – no, more than anger. He was far past that and approaching rage at light speed. It took him a moment, and he spoke again only when he was reasonably certain he could control his actions. "Mason is unaccounted for." His tone was even, but he could not keep the edge out of his voice. "We need to find him immediately. I need the main monitor to search all areas of the base. I need it now."

Dwyer folded her hands in her lap. Her smile remained in place. She nodded at Wright.

"Colonel Hansen, we'll find Mason," Wright said from his position next to the hatch. "When we do, we'll inform you of his location."

Hansen did not take his eyes from Dwyer. She remained mute. Her eyes betrayed her excitement, but there was something else there as well. Something she tried to keep from him, but she was not quite skilled enough to do it successfully. Fear? No, not exactly. Apprehension? That was closer to the truth. He made her nervous. For the first time since her arrival, she was uncertain about Hansen. She seemed to realize how close he had come to losing his cool, and it surprised her. He took it for what it was worth.

He turned and walked to the hatch. He stopped and regarded Wright. Armstrong's latest commanding officer managed to keep the hatch between them. Unlike Dwyer, Wright's eyes held no excitement. He was frightened, and he did not bother to hide the fact.

"Make sure you do," Hansen said. He exited the room.

Wright sealed the hatch behind him.

****

"That's it. We're fucked."

Hague turned away from the nav console and threw his hands into the air. He kicked at a broken piece of what used to be the pilot's console on the deck in front of him. It sailed slowly across the bridge. It bounced off one of the forward windows, made it almost to the captain's chair before it settled slowly to the deck. It bounced once in slow-motion and then lay still. "Goddamnit!" He gripped the back of the captain's chair with both hands and squeezed.

"Now we know why the rescue team was sent out here," Narita said. He remained seated at the nav console. "And why they didn't bother to recover the bodies of the crew. It wasn't their mission."

"Motherfuckers," Hague said. He released his grip on the captain's chair and planted his hands on his hips. "Now what do we do?"

"What *can* we do? The data is gone." Narita stood and began to pace back and forth in front of the nav console. A rail separated the port and starboard workstations from the center of the room. Narita kept one hand on the rail, used it to push himself along the deck. He ducked under a hanging power cable, turned, retraced his steps. After a few moments, he stopped and turned to Hague. "Wait a minute. Wait, wait, wait."

Hague's brow furrowed. "What is it?"

Narita moved as quickly as he was able back to the nav console. He quickly unhooked the power generator from the input jack. The monitor went black and plunged the bridge back into darkness. Narita bent down, retrieved his toolkit and made for the exit hatch.

"What the fuck, man?" Hague asked. But he was alone on the darkened bridge. He shined his light through the open hatchway, but Narita was already gone. "Narita, hold up." Hague followed him through the hatch.

Narita did not wait. He negotiated his way around the corpses in the corridor and reached the ladder. "Come on, old man, hurry." He moved down the ladder as quickly as the isolation suit would allow. In his haste, he nearly dropped his toolkit twice. He managed to hang onto it until he reached the access to B deck. He stood back from the ladder and waited for Hague.

Hague mumbled something unintelligible over Narita's helmet speaker. The engineer watched the older man's flashlight beam dance across the bulkheads around the ladder. In a few moments, Hague entered B deck.

"What's this all about?"

"Maybe nothing," Narita admitted. "Maybe everything. Follow me."

They stepped over the fallen water pipe and the two corpses. Farther down the corridor they passed another body. Narita did not stop to examine the unfortunate crewman who would spend eternity entombed within a wrecked ship on the lunar surface. Several access panels along the bulkheads had sprung open, most likely when the ship crashed. Narita hoped that was the reason.

He shined his flashlight onto the deck and smiled. "No footprints. Doesn't look like they made it down here. That's good, that's good." He did not know if he spoke to Hague or himself. He continued down the corridor.

He stopped in front of a hatch on the starboard bulkhead. "Yes!" He tugged on the hatch. Nothing. He tugged on it again, received the same result. Hague caught up to him, and Narita said, "Help me with this."

Hague shined his light on the hatch. The stenciled lettering read:

OPERATIONS MAINFRAME

Narita shifted his grip on the hatch handle to allow Hague a grip on the wheel. Together, they pulled for all they were worth. Narita was willing to bet the hatch metal would shriek its protest had they not been in near-vacuum. As it was, he heard nothing. After a moment, during which the young engineer feared the hatch would remain stuck forever, it swung open slowly. It did not open all the way, but Narita was confident he and Hague would be able to squeeze through.

"It's buckled to the frame," Hague said needlessly.

"Doesn't matter. Follow me." Narita squeezed through the opening and entered the mainframe room. His flashlight beam revealed a bank of computers that lined every inch of the bulkheads. The room was about the size he had expected and laid out as he remembered.

"How'd you know about this?" Hague asked as he entered the room.

"I toured the *Icarus* at the GSA Museum when I was a kid. Same ship, more or less."

"Okay, but what are we doing here?"

"You'll see.'" Narita walked about the room, shining his flashlight on each separate computer bank. He stopped when he got to the one labeled **NAVIGATION AND HELM.** "This is the one." He placed his toolkit on top of the computer bank and opened it. The portable generator made another appearance. He began to link it to the computer. "Problem is, these systems are all linked. We don't have enough oxygen in our suits for me to waste time isolating this one. That means this generator will temporarily power the ship's entire mainframe."

"So? I don't get it."

Narita continued to work. "It wasn't built to run a system this size. We'll have three or four minutes, at most, before it's out of juice."

"Three or four minutes for what? The data is gone. Why are we down here?"

"Yes and no." Narita made the final connection.

The overhead lights blinked a few times and came on. One of them sputtered, sparked and went out. The rest remained intact. Every computer bank in the room came alive. Lights flashed and blinked. They would be able to hear the hum of the circuitry if not for the vacuum. Narita deactivated his flashlight and placed it on the deck at his feet.

He pushed the button that activated the small monitor built into the computer. The screen lit up with snow. Narita began to press buttons and flip switches. He worked the controls as quickly as the bulky gloves of his isolation suit would allow.

"Now would be a good time to pray," he said.

After a few moments the snow disappeared. It was replaced with an image of the solar system. A red line crossed the image. It originated at Earth, looped around Uranus and ended on the moon: The final voyage of the *Daedalus*.

Narita did not attempt to hide his smile. "Got it." He stood back and folded his arms across his chest.

Hague approached him and got his first look at the image on the monitor. "Holy shit! How'd you do that?"

Narita's smile broadened. "Like I said, they never made it down here. They probably thought wiping the nav computer on the bridge would be enough. But I'm guessing they used some type of magnetic pulse generator. It took care of the nav computer, but it didn't touch the mainframe."

"Lazy fuckers."

"They were probably on a time limit," Narita said. He took another device from his toolkit. He hooked it into the computer bank's open port. He activated the device, and its tiny screen lit up. He inputted a command and watched the screen intently. Images and lines of code appeared and scrolled up. He smiled again. "The old isolation suits had even less oxygen capacity than ours. They must have used most of theirs getting to the bridge and back. And they probably thought that was sufficient to cover their tracks."

Hague eyed the large computer dubiously. "Okay, but how do we get this heavy bastard back to Armstrong? Or even out of this room, for that matter?"

"Don't need to. All we need is the memory core." He rooted around in the toolkit until he found what he was looking for. "Going to remove that now. We're in business."

Hague's eyes narrowed. He moved a few steps closer to the monitor. He reached out a gloved hand and planted one finger on the screen. "What is that?"

Narita did not look up from his work. He had already opened the access pancl on the face of the computer bank. "What's what?"

"This smudge near Neptune. Is it a bad spot in the memory core?"

Narita shook his head, continued to work on the computer bank's innards. "No. That's a comet. McEnerney-1970 is my guess."

Hague's eyes went wide. "Am I sensing a correlation here?"

"Why not? I am." Narita pulled the memory core from the computer bank. The image on the monitor winked out. A moment later it was replaced with the old GSA logo. "That's it, and not a minute too soon. Generator is about dcad."

Narita disconnected the power generator from the console. The room returned to darkness. The blinking lights on all the computer banks died and remained dead. He reactivated his flashlight and placed everything back inside the toolkit. "We're out of here." He started for the hatch.

"Outstanding." Hague clapped his hands together. Dust particles floated from his gloves and drifted lazily to the deck. He eyed the dark monitor of the navigation mainframe a final time. Then he followed Narita through the hatch.

****

Hansen looked up when Thorpe, Mikhailov and McKnight entered the main control room. He had resumed his seat at the main monitor, mostly because he had nothing else to do. With their arrival, he stood and faced them.

Thorpe was clearly the most distressed of the three, and why not? It was his friend and colleague who was missing. All three were out of breath, but Thorpe wasted no time.

"We have to find him, Mike." He looked at the main monitor as if seeing it for the first time. His brow furrowed at the GSA logo. "Why aren't you looking for him?" His tone was not accusatory, not precisely. But it held an edge he had never before heard from Thorpe. He moved around Hansen and started pressing buttons on the control console.

"That won't work."

"What the fuck?" There was more confusion in his tone than anything else. He punched the same buttons and hit the same switches over and over again. "Main monitor is down?"

"Not exactly." He inclined his head toward his old office.

"You've got to be fucking kidding me!" He took an angry step toward the hatch to Wright's office.

Hansen's arm shot out and blocked him. "They're looking for Mason now, Thorpe. Settle down." He looked at McKnight and Mikhailov. They looked as furious as Thorpe, as he himself was.

"Settle down? Are you serious? That twat and her little sidekick are looking for Mason? You can't be serious."

Hansen took a deep breath. "They are. But that doesn't mean we can't look for him, too. We just can't do it with the main monitor. We'll split into teams—"

"This is bullshit, Mike," McKnight said. He stabbed an accusing finger toward Wright's office. "They can't cut us off like this."

"Mason could be in serious trouble," Mikhailov added.

"We're *all* in serious trouble," said a voice from the other side of the room.

They turned as one. Millman stood inside the hatch to the control room. He was out of breath and leaning on the bulkhead for support. His lab coat was gone, and the left sleeve of his work shirt was torn away. What looked like deep gouges on his bare arm dripped a small amount of blood onto the deck. He looked at them with wide eyes.

"*Very* serious trouble," he said.

Chapter 13

We Were Wrong

Millman leaned over Kehoe's corpse and began the incision. He cut a clean, straight line down the nurse's desiccated chest. No blood welled up from the wound, but he had become used to that. He had performed the same procedure on both Sullivan and Doyle, with the same result. He returned the scalpel to the tray and selected the chest spreader.

This is nonsense, he thought as he placed the surgical tool on Kehoe's chest. He had been through this a number of times. What, precisely, was he looking for? He would find no difference between this corpse and the others in the infirmary. They had all been subjected to the same procedures, the same tests. The results he had found in Doyle and Sullivan matched what the former had found when he examined the corpse of the woman from the starliner. He wondered what Dwyer expected him to find in Kehoe that wasn't shared by the others.

In the end he resigned himself to following her orders. As if he had a choice. One word from Dwyer and he would never work in xenobiology again, for the GSA or anyone else. He contemplated this as he cranked the chest spreader and watched Kehoe's torso open like an obscene parody of a flower. A puff of dust rose into the air from the chest cavity. Millman grimaced and turned his head away. Surgical mask or not, he wanted nothing to do with anything that had been inside the body. He waved a hand through the air and the dust obediently wafted away.

He caught sight of the silhouette that was Nixon in the opaque glass. The security chief leaned against the glass, arms folded across his chest and head down. He looked bored, or as bored as a silhouette could look. *I'll trade places with ya*, Millman thought. *I'd rather be standing around bored to tears than in here with this shit.*

The chest spreader reached its limit. Millman peered inside and was utterly unsurprised by what he saw. Kehoe's internal organs were withered and bone dry. He saw not a drop of blood anywhere. The man's heart had shrunk to the size of a plum; it lay there in his chest like a dead, black tumor. He reached for the portable scanner.

In the end, it was his total boredom that saved his life. Had he found something of interest in Kehoe's chest, he might have been too occupied with the discovery to hear the slight rustling of the sheet behind him. Millman turned. His eyes went wide. The scanner dropped from his numb fingers and clattered back onto the tray.

Doyle stood on the other side of the room. He took a hesitant, lurching step forward. His chest was open, and Millman could see the dead man's heart and lungs drop a few centimeters with the movement. Doyle's eyes were recessed back into his skull. They were large and gray and fixed on Millman.

He took a step back. He wanted to scream, tried to scream, but the sound died in his throat. Had his lungs not protested the lack of oxygen, Millman might never have noticed that he held his breath. He backed up another step, watched Doyle close the distance. Two more backwards steps and Millman felt the bulkhead behind him. The intercom was a meter or so away from his hand. He clawed at it, but his fingers found only empty bulkhead. He needed to look to find the intercom, but he found he could not take his eyes from the dead man.

Doyle shambled past the exam table that held Kehoe's body. He knocked over the tray as he went. Surgical tools went flying. They clattered off the deck and the bulkheads. He reached out with both arms, a man who longed for his lover. His mouth opened. His shrunken tongue worked behind his teeth, but he produced no sound. He reached for Millman.

The xenobiologist still could not scream, could not utter so much as a whimper. He saw his avenue of escape to his left. He dashed for it. He tripped over the body bag that held the remains of Sofia Nelson and crashed to the deck. The impact knocked the breath from his lungs. He gasped, rolled onto his side. His wide eyes fell once again on Doyle.

The dead man had reached the spot so recently vacated by Millman. He turned slowly and looked down. Their eyes locked. Doyle stepped to his right and reached for Millman. His gray, skeletal fingers opened and closed slowly. It could have been his imagination, but Millman could swear he hard those joints creak with each movement.

Millman turned, down on all fours, and scrambled over the body bag. He thought at first he had imagined it, but when he saw the movement repeated, his horror turned to terror. The body inside the black plastic bag moved. It strained against its confinement.

Millman flashed back to a tour he had served on a hospital ship in the early days of the Brazilian Conflict. One of the patients had snapped under the horrors of combat and had been declared clinically insane by the ship's psychiatrist. The man had been placed in restraints, and he had struggled against them with all his might. He thrashed every which way, screamed nonsensical words and did his best to escape. The jerking movements of the person within the body bag looked identical to the insane man he had watched so long ago.

Millman flopped onto his back and scrambled away from the body bag. Doyle reached it a moment later. Millman fully expected the dead xenobiologist to reach down and open the bag. He did not. Doyle stepped over it and continued his advance on Millman. The body bag continued to thrash about.

Doyle reached down and closed his fingers around Millman's arm. His desiccated intestines spilled from his body and landed silently on the deck. Tiny plumes of dust rose from the entrails. The fingers around Millman's arm tightened.

Millman tried to scream, tried to make any sound at all. He could not. He pulled back, turned away. He managed to get his feet under him. He surged forward, a linebacker who had just recovered a fumble. He heard his lab coat begin to tear. Doyle did not release his grip. Millman pin wheeled his arms, felt Doyle's grip loosen slightly. He was out of the lab coat and regained his balance. Doyle held the lab coat out in front of him, as if he knew he should recognize the object. He regarded the lab coat for another moment before he discarded it and resumed his march.

Millman put the exam table between himself and the dead man. The hatch was at his back. He calculated the odds of getting to the hatch controls and opening it. He knew he could make it. He kept his eyes on Doyle and reached back blindly with his right hand.

His other hand was seized and yanked downward. Millman lost his balance and collapsed across the exam table and Kehoe's body. He gasped and instinctively pulled away. It was not Doyle who had grabbed him, nor had the woman from the *Sovereign* freed herself from the body bag and joined the pursuit.

It was Kehoe.

Millman was nearly nose to nose with the dead nurse. Kehoe's lips pulled back from his teeth. "I need you," he said. His breath was faint, barely enough to register against Millman's cheek. The air coming up from Kehoe's lungs was cold. Millman found he could not smell anything, for which he was grateful. He had no desire to smell the rot that had overtaken Kehoe's shriveled lungs.

Millman pulled away with everything he had. Kehoe sat up enough to get his other hand farther up Millman's arm. The nurse did not quite get a strong enough grip, and Millman all but threw himself away from the talking corpse.

Kehoe's fingers gouged their way down Millman's left arm. His shirt sleeve tore and blood welled up from the wounds. Millman pulled back and inadvertently pulled Kehoe into a standing position beside the exam table. That was when Doyle reached them.

Four hands pawed at Millman. His mind went blank, and it was the merest instinct that triggered his leg muscles. He hurled himself and the two dead men at the opaque glass behind him. At the last moment before impact, he finally found his voice. He screamed.

****

Nixon was bored – no, more than bored. He was nearly comatose. He was unsure how long he stood outside the infirmary. He had put off looking at the chronometer on the bulkhead next to the intercom. He felt if he knew the time of day (or night), he'd begin to lose his mind.

It wasn't the first time he found himself bored with an assignment. His early military career had consisted mostly of guarding the stockade and, on thankfully rare occasions, dealing with paperwork. He considered himself disciplined, a career military man who could easily take the good with the bad. He had never once complained about an assignment. He had even requested the post at Armstrong. He felt if he could handle the doldrums of life at an isolated facility, he would be able to handle anything.

Since the start of his tour, he had been required to use his authority only once. That had been when a technician got a little too rough with Brodeur, the base psychologist who had preceded Mikhailov. The techie, a fat, alcoholic simpleton named David, had departed Armstrong a few months earlier than he had planned, and with fewer teeth than when he arrived. The downside was Brodeur was too injured to finish her tour. Nixon had not arrived on the scene in time to prevent her injuries. Aside from the one unfortunate incident, his tour on Armstrong was uneventful.

Until the goddamned starliner with its full complement of corpses showed up.

But all the activity since the arrival of the *Sovereign* and the GSA team had gone the way of David and Brodeur. And he was stuck babysitting the limp dick on the other side of the bulkhead.

Nixon rubbed his eyes and hoped for something to happen. Nothing serious. He did not want a repeat of what had happened in the holding area or the security office. But *something*.

The scream was muffled enough that, for a split-second, Nixon did not recognize it for what it was. His first thought was it originated somewhere far off, or perhaps it had come from the intercom. He did not have time for a second thought. The window at his back exploded. The scream was suddenly louder, and Nixon was struck with enough force that he sprawled on the deck. He landed hard enough to knock the breath from his lungs. Tiny bits of glass embedded themselves into his palms. He managed to rise to his knees. The noise filled the corridor behind him. He turned and looked.

Millman was flat on his back. The scientist struggled with someone who had landed on top of him. His hands were locked on the other man's shoulders. Gray, skeletal fingers closed around Millman's throat and his screams stopped. He turned his head. He made eye contact with Nixon. The security chief saw the desperate panic in Millman's eyes.

Nixon jumped to his feet and rushed the man who pinned Millman to the deck. He grabbed the man by his bony shoulders and pulled him back. *Christ, he weighs nothing.* The man lost his grip on Millman. Nixon spun him around and threw him across the corridor into the opposite bulkhead. He landed hard, bounced off the bulkhead. His intestines spilled out from his body and landed on the deck with an unpleasant sound. He raised his head and regarded the security chief. That was when Nixon got his first look at the man.

"Kehoe?"

The word did not register. Nothing registered. Nixon's mind went blank. It could not possibly be Kehoe. Kehoe was dead. Yet the thing that stood only a few meters from him was unmistakably the nurse. His chest was wide open, its sides separated by the chest spreader that hung from the skin. Kehoe shifted his weight off his broken ankle. The chest spreader came loose and clanged to the deck. Kehoe took a stutter-step toward him.

"We're dead, we're fucking dead," Millman rambled.

Nixon turned toward him. His eyes saw the movement behind Millman, and he raised them to the shattered glass. Doyle and Sullivan stood behind the remnants of the window. Their recessed eyes moved from Millman to Nixon.

"I need you," Doyle said to him. The voice was rough, the voice of a lifelong smoker in the final stages of throat cancer. It barely registered as language. Doyle began to pull himself through the new opening in the bulkhead.

Nixon turned, saw Kehoe was only a few meters away. The nurse advanced slowly. His arms were outstretched, as if he beckoned to Nixon. One foot dragged across the deck. His mouth worked but no sound came from him. Nixon was grateful; he had no desire to hear that voice again.

He grabbed Millman by his arm and hauled the man to his feet. Doyle got his first leg through the opening. His bare, gray foot landed on the deck soundlessly. Bits of glass must have embedded themselves into the soles of the dead man's feet, but if they did, he gave no indication. His eyes never left Nixon.

Nixon shoved Millman down the corridor hard enough the scientist nearly lost his footing. "Get outta here," he shouted. "Warn everyone what's happening."

"What about you?" Millman asked.

Nixon slammed his fist into Kehoe's mouth. The skin and bone gave way and Nixon's fist disappeared into the skull. An explosion of dust nearly choked him. He pulled his fist back. Kehoe staggered back against the bulkhead. Some of his teeth bounced onto the deck. "I'll be fine. Go!"

Millman bolted down the corridor.

Nixon spun just in time to see Doyle reach for him. Behind the dead man, Sullivan began to pull himself through the shattered window. Nixon put everything he had into his next swing.

****

"We're in seriously deep shit."

Millman spoke matter-of-factly, with no emotion. He may as well have stated a finding that was obvious and foregone. Blood continued to drip from his wounded arm.

Mikhailov and McKnight rushed to him and helped him into a seat at one of the control stations. Hansen watched them and then hit the intercom switch nearest him. "Nix, report immediately."

"He's dead, Colonel," Millman said. His tone remained flat. "He can't answer you."

Hansen glared at him. "Captain Nixon, respond." The intercom replied with silence. All eyes fell on Hansen. All except Millman's; he kept his eyes lowered.

Mikhailov moved to the rear bulkhead. She unhooked the first aid kit and brought it back to Millman. Hansen had had enough. He walked quickly and purposefully to Millman. He shouldered Mikhailov out of the way and grabbed the scientist by his shoulders. Millman's eyes went wide as he focused on Hansen. The fear had returned and taken up what could be permanent residence behind those eyes. Hansen did not care.

"You'd better start talking right fucking now, Doctor."

Millman stammered. Hansen shook him. The scientist moaned with pain. His hand tried to cover the wounds on his arm. Hansen allowed him that much, no more.

"We were wrong," Millman said. His voice was no longer emotionless. He sounded frightened. "We were so fucking wrong." He took a deep breath, held it, released it loudly.

"Wrong about what?" Hansen asked.

"About *everything*!" His eyes moved from Hansen to the others in the room. "Don't you get it? They got up and *walked*! They weren't dead. They never were."

"*They?* As in, more than one?" Mikhailov asked. She hovered over Millman with the first aid kit. She had not yet opened it.

Millman looked at her. "Yes, more than one. Potentially *a lot* more than one."

"What the hell are you talking about?" Thorpe asked.

Millman swallowed. "Your friend, the one who's missing, you can forget about him. He's dead, too."

Thorpe took an angry step toward him.

Hansen's eyes narrowed. He pulled Millman to his feet. He ignored the loud moan. "Listen to me, Doctor. Take a deep breath, get your shit together and *talk to us*. What are we dealing with?"

Millman did as ordered. He closed his eyes and took a deep breath. Hansen could see and feel some of the tension and panic leave the doctor's body. For a moment, he was thankful, but only for a moment.

Millman opened his eyes again. "We thought this alien life-form was jumping from body to body, right? As it burned out one host, it would find another. But we were wrong. They're not doing that at all. The closest analogy would be, well, they're procreating. Within us."

"Holy God," McKnight mumbled.

"God has fuck-all to do with this," Mikhailov said.

"You're right about that," Millman said. He continued. "These things burn through their host bodies, but for all we know, that's how they like them. In fact, I'd go so far as to theorize they prefer a colder body temperature. It would make sense, given their natural habitat."

"The comet," Hansen said.

"Yes."

"That will be quite enough, Dr. Millman."

Everyone turned in the direction of the voice. Hansen was not surprised, nor was anyone else, he wagered, to see Dwyer and Wright emerge from the office. The woman walked purposefully, arms at her side. Her scowl, which Hansen had glimpsed a few times, was back with a vengeance. She did not look at him or any of the others. Her gaze was fixed on Millman. Wright followed a few paces behind her.

"You're discussing classified matters, Doctor. You will cease and desist immediately. Accompany me to Major Wright's office for full debriefing." She stopped in front of Millman. Even from the side, Hansen could see her eyes drill their way into Millman's. The doctor cringed.

"Ms. Dwyer—"

"Colonel Hansen, one more word from you and you will be placed under arrest. Am I clear?"

Hansen looked at Wright. The man seemed unconvinced, but he placed his hand on the butt of the gun in his holster.

"Look, lady—" Mikhailov started but was unable to finish.

Wright pulled the weapon from its holster and thumbed off the safety. He pointed it toward the ceiling, arm cocked. He glared at Mikhailov.

"That'll be enough of that bullshit," Dwyer said. "Dr. Millman, with me." She started to turn.

Millman did not move. "They have a right to know."

Dwyer remained with her back to everyone. "No, they do not."

Millman looked from Dwyer to Hansen. "It came from the comet, as you know. McEnerney-1970."

Dwyer turned at last. She favored Millman with a withering look. "How *dare* you? You are under *my* authority—"

"The GSA detected the comet and diverted the *Sovereign of the Stars* so she would get close enough for detailed sensor readings." Millman spoke quickly. His words threatened to blend together. "They knew there was an alien life-form somewhere inside the comet. They *knew*, and they didn't tell anyone."

Dwyer's eyes swam with rage. Her hands shook. "One final chance, Dr. Millman. If you shut up right now, I'll see to it you don't spend the rest of your life in a federal penitentiary."

Millman ignored her. It seemed to Hansen that once the man started to speak, the barriers placed on him by Dwyer crumbled to dust. The words poured from him quickly and easily; the only break was when Millman paused to take a breath. It was like watching a horse that had been penned its entire life suddenly set free.

Hansen's eyes darted from Millman to Dwyer, pausing for the briefest moment on Wright. The major appeared stunned, but he kept his weapon in the ready position.

"When they lost contact with the *Sovereign*, they reviewed her telemetry. They knew *precisely* what had happened. They—"

"*Now*, Major Wright!" Dwyer shouted.

Wright brought the gun level with Millman and aimed it at the doctor's chest.

Hansen might have shouted something, but he was not certain. He threw himself at Wright. He tackled his former second-in-command around his waist. Wright backpedaled and lost his balance. The gun went off. The report was deafening; the gun had been very close to Hansen's right ear when Wright pulled the trigger. The two men collapsed to the deck. Hansen, nearly deaf in his right ear, nonetheless thought he heard a woman's high-pitched scream from somewhere behind him.

His right fist swung an elegant arc through the air and connected solidly with Wright's jaw. His left hand grabbed at Wright's wrist, and he squeezed with everything he had. The major hung onto the weapon, although he was most likely unaware of it. Hansen pounded Wright's hand on the deck until the man's fingers opened. The gun flew through the air and landed somewhere far away. Hansen landed another blow across Wright's jaw. Wright howled with pain. Hansen hit him again.

There was a fair amount of commotion behind him. He rolled off Wright, rose to his knees and looked in the direction of the noise. He expected to see Millman with a gunshot wound. At first, he thought that was precisely what he saw. The scientist was on the deck, on his stomach. But his hands covered his head, and the only blood Hansen could see was on the doctor's arm.

Then he saw McKnight. The pilot sat on the deck, both hands clutching his abdomen. Blood seeped from between his fingers. Mikhailov knelt beside him. She had managed to open the first aid kit. She fumbled through it with one hand while her other supported McKnight's back. The pilot looked at Hansen with eyes full of surprise and pain.

"Don." Hansen was on his feet in an instant. He reached McKnight's side and took over for Mikhailov. She directed her full attention to the first aid kit.

"Son of a bitch," McKnight said through clenched teeth. He pulled one hand away, looked at the blood dripping from his fingers. "I don't fucking believe this."

"It's all right, Don, it's all right." Hansen tried to keep the calm in his voice. He thought perhaps he even succeeded. Not that it would make a difference. The blood was nearly black; the bullet was in his liver. "We're gonna get you fixed up good as new." It was a lie. He hoped McKnight did not pick up on the tremor in his voice.

Mikhailov pulled a roll of bandages from the first aid kit and began to unspool it. She glared at Dwyer as she did so. Hansen moved out of the way to allow Mikhailov to do her thing.

He stood. "Everyone else okay?" Thorpe had recovered Wright's weapon. He stood over the major, who rocked slowly back and forth on the deck. Wright rubbed his jaw and occasionally ran his sleeve across his nose, which bled quite profusely. Thorpe did not aim the gun at Wright, not exactly, but he certainly pointed in that direction.

Millman rose to his knees, apparently only just aware he had not been shot, and that no more bullets would be coming his way. He looked tentatively from Dwyer to Hansen. Dwyer had not moved during the commotion. She remained in place as if rooted to the deck. Her eyes were wild, but there was still rage there. Oh, yes, still plenty of that. But she also appeared uncertain. It was close to the same look she had displayed in the holding area after Duncan died.

"Millman, help McKnight." Millman crawled on hands and knees to McKnight and Mikhailov without making a sound.

Hansen approached Dwyer and grabbed her arm. She did not resist at first. He led her to one of the workstations. When he tried to sit her down, she struggled against him. "Get your fucking hands off me!" Hansen smiled inwardly, but said nothing. He forced her into the chair. She glared at him.

"Tell me everything you know."

"It's classified, Colonel. You already know far too much." The little girl was gone again. Defiance dripped from every word. "You and your crew are now in possession of knowledge about a hundred levels above your pay grade. Heads will roll when we get back to Earth. You wait and see."

Hansen slammed his fist on the control panel in front of Dwyer. She jumped back in the chair. Her eyes went wide, but only for a moment. She regained control quickly. "I'm not asking you. I'm *telling* you. Start talking."

"Fuck you." She continued to glare at him.

"You *bitch*," Mikhailov said. Hansen turned and saw Mikhailov get to her feet. Millman had laid McKnight flat on his back and was working on him. Mikhailov took a few steps toward Dwyer. "You're responsible for all this." She swung her arm in an inclusive arc around the room.

Dwyer's eyes narrowed. "Who do you think you're speaking to? You're in enough trouble as it is, doctor. The best thing you could do right now is to shut your fucking mouth."

Mikhailov moved fast enough that even Hansen was unprepared. She plowed past him and threw herself at Dwyer. Mikhailov wrapped her hands around Dwyer's throat and both women tumbled to the deck. They became a tangle of arms and legs. Fists flew. One landed on Hansen's leg as he moved in to separate them. It was difficult to tell who was who. After a few moments, he was able to get a solid grip on Mikhailov's right arm. He hauled her off Dwyer. Dark hair dangled from Mikhailov's fingers. Her face was red, but she appeared uninjured. Dwyer's nose and mouth bled and turned the front of her blouse to crimson. She coughed several times and spat blood on the deck.

Hansen pushed Mikhailov away. At first, he thought she would simply run around him again and have another go at Dwyer. But she seemed satisfied, at least for the moment, in her triumph. "There's more where that came from, bitch," Mikhailov hissed. "Remember that the next time you open your mouth." Dwyer did not reply, and Hansen led Mikhailov away.

Wright pulled himself onto one of the empty chairs and sat down. He continued to rub his swollen jaw; the other dangled lifelessly in his lap. He looked at Thorpe, who maintained his position overlooking Wright. The geologist also maintained his grip on the gun.

Hansen and Mikhailov rejoined Millman and McKnight. The pilot remained on the deck, flat on his back. Blood drenched his clothes and the bandages that had been applied to the wound. His chest rose and fell, but the breaths were shallow. His eyes were open, and he stared at the ceiling.

"Report," Hansen said.

Millman did not look up from his work. "It's bad, Colonel. Very bad. He needs medical treatment right away."

"Can you help him?"

"Maybe, but not with a first aid kit. Not for this kind of wound. He needs the infirmary. But that's not an option."

"The triage center in C-ring," Mikhailov said. She sniffled and wiped tears from her eyes. "Isn't it set up to handle emergency cases like this?"

"If we carry him that far, we'll kill him." Millman shook his head.

"The infirmary it is," Hansen said. He looked at both Mikhailov and Millman before he returned his eyes to McKnight. The color had drained from his face. His eyes had closed. "We have no choice."

"Colonel, maybe you didn't hear me," Millman started. "We *can't* go back there. Those things are all over the area."

Hansen glared at Millman. "I am not going to let this man die." His voice dropped several octaves. "And neither are you."

He walked to his former office. The hatch was open, most certainly because Dwyer and Wright had seen no reason to close it when they entered the main control room. He stepped through the hatch and moved to the large panel on the bulkhead. He licked his lips and hoped the scanner would still recognize his palm print. It did. The locker swung open. Hansen reached inside and pulled out the remaining gun and holster. He closed the locker and returned to the control room.

He handed the gun and holster to Mikhailov. She accepted them without comment and absentmindedly strapped on the holster.

He looked at Thorpe. The geologist did not look comfortable with the gun in his hand. He looked even less comfortable standing guard over Wright and Dwyer. Hansen nodded to him. "Keep an eye on them, Thorpe. Don't let them out of those seats. We'll be in the infirmary. I'll keep you apprised of the situation."

Thorpe shuffled his feet. "Roger that, Colonel."

Hansen bent down and picked up McKnight's legs. He looked at Millman. "On three.

Chapter 14

The Once-People

Nixon moved as quickly as he was able. His right knee threatened to buckle, and he was forced to pull himself along the bulkheads. He left handprints in blood in his wake. He was out of breath, and his knee screamed at him with every step. The adrenaline that had allowed him to break away from the three once-men outside the infirmary was nearly spent. He felt cold, but that was not the only reason his muscles trembled.

He could have seen it coming, *should* have seen it coming. He flashed back to the security office. He had been livid when he discovered Hasegawa's body was gone. He had assumed Millman had dragged the dead woman from the room. The evidence of his eyes was overruled by the logic center of his brain. It had not occurred to him until he had broken away from the once-men outside the infirmary. Had Millman, or anyone else, dragged Hasegawa's body from the infirmary, they would have left streaks of blood starting from where she had slid down the bulkhead. There had been no streaks, only a single set of footprints. He doubted Millman would have been so clumsy as to step in Hasegawa's blood and track it across the room. And the footprints had been too small for Millman, anyway, but the perfect size for Hasegawa. It should have been obvious, but he had failed to see it. It brought him unmistakably to a single thought: *She walked out of that room on her own.* Only it wasn't truly her, was it? No. It was not. Not anymore. His run-in with Kehoe told him that much.

He stopped at the connecting corridor between B- and C-rings and tried to catch his breath. His heart hammered away inside his chest and threatened to burst through his ribs. It would not have surprised him had it done precisely that. Sweat dripped from his hair and stung his eyes. He blinked it away. He leaned down and rubbed his right knee. Pain shot up his leg. He groaned. *Has to be broken.*

He saw the shadow on the bulkhead down the corridor. It shambled closer to him, although it did not move quickly. A moment later, another shadow joined the first. Then, a third. "These guys don't give up," he said breathlessly. And why would they? It wasn't as if they got tired. Being dead, it seemed, had its advantages. *At least Millman got away*, he thought.

He pulled the gun from his waistband and popped out the clip. Empty. He pulled back the slide. A single round occupied the chamber. He had grabbed the gun from a weapons locker near the security office. He had, apparently, nearly emptied the thing into the three men *(once-men)* behind him. Pieces of flesh and bone had flown off the corpses, each accompanied by a plume of dust. Not one of them had broken stride. Nixon stuffed the gun back into his waistband. If it came to it, he would use the last bullet on himself. He found the odds of that happening increased by the minute.

The shadows grew closer. Nixon could see the first of the once-men, Doyle, he believed, round the bend in the corridor. Sullivan and Kehoe would be right behind him. Nixon entered the connecting corridor that led to C-ring.

His mind raced. If he could get far enough ahead of them, he could circle back and rejoin Hansen and the others. Just as quickly, he knew that was not possible. He could not outrun them, not with his knee likely broken. They had closed the distance slowly but steadily. He needed another plan.

If his security codes had been neutralized, and he believed that to be the case, he would be unable to lock the hatches behind him. He could not simply lock them inside a room. The only areas in C-ring, in the entire base, for that matter, large enough to even make that attempt were the three hanger decks. He disliked the idea of leaving them with the transports, anyway. If the situation changed and they were able to evacuate the base, it would be difficult to fight their way past the once-men.

Pad three. He thought of the starliner on pad three. If Wright had not gotten around to neutralizing the codes for the airlocks, his plan could work. All he had to do was get them inside the docking sleeve, seal the hatch behind them and retract the sleeve. The sudden decompression would send them shooting out onto the lunar surface. It would most likely mean he would have to board the starliner, if only long enough to get the three once-men to pursue him. He was less than thrilled with the prospect of another visit to the *Sovereign of the Stars*, but he saw no other way.

Nixon made for airlock three.

****

"I saw the telemetry, but I didn't have time to study it in detail. I wish I had."

Hansen moved as quickly as Millman would allow him. They carried their burden down the corridor and toward the infirmary. Mikhailov walked ahead of them. She held the gun with both hands and pointed it at the deck. Since their departure from the main control room, they had seen nothing, heard nothing. In his time on Armstrong, Hansen could not remember the base so quiet. Aside from their footfalls, and the occasional semi-conscious moan from McKnight, the corridors were silent.

"Keep talking," Hansen said.

"It looked like something from the comet, well, it reached out toward the *Sovereign*. I know how that sounds, believe me. Doyle thought I was misreading the telemetry, but I'm telling you, that's what it looked like to me. There's a hull breach on her port side. I think that's where this thing gained access to the ship."

"We figured that part out already." Hansen was too concerned with McKnight to bother infusing his tone with the appropriate note of impatience.

They rounded a bend in the corridor and continued moving. Mikhailov scanned every bulkhead and hatchway they passed.

"So the GSA sent that ship to pick up this life-form?" Mikhailov asked.

Millman shook his head. "No. They probably only wanted detailed scans of the comet. I don't think they knew what was going to happen. But when it did, and they saw the telemetry, they realized they had this life-form isolated aboard the *Sovereign*. That's when Dwyer put my team together."

"This makes no sense." Mikhailov made another turn in the corridor. "How'd they even know about it in the first place?"

"Because they had already seen scans from its previous course through the solar system," Hansen answered. "Isn't that right?"

Millman nodded. "That's right. When Dr. Garrett McEnerney discovered the comet, he worked out its course and calculated the time until its next appearance. Seventy years later, and seventy years ago, the GSA sent another ship for a fly-by of the comet. The readings they sent back suggested the presence of a biological organism either within the comet, or on its surface."

"The *Daedalus*." Hansen did not sound surprised.

"Right again." Millman shifted his grip on McKnight.

"This happened before?" Mikhailov sounded incredulous.

"No. The *Daedalus* crashed all on its own. There is no indication whatsoever they made contact with the alien life-form. But they had the scans, and the GSA recovered them."

They reached the infirmary. Mikhailov stopped and gasped. The deck was littered with broken glass and a spattering of blood. The far bulkhead was dotted with handprints in blood. A chest spreader lay on the deck.

"Get inside and open the hatch," Hansen said. He laid McKnight on the deck as gently as he could. Millman did the same.

Millman approached the opening in the bulkhead so recently occupied by the window. He gasped and stopped dead in his tracks. Hansen rushed to his side and motioned Mikhailov over. He looked inside the infirmary. It was wrecked, as he expected. Instrument trays were knocked over. All manner of surgical tools lay scattered about the room. His eyes moved quickly, scanned for any sign of threat. He found none. Nor did Mikhailov, who, after a moment, lowered her weapon.

"What is it?" Hansen asked.

Millman licked his lips. "The body bag on the deck," he said after a moment. "It's empty."

Hansen had noticed the body bag when he looked into the room, but saw no significance to it. He looked at it again. It appeared to be shredded. There was a light coating of dust on its surface and more of the same on its insides. His eyes narrowed when he noticed the zipper was still intact and closed.

"I take it it's not supposed to be?" Mikhailov asked. The edge of nervousness crept into her voice again.

Millman swallowed hard and negotiated his way into the infirmary. A moment later, he opened the hatch. He assisted Hansen with

McKnight. They laid the pilot on the nearest exam table and Millman went to work.

Hansen noticed the doctor had avoided Mikhailov's question.

****

They were closing on him fast. His broken knee slowed him down, and his adrenaline was at low ebb. But it was more than that. *They're getting faster.* He was convinced of it. When he fled the infirmary, he had managed to put some distance between them and himself. The gap had shrunk considerably since then, and he knew it was not simply because he was winded and wounded. Their close proximity would be easier to take if that were the case.

He had nearly collapsed more than once. Somehow, he kept going. The three once-men were no more than ten meters behind him. He could hear their bare feet shuffle across the deck, could hear the creak of their muscles and bones. They had not spoken, a fact for which Nixon was ecstatic. But he thought they would when they caught up to him. And catch him they would, if his plan failed. He simply did not have enough left in the tank for much more.

He limped his way around the next bend in the corridor. Ahead of him was airlock three. Beyond the airlock was the docking sleeve and the *Sovereign of the Stars*. Thirty meters, at most. He pulled himself along the bulkhead. He no longer left smears of blood behind him. The small cuts to his palms had stopped bleeding a few moments before. *Thankful for small favors.* He neared the airlock.

It was the sound that told him he was in trouble. It was low, rhythmic pounding. His first thought was one of the generators was acting up, but he quickly tossed that idea. The sound wasn't in the bulkheads or in the conduits within the ceiling. It was from up ahead, from the airlock. Nixon slowed down. His shoulders slumped. He reached the airlock a moment later. He put his face to the glass window. He knew what he would see before he saw it.

The outer airlock hatch was open. A face that looked most similar to the faces of the once-men peered at him from the other side of the small window. It had been female once, but that had been long ago. The once-woman in the expensive blue dress pounded her decayed fist on the inner airlock hatch. Small plumes of dust accompanied each impact. Behind her, and occupying most of the space inside the docking sleeve, were more once-men and once-women. Nixon estimated they numbered perhaps a dozen. Some were dressed in elegant gowns and tuxedos, others appeared to be crew members. One of them wore the uniform of a ship's officer. Their mouths worked, but Nixon could hear nothing. He did not need to activate the intercom to know what they said to him.

Nixon's face fell. He leaned against the bulkhead next to the airlock hatch and released a long, slow breath. He raised his head in time to see Doyle and his companions were no more than ten meters from him. Their arms were outstretched. "I need you," Doyle said at last.

"Doesn't everybody," Nixon replied.

He spared another glance at the small window in the hatch. The once-woman's face was still there, still pressed against the glass. Her shriveled dry fists still pummeled the hatch. If he could get past her and her shipmates, he could do it. It was impossible, of course. Even had his knee been in perfect shape, he could not have fought through so many. To say nothing of any other once-people inside the *Sovereign.* It would be so much easier if they could have lowered the starliner into the hanger…

"The hanger," he said aloud.

The hatch that led to hanger three was to his left. He looked at it, then at the three once-men who approached. They were no more than five meters from him. Nixon dashed for the hatch. His knee barked and promised severe pain for days to come. Nixon ignored it. He ducked under Doyle's arms and opened the hatch.

He moved too quickly. On the other side of the hatch was the staircase that led to the floor of the hanger. His momentum carried him through the hatch. Nixon lost his balance. His knee gave, and his feet went out from under him. Nixon tumbled down the metal stairs. Each collision brought new pain. He kept his senses enough to tuck his broken knee into his chest as best he could. It spared him more than one impact, but he could not protect it completely. It hit one of the stairs and sent lightning bolts up his leg. Nixon screamed. He landed hard on the floor of the hanger and remained still for a moment.

His vision was obscured by more stars than he had ever seen. They blossomed into multi-colored flowers behind his eyes. His head pounded and his knee felt like it was on fire. He choked down another scream and pounded his fist on the deck. The fresh pain brought his mind into focus. He opened his eyes.

His vision was blurred at first. The flowers had become a prize-winning garden and blotted out nearly everything else. He opened his eyes as wide as he was able, blinked a few times. The flowers faded but did not vanish altogether. It was enough. He pushed himself to his feet. His broken knee sent a jolt through his body. He could feel the bones grind together. He saw the control room and limped toward it.

He found his gun a few meters away from his landing spot. He scooped it up without much thought and stuffed it back into his waistband. The control room was no more than twenty meters away. Each step felt like miles. He stifled a moan and continued. He caught movement out of his right eye and he turned his head. Doyle and

Sullivan shambled slowly down the stairs. Kehoe stood poised on the top step, as if unsure how to navigate this sudden obstacle with a broken ankle. Their eyes remained fixed on him. Nixon ignored them.

He reached the control room and opened the hatch. The workstations were dark, powered down. He activated them with the push of a button. Lights blinked and came to life. The monitor screen lit up with a cartoon image of Duncan sitting in the saddle and riding a rocket through space. Nixon swallowed hard and choked back a tear.

He looked out the control room windows. Doyle and Sullivan had reached the bottom of the stairs. They performed a uniform turn in his direction. "Shouldn't you guys have exploded already?" They made no reply. They simply started in his direction. Beyond them, he could see Kehoe had finally figured out how to negotiate the stairs with his broken ankle. He took them one at a time, slowly, but somehow seemed to move quickly all the same.

Nixon pressed buttons and flipped switches. He eyed the elevator in the hanger. It rested it its spot on the ceiling. Atop it sat the most expensive and luxurious starliner ever built. It was also his salvation. He couldn't get to the *Sovereign*, so he would bring the *Sovereign* to him. All he had to do was open the landing pad above and drop the elevator. The hanger would decompress and deposit the three once-men onto the lunar surface. The *Sovereign* would take damage, but Nixon did not care. He had come to hate the fucking ship, anyway.

He alternated his gaze between the controls in front of him and the three once-men closing on him. He needed only seconds. Their slow gait promised to oblige.

The monitor indicated all systems ready. Nixon eyed the landing pad control button. He waved to Doyle and his friends and smiled. "Fuck you," he said to them. He stabbed the button.

Nothing happened.

Nixon's smile vanished.

****

"I can still save your career. In fact, I can make you a hero when we get back to Earth. All you have to do is hand the weapon to Major Wright. What do you say, Doctor?"

Dwyer sat in the chair but did not move. Her eyes followed Thorpe as the geologist paced slowly back and forth. He was nervous, even scared. That much was obvious. Every few moments he would bring his free hand to his mouth and chew his fingernails. His eyes darted about. His hands trembled slightly. The gun remained pointed at the deck, unless he swung that arm back and forth. If the weapon were not present, Dwyer would classify the man as part of the endless stream of small-minded fools she was forced to deal with from time to time. That was not quite accurate. She would not deal with him at all. But he had the gun.

Thorpe did not answer her. He seemed to take no notice of her at all. He continued to pace in front of Dwyer and Wright.

Dwyer spared a glance at Wright. The major sat in the chair next to her. He wrung his hands together and glared at Thorpe. *Scared, but still useful*, Dwyer thought. She had sized up Wright pretty accurately when he greeted her in the hanger. A career military man who held no gods before his chain of command. Brainless but loyal. She was used to dealing with such people. But Wright was not the problem at present.

"Think about your future, Doctor. What do you want people to say about you? That you came through when it mattered most? Or that you refused to help innocent people in a life-and-death situation?"

Thorpe continued to pace.

"Listen to her, Thorpe," Wright said.

Dwyer raised an eyebrow. Had Wright taken the initiative? She had not expected anything of the sort. Her eyes narrowed, and she regarded the major with renewed interest. He periodically shook his right hand and flexed his fingers. Every few moments he rubbed his jaw. His nose had stopped bleeding but his chin was coated with blood. He looked both beaten and pathetic, but he was all Dwyer had to work with.

"Hansen's going to get us all killed. That includes you. Give me the weapon so we can stop him and restore order here. It's up to you." Wright shifted in his seat. "Come on, make the right decision." He rubbed his jaw again.

Dwyer thought perhaps they were beginning to get through to the worthless little shit. He cast a nervous glance in their direction and slowed his pacing. His free hand shook when he raised it and ran it through his hair. He stopped in mid-motion when his eyes fell on the open hatchway to his left.

Mason stepped through and into the control room. He appeared unsteady on his feet, and Dwyer's first thought was the man was drunk. She discarded the idea a moment later when she got a good look at his eyes. They were not the half-lidded eyes of a man who had had one too many.

Thorpe noticed the new arrival as well. He shouted, "Mason!" and rushed toward his friend.

Dwyer stood slowly and watched the geologist close the short distance to Mason. Out of the corner of her eye, she saw Wright rise to his feet. The major had apparently come to the same conclusion she herself had; he started to shout a warning to Thorpe. Dwyer hissed at him, and he fell silent. She took a hesitant step toward the hatch to Wright's office.

Thorpe threw his arms around Mason and blubbered, "Man, where have you been? I thought you were dead." He held the man for another moment, perhaps awaiting a reply. He drew back from the embrace and placed his hands on Mason's arms, as if trying to determine if the man were real or a mirage.

Mason did not break the embrace, but he spoke, and Dwyer felt confident she knew precisely what he said. Thorpe recoiled, but Mason grasped his arms and held him close. He leaned in to Thorpe.

Dwyer should have picked that moment to bolt for Wright's office, and she would chastise herself later for not doing so. She would have made it easily. She found herself rooted to the deck by her own curiosity. She had yet to see the phenomena with her own eyes, and she felt compelled to witness it, at least once. Wright apparently did not share her enthusiasm for the moment, for he started for the hatch. She placed a hand on his arm and wrapped her fingers around it slowly but forcefully. He looked at her questioningly, but she merely shook her head. She did not want to miss a moment of what she had come to think of as The Exchange.

Thorpe gurgled something. His body went stiff, as if he had been struck by lightning. His finger convulsed on the trigger of Wright's gun. A single shot buried itself in the deck, and the sound reverberated around the room. His arms flailed as he squeezed off another shot. The bullet ricocheted off the deck before burying itself in the aft bulkhead. A moment after that, Thorpe dropped to one knee. The gun fell from his hand and landed on the deck.

Mason did not collapse. He was unsteady on his feet, making Dwyer again think of a man who had had too much to drink. Mason fell into the chair at the environmental control station. It rolled away and he fell to the deck. He landed on his back and his arms waved weakly at the console.

Wright lunged for the gun. He scooped it off the deck, straightened and pointed the weapon at Thorpe. He retreated slowly until he once again stood next to Dwyer.

"Hold it!" Dwyer said. "Don't fire!"

Wright kept the weapon aimed at Thorpe. His eyes moved quickly from Thorpe to Dwyer. "You want him in a holding cell?"

"Get Millman back here on the double," she said.

Wright moved for the intercom.

Thorpe turned his head in their direction. Wright froze in midstride. His hand hung suspended in the air inches from the intercom button. After a moment, he recovered enough to point the gun at Thorpe. "What's he doing?" Wright asked.

Dwyer could hear the fear in Wright's voice. Her opinion of the man plummeted even further, if such a thing were possible. Had he not been present when the engineer exploded? Had he not heard Millman's explanation? Did he honestly not know? If that was the case, he was even less intelligent than she had thought. If he did know the truth, and asked anyway, then he was truly a fool. Neither scenario filled Dwyer with confidence.

Thorpe took a step toward them. Wright backed away from the intercom and raised the gun. He kept it trained on Thorpe's chest while moving quickly to Dwyer's side.

"Ms. Dwyer, what the hell is going on here?"

The undertone of authority and confidence had left his voice. He sounded scared.

"Lower your weapon, Major. We need him alive."

Wright started to obey her. He must have noticed something in Thorpe's eyes or body language. The gun halted its descent and he brought it back up again. "Stay where you are. That's a direct order, Doctor Thorpe."

Thorpe did not stay where he was. He took another step toward them.

"Hold your fire," Dwyer said, but she retreated a step when she said it.

Wright continued to aim the weapon at Thorpe. Thorpe continued his slow advance.

Dwyer looked at Thorpe, then at Wright. She did not like what she saw from the major. He planted his feet, and his lips compressed into a thin line. It seemed impossible, but he was about to disobey her. *"Hold your fucking fire, Major!"*

The gun quivered in his hands. She was certain he was about to pull the trigger. At the last moment he lowered the weapon with a frustrated grunt.

"Fuck this," he said, and he turned in the direction of the hatch. He stopped and gasped.

Dwyer turned.

What had once been Dr. Hasegawa entered the main control room. She moved slowly. No, not moved. *Lurched.* She made a more or less straight line from the hatch toward Dwyer and Wright. Dwyer's breath caught in her throat. She turned to Wright.

The commanding officer of Armstrong base stood motionless, a statue of a man terrified beyond rational thought. His eyes remained fixed on the new arrival. He did not see Thorpe approach him from behind.

Dwyer did. Blood began to trickle from Thorpe's nostrils. He reached out for the major with both arms.

"I need you," he said.

****

Nixon stabbed at the button again. Nothing happened. He took his eyes from the three once-men outside the hatch and looked at the control panel. A red light flashed below the small monitor. Nixon pressed the button beneath the light. The monitor came to life. Its screen displayed a single message:

**ACCESS TO COMMAND
FUNCTIONS RESTRICTED TO
AUTHORIZED PERSONNEL ONLY.**

"Son of a bitch." It was a whisper, nothing more. His eyes flew across the control panel. It was a useless gesture. Without access to the command menu, he could not open the landing pad.

The once-men opened the hatch. Slowly, they entered the room. Doyle was first to step through. Sullivan and Kehoe shouldered each other out of the hatchway and succeeded in wedging themselves in place. It would have been comical under other circumstances.

Nixon pulled the gun from his waistband. He aimed it at Doyle and nearly pulled the trigger. He stopped himself. What was the point? He had shot him, shot *them*, several times. Yet here they were. Nixon put the barrel of the gun to his own temple. *Better to go this way*, he thought.

Doyle was no more than five meters from him. His gray arms beckoned to Nixon. Behind him, Kehoe won the struggle and stepped through the hatch.

Nixon pulled the trigger.

He heard the dry click and nothing more. *The fucking safety*, he thought, and he laughed aloud. He shook his head. He lowered the gun, looked at it. "Ain't that a kick in the balls." He thumbed off the safety. He very nearly brought the gun up to his temple again. Then he thought better of it.

He saw the button for the intercom and stabbed it. He did not know if Dwyer had restricted its use as well, but he hoped she had not. He shouted, "Mike, if you can hear me, grab on to something."

Doyle's hands wrapped themselves around Nixon's arms.

Nixon pointed the weapon at the control panel and pulled the trigger.

****

The elevator dropped rapidly to the floor of the hanger. The oxygen inside the large area wasted no time evacuating into the lunar atmosphere. The control room hatch flew all the way open. Sullivan, who was partly through the hatch, was ripped from it so suddenly and violently his right hand tore from his wrist. It maintained its grip on the hatch frame even as his body disappeared through the open space so recently occupied by the landing pad. He was not alone.

The windows inside the control room buckled to their frames and exploded. Sparks flew from the damaged control panel and followed the bits of glass out through the opening in the hanger's ceiling.

The sudden torrent of air escaping the hanger acted against the belly of the ship above. It shoved the *Sovereign of the Stars* violently to the side. Her starboard landing strut was suddenly required to support far more weight than had ever been intended. The metal would have screamed had there been atmosphere. As it was, it buckled silently at the joint. The starliner began to list to starboard.

The docking sleeve grew taut and then gave as the starliner pulled away. It tore loose from the hull of the *Sovereign of the Stars*. The sleeve became rigid for a single moment. The explosion of air blew the once-people inside the sleeve out onto the lunar surface. Some were propelled with such force and speed they crashed against the hull of the starliner and bounced off. Several smudges of dust marked their impact points. Desiccated pieces of human bodies rained onto the lunar landscape.

The starliner's three intact landing struts were pulled from the edges of the landing pad simultaneously. The ship's list to starboard quickly became unrecoverable. To the only two people who watched the unexpected and violent incident, the *Sovereign of the Stars* seemed to fall in slow motion. She crashed onto the lunar surface on her starboard side. Dust and debris billowed from the point of impact, some of which would not settle for hours.

Nearly every window inside the ship shattered with the force of the impact. The atmosphere within evacuated through the open hatch. Everything not bolted to the decks and bulkheads was blown through the hatch. Expensive works of art, hand-carved wood furniture, musical instruments and bodies were torn out of the ship. They would eventually find a resting spot on the lunar surface next to cutlery made of pure silver and gold, articles of clothing and bedpans.

Within the engine room, alarm klaxons wailed silently in the new vacuum. Warning lights flashed on nearly every control console. Indicator lights changed from green to red and screamed for attention. The air circulation system overloaded and shut down. Sparks flew from the station that monitored and maintained the starliner's artificial gravity generators. Chief engineer Watkins' monitor screen flashed a message no one would read:

WARNING WARNING WARNING
MAIN DRIVE ENGINES DESTABILIZED
WARNING WARNING WARNING

The ship's atmosphere was still in the process of evacuating when the drive engines exploded. Entire sections of the starliner's hull were blown in all directions. The fireball was brief but enormous. It spread out from the ship. Much of the debris hurled from within the starliner caught fire or simply vaporized. The spreading wall of flames destroyed the docking sleeve and blackened the interior of airlock three. The window in the inner airlock hatch shattered. Automatic isolation doors quickly descended from the ceiling and sealed off the area around airlock three. The outer walls of C-ring scorched under the extreme heat.

The fireball burned itself out quickly. Smoke rose from the wreckage of the *Sovereign of the Stars* and would not abate for hours. The explosion registered 7.0 on the Richter scale, recorded in the geology lab. No one would ever know.

The starliner herself lay on her starboard side in the lunar dust. Much of the hull aft of amidships had simply vanished in the violence of her death. Her port hull lay open, her interior spaces exposed to the near-vacuum of the moon's surface. The scorched portion of her hull, which had once been penetrated by an alien life-form, was gone forever.

The *Sovereign of the Stars* became the newest and largest wreck on the moon.

Chapter 15

Trapped and Isolated

"We just crossed the threshold of the jamming signal. How's the core look?"

Hague looked at Narita in the passenger seat of the LST. The engineer held the computer core in his lap. He had attached a portable scanner to its single port. Lights on the small scanner flashed their slow sequence. They meant nothing to Hague; they would mean everything to Narita.

The engineer played with one of the control knobs on the scanner. "Looking good so far. All data intact."

Hague slapped the steering yoke. "Told you I knew what I was talking about. Am I a fucking genius or what? We're as good as home."

"I'll celebrate when we actually land at Grissom."

Hague frowned but said nothing. The wide-eyed kid he had brought to Armstrong at the start of the last rotation had vanished. Back then, Narita had been full of excitement. He all but hugged Duncan when introduced to her, so excited was he at the posting. He laughed easily and honestly. But that kid was no longer in evidence. He sounded tired to Hague, tired and old. He hoped that kid would return someday, but he had his doubts. With everything that happened in the past few days, he doubted anyone would return to being the person they had been pre-*Sovereign of the Stars*.

He returned his attention to his instruments. "ETA four minutes." He did not expect a reply, nor did he receive one. C-ring came into view a moment later when Hague guided the LST down and through a small impact crater. When the transport crested the top, the first thing he saw was the *Sovereign of the Stars*. It loomed above the base and the landing pad. The curvature of C-ring should have hidden it from view, but the damned thing was so massive it towered above everything around it. The steel hull reflected the sunlight quite effectively, even through the shield on Hague's helmet. He squinted and cursed it silently. Hague could see the outline of the garage door on the skin of C-ring. He turned in that direction.

Quite unexpectedly, the *Sovereign of the Stars* tilted to one side. He thought at first he had imagined it. A moment later, the top edge of the docking sleeve tore away from the hull. The ship teetered. "What the hell is that?" he shouted.

Narita had packed away the portable scanner and zipped the toolkit shut. He winced when Hague's voice nearly overloaded the speaker in his helmet and looked up.

What appeared to be bodies flew out from the docking sleeve. They tumbled across the night sky. Objects exploded out of the *Sovereign*'s open airlock hatch, accompanied by frozen oxygen. The great vessel's list to starboard increased until Hague knew it could not right itself. It fell over slowly, as if reluctant to surrender itself to the inevitable. It impacted the lunar surface and a great cloud of dust obscured the starliner from his vision.

"Jesus Christ," Hague said.

"Oh my God," Narita added. "What happened?"

The dust cloud raced toward them. Hague braced himself against the yoke and slammed his foot on the brake pedal. The LST skidded to a stop after a few moments. Moon dust flared in front of the transport's tires. The cloud was nearly upon them.

"Get down!" Hague grabbed Narita around the shoulders and forced the engineer down across the console between their seats. Narita hugged the computer core to his chest. Hague threw himself on top of him.

The dust cloud enveloped the LST. It rocked slightly on its suspension. Wind such as Hague had never felt on the lunar surface tore at his isolation suit, at his helmet and gloves. He gritted his teeth and held onto Narita as if he were a drowning man suddenly thrown a life preserver. The wind was silent in the near-vacuum, but Hague's mind came up with a sound he thought would be pretty accurate had this occurred under an atmosphere.

The wind lessened in intensity after a few moments. It was a moment longer before Hague felt safe enough to raise his head. His faceplate was covered with dust. He wiped some of it away and tapped Narita on the shoulder. "It's okay, it's over."

Narita started to rise.

That was when the starliner exploded.

****

Hansen nearly lost his balance. The deck beneath his feet shook, then it heaved violently. He grabbed onto the side of the exam table with one hand and placed the other on McKnight's chest. The ceilings lights flickered, went out and then came back. He heard Mikhailov shout something, and he was certain he heard her crash to the deck. On the other side of the exam table, Millman went down as his knees buckled.

"What the hell's happening?" Mikhailov shouted from somewhere behind him.

The damaged power cables that dangled from the ceiling swayed like tree branches in a hurricane. They dropped another meter. Hansen leaned over McKnight and tried to shield the unconscious man. Sparks flew from the intercom panel and showered Millman as the scientist rode out the tremor. His hands flew up and covered his face. The instrument tray rolled a few meters then tipped and landed on its side. Surgical tools flew in all directions.

The quake lasted only a few moments. When the tremors subsided, the first thing Hansen did was check McKnight for a pulse. He found one. It was weak and erratic, but unmistakable. *Still alive. Thank God for that.* He turned his attention immediately to Mikhailov. She had indeed lost her footing. She sat on the deck and cradled her left wrist. Surgical tools lay scattered on the deck around her. Hansen extended a hand. She took it wordlessly.

"You okay?"

Mikhailov rubbed her wrist. "I'm fine, Mike. What was that?"

"It wasn't seismic activity, I can tell you that," Millman said. He pulled himself to his feet. "Not in this area."

"Nix," Hansen said. He ignored the look of horror on Mikhailov's face and said, "Keep working on Don." He started for the intercom, stopped. The bulkhead around the panel was scorched. A tiny flame sputtered at its top. He moved quickly into the corridor and found the nearest intercom. He hit the switch. The indicator light remained dark. He hit it again, received the same result. "Comm is down in this section," he called over his shoulder. He reentered the infirmary.

"What did you mean when you said 'Nix'?" Mikhailov continued to massage her injured wrist.

"I thought I heard him say something just before the quake," Hansen said. "I didn't pay attention because of Don. Offhand, I'd say Nix was the source of whatever that was. I want you two to stay here. Do whatever you can for Don. I'm going to the con."

"Wait, Mike," Mikhailov said. When Hansen turned to her, she swallowed hard. "I'll go. You're better at this than I am." She indicated McKnight. "I'm pretty fucking useless here."

Hansen considered. Her eyes told him she did not want to go to the main control room by herself, but she seemed determined. She even stood a little straighter than usual. She stuck out her chin and squared her shoulders. It would have made him laugh under different circumstances. "Okay, go. Find out what happened and then double-time it back here. Understood?"

Mikhailov nodded. "Understood quite clearly."

She stepped through the hatch and looked in either direction of the corridor. She seemed satisfied with what she saw. She took a single step into the corridor before she stopped and reentered the infirmary. She unhooked the holster from her waist and held it out to Hansen. "Here. We both know I'm useless with this thing, anyway."

Hansen tilted his head. "Are you sure? You might run into trouble between here and there."

"I'll be fine." She smiled weakly. "Thorpe's holding down the fort. And besides, those things were last seen in this area, not the control room. You'll probably need this more than I will."

Hansen took the holster and strapped it around his waist. "Okay. Just be careful."

"Bet on it." She stepped through the hatch once again and rechecked the corridor in either direction. A moment later, she was gone.

Hansen watched her go and then returned his attention to McKnight.

****

Hague would have been thrown from the LST had he not been secured to the seat. The transport rocked violently. Its wheels jumped a bit and, when the quake subsided, the transport had swung a few degrees to the left. The fireball rose high into the darkened sky. It lasted only a moment before it burned itself out. Large plumes of smoke billowed up from behind the curvature of C-ring. He could just make out the bow of the *Sovereign of the Stars*. The ship, or what remained of her, rested on her side.

"Holy Mother of God," Hague said.

Narita looked at the cloud of smoke and whistled through his teeth. "Had to be her main engines, had to be. Nothing else could have exploded with that much force."

Hague slapped the LST into gear. The transport lurched forward. "Whatever it was, it's not a good sign. We have to get back there fast." He depressed the accelerator. The transport shuddered. Its left rear wheel spun and machine-gunned pebbles and dust away from them. The LST did not move.

"Come on, let's go," Narita said. He sounded both frightened and impatient. "Go, go, go."

Hague gritted his teeth and worked the transport's controls. "I'm trying. Something's wrong." He mashed the accelerator. Rooster tails of dust kicked up behind them. The transport remained in place.

"What the hell are you waiting for?" Narita's voice rose in pitch. He sounded close to panic.

"I think we lost the drive axles on your side." He tried the accelerator again. The transport lurched forward and to the left. He felt the vibration of the LST's engine through the pedals at his feet and the steering yoke. He took his foot from the accelerator and hit the main power switch. The indicator lights winked out and the engine died. Hague sat back in the seat. "That's it, we're not moving."

Narita released his restraints and dismounted the LST. He kept his toolkit held tightly in his hands. He took a single step away from the transport before he reached back inside and grabbed the remote control for the garage door. He looked at Hague, who remained in his seat. "Gotta go, gotta go."

Hague released his restraint and followed Narita. They were close enough to Armstrong that he could see quite clearly the outline of the garage door. He tried to focus on that, but he could not help himself from the occasional glance at the new debris field as they grew closer.

A writing table, its granite top broken and several pieces missing, was the first piece of debris they came across. Next to it lay a fifteen-meter section of the starliner's hull. It contained six portholes; the glass was missing from each of them. The severed hand belonged to a woman, if the long, painted nails were an indication. A diamond ring remained on one of the shriveled fingers.

Hague saw the first body a moment later. It had been a man once. Both legs were gone at the knees. His left arm was likewise missing in action. What remained of his clothes marked him as a passenger. His face was hidden in the dust. Hague was grateful for that.

The second body belonged to a young boy, no more than eleven or twelve years old. Clutched in his mummified hand was what appeared to be a toy spacecraft. Hague turned away. He did not want to see any more. He ignored the rest of the bodies they passed.

They reached the garage. He watched Narita aim the remote at the panel on the wall next to the door. The yellow light mounted on the wall just above the door began to flash. A moment later, the garage door began its slow disappearing act into the bulkhead. Hague tapped his fingers impatiently and stole several glances over his shoulder. The door seemed to move slower than usual, but it might have been his imagination. When there was enough room for them, both men moved as quickly as they were able into the garage.

"Let's repressurize the garage and get the fuck out of here." He took two steps toward the hatch when he noticed Narita. The engineer stood next to another LST. The computer core remained in his right hand. The toolkit fell from his other hand and landed on the deck without a sound. He stared at the open moonscape. "Narita?" Hague's brow furrowed. He approached the engineer. "Kid, what are you doing?"

Narita raised his left arm and pointed straight ahead. Hague looked.

The woman in the singed nightgown stood perhaps fifteen meters outside the garage. She moved slowly in the low gravity. Her eyes, deep inside their sockets, seemed fixed on Hague. She wore plush slippers that might have been pink; they disappeared almost entirely into the moon dust with each step she took. Her skin was withered and appeared ancient. She wore no protective clothing, yet seemed untroubled by the near-vacuum around her. She raised her withered right arm and pointed at them. Her mouth worked silently.

Behind her, Hague caught sight of three more people. A woman in the tattered uniform of a chef rose to her knees. Dust and a small piece of debris from the starliner fell off her back and from what little hair had not been singed from her head. She regained her feet and took a slow, halting step in their direction. Behind her, two children, a boy and a girl, also began their trek to the garage. The children held hands.

"Fuck me," Hague said.

The obscene quartet made slow progress toward the open garage door. They did not walk so much as they *shambled*. It looked unnatural, and not solely because of their lack of isolation suits or the mummified appearance of their bodies. There was much more to it than that.

Hague felt a rumble in his stomach and he prayed he would not vomit inside his helmet. He reached the wall panel and hit the button that activated the garage door. The door obligingly began to slide closed. It moved slowly, too slowly for Hague. He thought perhaps there was a malfunction in one of its motors. The dead people outside the garage continued their slow advance. They were no more than ten meters from the threshold. Hague calculated the speed of the door against the speed of the people outside. It would be close, too close.

He grabbed Narita and pulled the engineer across the deck. They reached the hatch and turned. The woman in the nightgown had one foot across the threshold when the door closed on her. Her head and the right half of her body had made it inside; the rest of her remained on the other side of the door. Her arm waved at them. Her foot lifted from the deck and then set down again. Dust plumed up and off her slipper (it was indeed pink) with each impact. Her mouth opened and closed, her eyes drilled into them.

For a moment, Hague thought the door would not seal itself. Without a clean seal, they would be unable to repressurize the garage or open the hatch and reenter Armstrong. *That would prove our luck is holding*, he thought. *To make it all the way there and back and be stopped here? Like this?* He nearly laughed. It was only for a moment, however. The door closed itself completely, and the seal was complete. The right half of the woman's body landed on the deck in a plume of dust.

He watched Narita activate the environmental controls. Almost against his will, Hague walked across the garage to the dead woman. She was not dead. She lay on the deck, flat on what remained of her back. Her eyes were open and focused on Hague. She reached up with her arm. The half of her nightgown that made it inside the garage had fallen away. Hague got a good look at her withered body. He should have seen blood and internal organs and bone. Perhaps it was the lighting in the garage (although he knew it was not), but the woman's insides appeared to be uniformly gray. He could make out what he took to be some of her ribs, but he could not identify the rest of what he saw.

He yanked off his helmet and vomited onto the deck. It was an impulse move; he was not even aware the garage had repressurized. Later, he would berate himself for such stupidity. At present, all he could do was void the contents of his stomach.

****

Mikhailov reached the connecting corridor between A-ring and the command module. She paused for a moment, out of breath. She leaned against the bulkhead and thought, *I need to quit smoking.* Then she took out a cigarette and fumbled through her pockets for her lighter. She remained that way for another moment, leaning against the bulkhead and searching for her elusive lighter. She found it, brought it out and flicked it to life. She brought it up, but the flame stopped inches away from paydirt.

Shouts, panicked shouts, reached her ears. She knew from where the sounds originated. She ditched her unlit cigarette and ran the rest of the way. She reached the hatch to the control room and looked inside.

She heard a gunshot. The bullet buried itself in the bulkhead next to her head. She shrieked and dove to the deck. Her hands covered her head and she felt warm blood on her cheek. She felt the wound with her fingers and decided it was superficial. *Probably caught a small splinter of the bulkhead. Big deal. Get on your feet, bitch.*

She rose to her knees and heard more shouts from inside the control room. "Hold your fire!" She had no idea if anyone heard her. She peeked inside the room, ready to retreat in a hurry if she heard another gunshot.

The first thing she saw was the main monitor screen. At first she thought a transport had crashed just short of the landing pad. The twisted and ruined hull belched smoke slowly into the lunar sky. But the ship was far too big to be a transport. The identity of the wreck came to her all at once. She gasped.

Her eyes moved away from the monitor. Wright stood near the room's center. He held the gun with both hands and aimed it squarely at Thorpe. Her first thought was Wright had somehow managed to wrestle the gun away from Thorpe and was about to shoot him. She very nearly screamed for Wright to stop, but she caught herself in time. Something was clearly wrong with the geologist; he moved slowly, and there was an unnatural quality to his gait. His eyes reminded her of Duncan's the night the engineer attacked her in her quarters. Behind Wright, directly behind him, stood Dwyer. She had both hands on Wright's shoulders, and moved her feet in time with his. She clearly wanted to keep the major between herself and Thorpe.

Not just Thorpe. Two others were inside the control room as well. It took her a moment, and when she recognized them, her jaw dropped and eyes went wide. Hasegawa stood perhaps ten meters away from Thorpe. A few meters farther away, Mason struggled weakly to get to his feet. They all moved slowly toward the center of the room. Their arms were outstretched, as if they beckoned to Wright and Dwyer. Mason appeared much as Thorpe, but Hasegawa most closely resembled the woman from the starliner. Her lab coat, saturated with blood from the gunshot wounds that took her life in the security office, hung from her shrunken frame.

Smoke drifted lazily from the environmental station. Mikhailov guessed, correctly as it turned out, that Wright had missed his target and shot the workstation. As Mikhailov watched, Wright fired another round. It connected solidly with Thorpe's chest. Blood trickled out of the wound but stopped itself almost instantly. The hole in his shirt and the small red stain were the only indications anything had happened at all. Thorpe did not seem to notice. He continued his slow advance.

Mikhailov got to her feet. "Wright, Wright, over here. Come to me."

Wright and Dwyer whirled in her direction. The gun swung her way again. Mikhailov backed away instinctively. No shot was fired.

"We're trying!" Wright shouted. "They're between us and the hatch! Help us!"

"How?" Mikhailov peeked around the corner. Thorpe and Hasegawa seemed intent on reaching Wright and Dwyer. Mason, who had finally managed to regain his feet, turned in her direction. His head lolled to one side, his skin was pulled tightly around his bones. Upon closer inspection, he more closely resembled Hasegawa than Thorpe. His mouth was open, and he produced a sound Mikhailov had never heard from a human being. She retreated a meter farther from him and cursed her decision to relinquish the gun to Hansen. "I don't have a weapon."

"They don't care about weapons," Wright answered.

"*Help us you fucking cunt!*" Dwyer screamed.

Wright squeezed off another shot. It hit Hasegawa squarely in the throat. Dust followed the bullet out of the exit wound. She backed up a single step, paused and then resumed her march. Her neck was nearly gone; even from her vantage point Mikhailov could see where the top of Hasegawa's spine met her skull.

"I'm almost out of ammo and they keep coming! Mikhailov, help us!"

Mason reached the hatchway and peered through it. Mikhailov locked eyes with him. The breath left her. She slid back along the bulkhead slowly, as if her muscles had forgotten how to operate properly. Mason stepped through the hatchway. He reached for her. "I need you," he said.

Mikhailov lost the power to produce sound, but as compensation she found she could move again. She whirled and took two steps away from the control room when she stopped dead. Sofia Nelson stood in the center of the corridor twenty meters away. She had something small grasped in her fingers. She turned over the object, seemed to study it. It took Mikhailov a moment to recognize it as the cigarette she had dropped. The dead woman's eyes remained focused on it. She tilted her head like a dog given an unfamiliar command by its master. After another moment, she put it between her lips. Her cheeks hollowed.

Mikhailov shrieked. She spun, saw Mason was nearly on top of her. She sprinted down the corridor toward Nelson. Tears spilled from her eyes and threatened to blind her. She reached Nelson in seconds. The dead woman ignored her. She continued to stand in the center of the corridor and tried to smoke the dead cigarette. Mikhailov pulled her arms in as much as she was able. She snaked her way around Nelson. She was convinced the dead woman would reach for her, but she did not. When she had cleared the obstacle, she cried out again and bolted down the corridor.

****

Nelson looked up, watched her go. Slowly, she pulled the cigarette from her lips and regarded it again. She dropped it to the deck and stepped on it with her bare foot. She looked at it for several more moments.

Mason reached her and nudged her out of his way. Nelson lost her balance and would have gone down had she not been close enough to the bulkhead. She sagged against it, steadied herself and regained her balance. Her eyes found a new object on the deck near her feet. She bent down and picked it up and held it in front of her eyes. She did not know what the object was, and it took her only a moment to decide it was of no interest to her. She dropped it to the deck and followed Mason down the corridor.

The top of her skull remained on the deck where she dropped it.

****

"That fucking bitch left us!" Dwyer shifted her gaze from the two dead people in the room to the open (and empty) hatchway. Hasegawa stood between it and them. "I gave her a direct order and she left us! I'm going to kill that cunt when I see her again!"

Wright ignored her and fired his weapon again. The bullet struck Thorpe in the chest, centimeters from a previous wound. Dust plumed from the new hole in Thorpe's body. There was no blood. The geologist gave no indication he even noticed. "We're running out of room, here. We're gonna have to make a break for it."

Dwyer shifted her grip on Wright's shoulders. They turned in a slow half-circle. "Don't be a fool, we'll never make it." She eyed Thorpe; he was closest. The geologist had suffered several gunshot wounds to his chest and abdomen. Strangely, those wounds no longer bled. But his nose and his mouth did. Blood trickled from his nostrils and the sides of his lips.

"I'm open to suggestions," Wright said.

Her opinion of Wright, hardly glowing to begin with, plummeted. "I suggest you kill these things and restore order to this facility, *Major.*" She was careful to keep Wright between her and the two dead people. But their circle was tightening at an alarming rate. She estimated she had no more than thirty seconds before either of them reached her. She could not allow that to happen.

"Kill them, don't kill them. Make up your mind! And by the way, how do you suggest I do that?" There was an edge to Wright's voice she had never before heard. At least, not when he addressed her. *The situation got the better of him. Even he's turning against me.* It made her decision that much easier.

She removed her hands from his shoulders and placed them on his back. She shoved with everything she had. Wright, unprepared for that particular maneuver, stumbled forward, nearly into Thorpe's outstretched arms. He screamed. She bolted for the hatch to his office. She ducked Hasegawa's arm when the dead woman tried for her.

She reached the hatch and entered the code quickly. The hatch sprung open. Dwyer dove through and kicked it closed behind her. She quickly locked it and put her back against it. She heard Wright scream from somewhere beyond the hatch. She paid no notice.

She felt the familiar tightness in her chest. The breath rattled in her throat, and her heart hammered within her ribcage. She gasped in as much air as she was able. Her vision began to blur at the edges. She fumbled through her pockets until she came across her inhaler. Her hands shook, and she very nearly dropped it. She took a long pull from it, felt the medicine make its way to her lungs. She breathed easier.

She willed her heart to cease its rapid beating and slow down. She became aware of the sweat on her brow. Her arms were covered with gooseflesh. She berated herself silently. Such symptoms were for lesser people. She would find a way out of this, of course she would. She was Lindsay *Fucking* Dwyer. She was the next president of the GSA.

It was time to reestablish those credentials.

****

Wright bolted for the closed hatch. He was forced to fire another round at Hasegawa when his course took him too close to her. The bullet lodged itself in her abdomen. She did not react. He aimed for her head and pulled the trigger again. He found himself entirely unprepared for the result. Hasegawa's head snapped back, dust exploding from the back of it; her hair blew back as if she were facing a strong wind. She staggered back and collapsed to the deck. She did not move.

Wright blinked at her for a moment. Was it that simple? He thought perhaps it was. In retrospect, he had been foolish not to have attempted a headshot when it became clear aiming for center mass was ineffective.

He looked at Thorpe in a whole new light. The geologist continued to close the distance between them. The man's eyes, previously dark brown bordering on black, had turned gray. He reached out for Wright with both arms. It was still terrifying, but less so now that Wright knew how to handle him. He brought up the gun, aimed it squarely at Thorpe's head and pulled the trigger.

Nothing happened. He panicked and pulled the trigger several more times. The hammer continued to strike empty air. He looked at the weapon as if unwilling to believe it had betrayed him. He threw himself at the hatch to his office and pounded on it with both fists. "Dwyer, open the hatch! Let me in now! I know how to kill them but I need more ammo!" He looked over his shoulder. Thorpe changed course and made for Wright. He was no more than six meters away. Wright pounded on the hatch again. *"Dwyer!"*

It dawned on him she would not open the hatch. He put his back to it and replaced the weapon in its holster. He looked at Thorpe and gauged the time it would take him to input his code and open the hatch versus the speed at which the geologist advanced. He would not have enough time unless Dwyer's relented and let him in. Thorpe was simply too close. The geologist had once again raised his arms. Combined with the manner in which he lurched about, Wright thought of sleepwalkers. Except for Thorpe's eyes, which were wide open and focused solely on him.

Wright eyed the open hatchway to his left. Mason had gone that route, distracted by Mikhailov. The psychologist screamed even after she had abandoned him and Dwyer. That meant there were probably more of these things in that direction. It also meant Mikhailov was most likely dead. In addition, the odds were very good he would die if he followed her. That left him a single option.

He ducked under Thorpe's arms when he reached for him. He dove for the base of the stairs that led to the engineering loft. He took them three at a time. At the top of the stairs, he turned and looked down into the main control room. Thorpe stood at the sealed hatch to his office. Slowly, he turned. He looked about the room, obviously confused as to where Wright had disappeared. It took him a moment to locate the major. His expressions did not change when the two of them made eye contact; he simply shambled for the stairs.

His intelligence is gone. The revelation hit Wright with a sickening thud. He should have realized it sooner – before he had decided on a course of action that left him trapped on the engineering loft. Trapped and isolated.

Thorpe reached the base of the stairs.

****

Hague very nearly ran past the infirmary before he noticed the activity inside. He skidded to a stop, slipped on the broken glass that littered the deck and went down. He cursed his clumsiness and regained his feet. He moved around to the hatch, saw Hansen and Millman working on someone laid out on the exam table. The rest of the room was all but destroyed.

He entered the infirmary. "What the hell happened here?"

Hansen and Millman looked up, but only for a moment. They quickly returned their attention to their patient. "McKnight's been shot," Millman stated matter-of-factly. The front of the doctor's shirt and trousers were covered with blood.

"What? Who shot him? And where is everyone else?"

"Did you get what you needed from the *Daedalus*?" It was Hansen who asked the question. He, too, concentrated on McKnight. He, too, was covered with blood.

"Got it. Narita's on his way to hanger two as we speak." He stepped closer to the table. "How can I help?"

He got his first good look at McKnight and suddenly felt the question was rather superfluous. The pilot was bathed in blood from his chest to his knees. All the color had drained from his face. He did not appear to breathe, but the single functioning monitor attached to him indicated a heartbeat. It was weak and highly erratic.

"We're finished," Millman said. "As finished as we can be, anyway. I just have to sew him up now."

"What are his chances?" Hansen asked.

Millman paused long enough to lock eyes with Hansen. He shook his head almost imperceptibly. "The bullet has been removed but he's lost too much blood." He paused. "Ten-ninety. At best."

"I don't want to pile on the bad news, but I will, anyway." Hague waited until Hansen acknowledged him with a look of desperate anticipation. "The *Sovereign of the Stars* exploded a few minutes ago. It just tipped onto her side and blew."

"That was Nixon," Hansen said, his voice neutral.

Hague swallowed and shook his head. "I'm sorry, Colonel, but that's not the worst of it." He licked his lips, tried to find a way to tell them what he and Narita had seen without coming across like a man who had lost his mind. He decided there was no such way in the English language, or any other language, for that matter. "There are people out there, outside the base. They came from the starliner." He swallowed. "They're wandering around out there without isolation suits or any other kind of protection. They came after us. One of them got cut in half by the garage door and she was still alive."

"That's not as surprising as you might think," Hansen said.

"Those have to be the people who were secured behind the blast door on the engineering deck," Millman said. "Sullivan and I opened that door but they weren't up and about yet."

"Narita and I didn't see them, either, and we were there for a while." Hansen could not keep the disbelief from his voice.

"Then you got very, very lucky, Colonel. I'm sure they had reanimated by then. If I were you I'd play the fucking lottery when we get back."

Hague had a follow-up question, but it died in his throat. He turned at the sound of rapid footfalls in the corridor. He backed away from the exam table and poked his head through the open hatchway. His trepidation that it might be Wright vanished when he saw Mikhailov round the bend in the corridor. He started to smile and step across the threshold when he caught sight of Mikhailov's expression. His smile vanished, and he rushed to her.

She collapsed into his arms. He dropped to one knee and lowered her to the deck. Her breaths came in short, deep gulps. Her eyes were wild. She gripped his arms with enough strength to make him wince. "We have to... have to get out of here right now. *Right now*, Robert! They're right behind me!

Hague looked the way she had come. He expected to see Wright, possibly Dwyer, but the corridor remained empty. "There's no one here, Galina. It's okay, calm down. I'm here."

"They're right behind me!" she shrieked.

He looked up again, saw nothing.

"Hague, get in here," Hansen called from inside the infirmary.

Hague helped Mikhailov to her feet and took her by her hands. He guided her into the infirmary. She did not fight him, which was fortunate. He was exhausted and in no condition to wrestle her.

"Help us," Hansen said. He held a stretcher next to the exam table. Millman had already lifted McKnight and held the unconscious man by his shoulders. Hansen handed the stretcher to Hague and moved to the opposite end of the table.

Hague took the stretcher and offered the other handle to Mikhailov. She took it without a word. They braced themselves for the weight about to be applied to the stretcher.

"One, two, three," Millman said. Both men lifted McKnight from the table and placed him on the stretcher. It sagged a bit on Mikhailov's side, and Millman moved around the table quickly and took the stretcher from her. Mikhailov moved to the side wordlessly.

"Okay, pad two," Hansen said. He took Mikhailov by her arm and stepped into the corridor.

Mikhailov followed him out, paused just outside the threshold and screamed.

Through the shattered window Hague saw two people enter his field of vision. The dead woman he did not recognize, but she appeared the same as the people he had encountered after the starliner exploded. The top half of her head was gone. He could see, more clearly than he would have liked, the crest of her brain. The man was Mason.

Hansen raised his weapon and fired. He put two bullets into both Nelson and Mason. Neither broke their stride. "Let's go, let's go," Hansen shouted.

Hague and Millman moved toward the open hatch as quickly as they were able.

****

Dwyer sat in the chair behind Wright's desk and tapped her fingers. She watched the image on the small monitor with a mixture of amusement and disgust. Wright stood on the engineering loft and hurled the fourth and final chair down the stairs. It joined the other three near the bottom. She had to admit, he had created an effective barricr for the dead man to overcome. For the moment, anyway. She doubted the barricade would last long. When Thorpe got through it, and he would, Wright was a dead man. And she would watch him die from within his own office. It wasn't that she wished him dead, or would take any joy from it. But she could not risk herself simply to save one man, an unimportant man, at that. In truth, she could not think of a single person for whom she would risk her life. Her calling was far greater. She needed to remain alive so she could answer that call. It was that simple.

She pressed a button and the image on the monitor changed. She recognized hanger two immediately. What she did not know was why Narita emerged from the control room and made his way toward the old transport. He had something in his hand, something she could not identify. *Probably some engineer's trick to override the jamming signal*, she thought. *Good luck*. He entered the transport and vanished from her view. She smirked. It was a fact some people were simply incapable of learning.

The image changed again and she saw empty corridor. Another touch of the button and she looked inside the sealed area around airlock three. A pair of left hands poked through the broken window, as if they belonged to blind people who suddenly found themselves in unfamiliar surroundings. She could not see the owners of those hands, which was fine with her. It was not that they frightened her, although they did. They were simply…*dirty*. She wasted no more time on the airlock.

The camera inside the security office afforded her a view of Sanchez staggering toward the open hatch. *Him, too*, she thought, and nearly laughed. This was becoming quite absurd.

The image of the infirmary was blacked out. At the bottom of the screen appeared the words: **CAMERA OFFLINE AREA A4**. She scowled and changed the image again. Another empty corridor, this one inside B-ring. *Where are you, Hansen?* She changed the image again.

It was one of the connecting corridors between B- and C-rings. Hansen and Mikhailov moved steadily through the corridor. A moment later, Hague appeared. He manned one end of a stretcher upon which McKnight lay. Even on the substandard image on the monitor, the man appeared dead. Millman had the other end of the stretcher. *Fucking traitor*, she thought. *Wait until we get back to Earth.*

She pressed a few buttons on the control panel. The monitor's image changed to the GSA logo. *Time to call in the professionals*, she thought. She entered her code and waited. Nothing happened. The logo remained in place. She entered it again, received the same result.

"What is this?" she asked of no one. Her brow furrowed. She tried again. The GSA logo stared back at her. "No." She slammed her fist onto the desktop. A cup of cold coffee vibrated its way off the desk and splashed on the deck. She did not notice. "Cromwell, you son of a bitch." Her voice was a decibel above a whisper. "I'll get you for this, you fucker. I swear I will."

She screamed suddenly and loudly. She swept her arms across the desk. Everything save the monitor flew through the air and made varying degrees of noise when they landed. She sat forward, chest heaving and lungs taking in giant gulps or air. She knew she could use another pull on the inhaler, but she did not retrieve it from her pocket. She had but a single course of action left to her. She swore vengeance on Cromwell and opened the facility-wide intercom.

"Hansen, this is Lindsay Dwyer." She choked on the words, but forced them from her lips. She could not hide her frustration, though; that was simply beyond her abilities. "Major Wright and I are trapped inside the main control room. We need your help."

Chapter 16

Time's Short

Hansen paused when they reached the open hatch to hanger two. He looked inside. He saw no one at first. He narrowed his eyes and could just make out Narita in the cockpit of the transport. "It's clear," he said, and he stepped through the hatchway. He stopped on the other side and helped Mikhailov through. She had recovered enough from her near-escape in the control room to move on her own, but Hansen guessed her adrenaline rush was gone. She shivered and moved more slowly than he would have liked.

"Mike, just to be clear, you're not going back for them, right?" Her voice was soft. Doubtless she had used a similar tone in her capacity as base psychologist. Under other circumstances, that voice could impart feelings of safety and stability, Hansen was willing to bet on that. Now, she simply sounded scared.

"Let's just get to the transport," was his only reply.

Mikhailov walked slowly down the steps to the hanger deck. When she reached the bottom, she waited for the others.

Hansen stepped aside when Hague arrived. He made it through the hatchway and managed to keep the stretcher level. "They're catching up, Colonel." Hansen did not need to ask who *they* were. McKnight appeared even closer to death than he had in the infirmary. His skin was nearly the color of snow. It contrasted with the darkening blood that saturated his clothes. Behind him, Millman reached the threshold.

"They're becoming acclimated to our atmosphere." Millman struggled through the hatchway. "The *rigor* is actually reversing itself. Pretty soon they'll be as fast as we are. Let's be somewhere else when that happens."

Hansen swung the hatch closed as soon as Millman cleared it. His hand moved to the control panel. Before he could activate the lock, the hatch handle swung up and impacted his left arm. The gun flew from his hand and disappeared somewhere over the rail. The hatch opened suddenly and knocked Hansen off balance. He teetered on the landing before he lost it completely. He crashed into Millman, who lost his grip on the stretcher. The stretcher caught Hague in the small of his back and pushed him down the stairs.

Hansen tumbled. He lost count of how many times he caught the sharp edge of a step on the way down. More than once, Millman landed with his full weight on top of Hansen. The breath was driven from his lungs, and he gasped. The fall seemed to last for several minutes, but it could have been his imagination. He impacted the cold concrete of the hanger deck and lay still for a moment.

Mikhailov screamed.

Hansen rolled onto his back slowly, with pain. He opened his eyes. At the top of the stairs, just inside the hatch, stood Mason. He placed both feet on the first step and looked at Hansen as if noticing him for the first time. Nelson entered the hanger behind him.

Hansen rolled back onto his stomach and rose to his knees. His left arm barked at him and promised him much pain tomorrow. Hansen ignored it. He started to rise, then dropped down again when he saw Hague kneeling on the deck next to McKnight. The pilot's body had come off the stretcher during the fall. He lay sprawled in an awkward position on the deck. Hansen crawled on hands and knees to them. He knew right away McKnight was dead. His neck appeared broken. He reached out for his friend. Hague grabbed Hansen's wrist and shook his head. Hansen's shoulders slumped. He closed his eyes and said a quick, silent prayer.

Hansen's head whipped about and his eyes scanned the hanger for his gun. It was nowhere to be seen. He rose to his feet and started in the direction of the stairs, where he was certain the gun had landed.

Millman groaned. He had come to a stop at the base of the stairs. Even from a distance, Hansen could see the white bone that had punched through the skin on Millman's right shin. Blood spurted from the wound and pattered on the deck. "Jesus Christ," the doctor said through clenched teeth.

Hansen forgot about the gun and he and Hague rushed to Millman's side, but Mikhailov got there first. She helped the scientist into a sitting position on the deck. Millman wrapped both hands above the wound on his leg. "This isn't my fucking day," he said.

"We'll deal with this on the transport," Hansen said. "Help me with him." He nodded to Hague. They each took a position on either side of Millman and lifted him from the deck. He gave a sharp yelp and squeezed his eyes shut. "Galina, get to Narita and tell him to start the prelaunch sequence."

"Right, Mike," Mikhailov said. She sprinted across the deck to the open hatch on the transport.

Hansen struggled under Millman's weight. He had the man's right arm across his shoulder. He watched the blood continue to spurt from the wound. They were moving slowly, much too slowly. He peeked over his shoulder and saw Mason had reached the bottom of the stairs. Nelson was only a few steps behind him. He did some quick calculations in his head, and he knew they would not make it to the transport before Mason and his new friend caught them.

"Gotta move, gotta move." He gritted his teeth and moved as fast as he was able.

"Colonel Hansen, I order you to report to the main control room immediately!" It was Dwyer's voice that came from the intercom. It filled the hanger and echoed off the bulkheads. "That's a direct order, Colonel! Acknowledge me, goddamn you!"

Hansen gritted his teeth and continued toward the transport.

Mikhailov appeared in the open hatch and made the thumbs-up gesture. Then her face fell. She dropped her arm and screamed.

Hansen had no time to look back. He would not have, even had he been so inclined. He knew what Mikhailov had seen, knew what he would see. He felt Millman jerk back and away from him. The doctor screamed. Hague spun and then backpedaled. He lost his grip on Millman. Hansen found he could not support the man by himself. Hansen's legs buckled at the knees. He went down.

Millman, no longer supported by either Hansen or Hague, fell backward onto the deck. He landed hard on his side. It was Mason who had grabbed Millman; the former geologist retained his grip on the scientist's back. Millman screamed nonsense syllables. His arms flailed, and he succeeded in landing several blows against Mason's head and chest. Blood spurted from the dead man's nose and two teeth flew from his mouth. If Mason noticed, he hid it well. He leaned down, until his newly-broken nose hung mere inches from Millman's.

"I need you."

"Mason, stop!" Hansen shouted. "Leave him alone!"

Mason ignored him. The once-man opened his mouth wide.

Perhaps it was his enhanced state of mind, or perhaps it was simply a case of proximity. Hansen was certain he saw something fall from Mason's mouth and enter Millman's. The xenobiologist ceased his struggles and lay still. Millman's chest stopped its rapid rise-and-fall while his arms, which were braced against Mason's shoulders, flopped to the deck. Millman's head lolled to the side. He appeared to be asleep, but of course, he was not. Blood continued to spurt from his wounded leg.

Hague shouted something. Hansen peeled his eyes away from the dead scientist. Hague backed up slowly, away from the corpse that at one time had been the third shift navigation officer of a starliner. Nelson closed the distance between them more rapidly than Hansen would have expected. Her feet were more nimble somehow. Her brain was a sickly off-white, and it seemed to pulse. Hansen could just make out the top portion of the organ above the cut-line in her head. His stomach protested the sight with a grumble that threatened to become more.

Nelson reached for Hague.

Hague pulled his arm back and then he put all his weight into the blow. His fist disappeared into a cloud of dust that exploded from the woman's head. Nelson's body staggered, her arms waved through empty air. Hague pulled his fist back, saw the dust that covered it. For the second time in less than an hour, he vomited.

The dust cloud began to dissipate. Nelson's body continued its herky-jerky dance across the deck. Hansen could see the woman's head had vanished completely. Her bare feet crushed brittle pieces of skull and teeth beneath them. The sound echoed off the concrete walls. The body twitched as if it had come into contact with a live electrical wire. What remained of its muscles convulsed. The body collapsed. It landed on the deck with a dry thud. It continued to twitch for several more moments before it lay still. It no longer moved.

"Did you see that?" Hague had recovered enough to admire his handiwork. Bits of vomit hung from his lower lip, but he wiped them away with his sleeve. "Do you believe that just happened?"

Hansen watched the body on the deck. For the first time since Hasegawa had pronounced her dead inside the infirmary, Hansen believed Sofia Nelson was truly gone.

He looked over his shoulder. Mason was back on his feet and had taken his first step toward Hansen. Millman lay on the deck. He appeared dead, but Hansen did not buy that for a moment. It was time to go.

"Board the transport," he said to Hague.

Both men ran for it.

****

Dwyer slumped in the chair at Wright's desk. On the monitor screen in front of her, she watched Hansen and Hague board the transport and seal the hatch behind them. They were actually desperate enough to attempt a return to Earth, even without the reentry data. She scoffed at them. They were in full panic mode, not thinking through anything. When they burned up during reentry to Earth's atmosphere, would they realize their mistake? Or were they too far gone to even think clearly? She supposed the latter, but hoped for the former. She wanted them to live just long enough to realize what fools they were. Had they listened to her, they could even now be back in control of Armstrong. Instead, they would cease to exist somewhere in Earth's atmosphere.

On the other side of the hatch and from his perch on the engineering loft, Wright shouted something. She did not catch enough of it to understand, nor did she care. It would be a simple matter for her to patch into one of the cameras inside the control room and see what had caused Wright's outburst. She decided not to. It was no concern of hers, after all.

She watched Mason reach the transport's hatch. He pounded his fists on it, but he did not appear to put much force behind the impacts. *Still acclimating to our atmosphere*, she thought. *But for how much longer? Not long, judging by how quickly they can move now*. She guessed it would be no more than a few minutes until he and his friend inside the main control room were as strong in death as they had been in life.

And she was stuck inside this fucking office.

She cleared her throat. "Colonel Hansen, Major Wright and I are in need of assistance." She tried to keep her voice level, calm. She felt anything but. "Acknowledge." She swallowed hard. When she spoke again, it was through clenched teeth. "Please."

****

Hansen grabbed the harness and pulled it down across Mikhailov's chest. She sat in the chair and stared ahead. Her eyes were wide and swam with tears. Her hands shook slightly. No, it was more than her hands. Her whole body quivered, as if she were cold. Her breath came in short, quick gasps. He placed a hand on her bare arm. It was intended to be reassuring, but he also wanted to be certain. Her skin was cold, clammy. *In shock*, he thought. *And why not? Join the club.*

He knelt in front of her and fastened the harness. "You okay, Galina?"

She continued to stare ahead. She jumped a little when the pounding started. Her eyes darted to her left, to the sealed hatch. "He's out there." Her voice trembled. "He's out there."

"And that's where he's going to stay." Hansen tried to sound convincing. In truth, he was not certain. He took her hands in his. They were as cold and clammy as her arm. He rubbed them. "I'm going to go to the cockpit now. Narita will join you back here in a minute, okay? Then we're going home."

She nodded absently. She winced with each thud from the hatch.

He gave her hands a final squeeze and stood. He walked away and resisted the urge to look over his shoulder. He removed the empty holster from around his waist and tossed it onto one of the unoccupied seats.

A moment later, he poked his head into the cockpit. Hague had taken the pilot's seat and was pressing buttons and flipping switches. Narita occupied the co-pilot's seat. He likewise worked the controls. "I'm going back to get Dwyer and Wright."

Narita's head whipped around. The look in his eyes spoke volumes about his opinion of Hansen's plan. Hague was more direct. "Are you out of your fucking mind?" He pointed out the window. "There's no way you'll make it to them alive, Mike. No way."

"I can't just leave them here. Get ready to launch. I'll be back as soon as I can."

Hague grabbed Hansen's arm. "You'll die out there. You know it and I know it."

Hansen nodded. "Maybe. But I have to try." He pulled his arm gently from Hague's grip. "Just get the transport ready."

"That's easier said than done, Colonel." Narita's tone made Hansen's heart skip a beat and stopped him in mid-motion.

"What is it?"

"I'd hoped I was imaging things, but I wasn't." Narita's hands flew across the control panel. Clearly, he saw something he did not like. He slammed his fist down on the seat's armrest. His eyes darted in Hague's direction. "Anything?"

Hague continued to work his controls. After another moment, he shook his head. "Nothing." He sat back in the seat and folded his arms across his chest.

"The computer core is no good?" Hansen asked. His eyes went to the small monitor in the center of the control console. It showed a return trajectory for Earth. It was precisely what he had hoped to see.

"The core is working perfectly," Hague said.

"Then what…?"

"We can't access hanger controls," Narita said. He slammed his fist on his armrest again. "We're locked out of the system." He sat back in the seat. "All that work for nothing." He stared out the windows at the hanger's control room.

"Dwyer locked out the con," Hansen said, almost to himself. "It didn't occur to me she had locked out everything else, too."

"Well, she did," Narita said. "I saw the lockout in the control room, but I thought I could still access hanger operations from here." He shook his head. "But I can't."

"The short version is, we can launch, we can fly, and we can even land. On Earth, no less." Hague ran a hand through his hair. "But we can't activate the elevator or the landing pad." He looked over his shoulder at Hansen. "We're not going anywhere."

****

Wright sat on the top step to the engineering loft. He waved his useless gun in a slow, elegant arc in front of him, a maestro conducting an invisible symphony. Behind him, the four control stations hummed and occasionally chirped at him. He ignored them. His eyes remained fixed on the man at the base of the stairs. Thorpe continued his struggle to get past the makeshift barricade in front of him. It may have been Wright's imagination, but he felt Thorpe moved more quickly than he had before, and with slightly more agility. He had managed to shift one of the seats, but it remained lodged against the railing. It would not stay that way forever. It was simply a matter of time, and he knew it. When he got past those chairs, Wright was a dead man. There was simply nowhere left to go.

His eyes moved again to the closed hatch to his office. He had heard Dwyer's calls to Hansen over the open intercom. The first two times she had called for help, he thought perhaps Hansen would obey her and come running. He no longer entertained such thoughts. Part of him took some satisfaction in Hansen's act of mutiny. He rather enjoyed the idea of Dwyer shouting orders to someone who simply ignored her. After all, she had sealed the hatch behind her and left him to die. "Karma's a bitch," he said to the closed hatch.

He glanced at the main monitor. It was synced to the controls in his office. He saw what Dwyer saw. The image had not changed in some time. It continued to display hanger two. The transport sat on the elevator pad, and the man who used to be Mason pounded on its hatch. He was curious, however, as to why they had not yet left. Were they seriously considering trying to rescue him and Dwyer? Wright doubted it. *He* certainly would attempt no such rescue. Not with one of those…*things* on the other side of the hatch.

His eyes were drawn to movement in the foreground of the image. Millman sat up quite suddenly and looked about. He seemed confused. His head turned slowly in the direction of the transport. He tried to stand, but his broken leg gave and he collapsed to the deck. He tried again, but he appeared to slip in the pool of blood that had collected beneath his broken leg. He went down again. He started to pull himself along the deck. He left a smear of blood in his wake. Two *of those things, now*, Wright thought. *The hits just keep on comin'.*

He returned his attention to his former crewmate at the base of the stairs. Thorpe was focused on the barricade. He wondered if the man even remembered why he felt the need to get through the thing. He had not so much as glanced in Wright's direction since he began his struggle to remove the seats.

"Wright, this is Hansen. Copy."

The voice came from the open intercom on one of the engineering stations. Wright glanced at it over his shoulder and then stood. He holstered his weapon. He walked slowly, almost casually, to the nearest workstation. "I'm here, Colonel."

"Wright, listen. I'm coming to get you and Dwyer. But it might take me a while to get there. What's your status?"

"Our status?" Wright laughed. "Fucked, that's our status." His eyes moved to the staircase once more. "Don't bother, Colonel. We'll be dead before you can get here. And besides, you won't make it out of the hanger. There are two of those things outside the transport just waiting for you to open that hatch."

"Colonel Hansen, you will disregard what Major Wright just told you." It was Dwyer. "Report to the con on the double!"

Wright cast a glance at the closed hatch to his office. "Belay that, Colonel. Just get out of here. As commanding officer of Armstrong Base, I order you to evacuate now."

There was a long pause, long enough that Wright thought perhaps Dwyer had figured out how to disable the intercom on her own. Then Hansen came back. "We can't access hanger controls." He sounded resigned. "We're locked out of the system. Can you restore my code clearance?"

Wright looked again at the image of hanger two. He fancied he could see Hansen through the cockpit windows, but he could not. The camera was simply too far away for that degree of detail. He took a breath.

"He'll do no such thing!" Dwyer shouted from within Wright's office. "Colonel, I order you to come help us!"

Wright frowned and glanced at the closed hatch again.

Hansen ignored her. "Major, can you help us?"

"Colonel, you will not abandon this facility! Do you hear me? That is a direct—"

"I can't do it, Colonel," Wright said. "Not from here. I'd need the terminal in my office or the one in the security office. I'm afraid neither is an option at the moment."

There was silence from Hansen and, thankfully, Dwyer. Wright took a moment to look down the stairs again. Thorpe had succeeded in shifting one of the chairs to the side. It was not altogether out of his way, but he had moved it enough to get his foot on the second step. He noticed Wright's presence as if for the first time and grunted. He started work on the second chair.

"But what I can do for you is open the landing pad." He glared at the hatch again. "How would that be?"

"Roger that." Hansen's reply was immediate. "We're standing by here. Tell me when you're ready to decompress the hanger."

Wright glanced at the ruined environmental control console below. Smoke continued to drift lazily from its remains. He licked his lips. "I can't do that. Environmental controls are shot to shit."

"You need us, Hansen" Dwyer said. The anger was gone from her voice, as was the pleading tone she had attempted earlier. The arrogance, however, had returned. In force. She may as well have added, *I told you so.* "Now get back here and help us."

Thorpe grunted some more and wrestled with the second and third chairs. He thrashed about. His face twisted with rage; it was the first show of emotion Wright had seen from him since he had joined Mason and the others. His eyes found Wright again, and he seemed to double his efforts to remove the barricade.

Wright watched his progress.

****

Mikhailov first thought Mason had started to pour on the speed and strength in his assault on the hatch. The pounding had certainly picked up in both rhythm and volume. It took her a moment to realize the rhythm had not simply changed, it had been *added to*. Someone had joined Mason. Her first thought was of Nelson, but she dismissed that. That woman was deader than anyone Mikhailov had ever seen. That left Millman. And since he was not shouting for help…

Mikhailov rocked herself in the seat as much as the restraints would allow.

****

Hague whipped his head around and looked at Hansen. "That's it, we're dead."

Hansen said nothing. He looked at the small monitor, at the plotted course that would take them home. Then he looked up and out the windows. The sealed landing pad above their heads mocked him. He was thankful the transport was not equipped with missiles; he thought perhaps he would open fire on the pad if it were. That would get them nowhere but dead, most likely.

He laid all the cards on the table and looked for a way out. The bottom line was Dwyer was correct. They needed her. He leaned across Hague and looked out the side window and into the hanger. He could just see two figures at the hatch below and behind him. One of them had clearly crawled along the deck. Hansen could see the smear of blood Millman had left in his wake.

"We can't go back out there," Hague said.

"We'll never get past them," Narita added.

"No, we won't." Hansen swallowed.

****

Thorpe managed to finally remove the first chair. He flung it aside with a grunt. It hit one of the workstations and bounced off. It landed on its side. With the first chair removed from the barricade, the second and third chairs did not present much of an obstacle. Thorpe hurled the second chair away, and then he shoved past the remnants of the barricade. His eyes fixed on the man at the top.

Wright watched his barricade crumble. His lips pressed into a thin line. He spared one more glance at Thorpe as he made his way slowly up the stairs. Wright strode purposefully to the nearest control console.

"Colonel Hansen, copy."

"We're here, Wright." The intercom crackled. It was nearly loud enough to drown out the sound of the footfalls on the steps. Nearly.

"I can't decompress the hanger, but I think I can still help you out. Are you listening?"

"Hanging on every word."

"I can open up the landing pad. After the atmosphere is evacuated, you should be able to take off. If Hague is a decent enough pilot, he can get the transport through the opening."

"Major Wright, you are relieved of all duties immediately!" Dwyer's shout nearly overwhelmed the intercom. It squealed and drowned out whatever she said next.

Wright watched Thorpe's hand grasp the top of the rail. In another moment, he would reach the loft.

"Time's short, Colonel. Make up your minds fast."

****

Hansen tapped Narita on the shoulder. "Get back there with Galina and strap yourself in. We're leaving."

Narita did as he was told without a word. When he was clear of the cockpit, Hansen took the co-pilot's seat. He pulled on the restraints and looked at Hague. "Can the transport withstand an explosive decompression?"

Hague nodded, but he continued to look out the side window. "I think so. We have enough mass, so it shouldn't move us. But Colonel, we have another problem." He looked at Hansen and hitched his thumb toward the window.

Hansen looked out into the hanger again. He looked past McKnight's body, past the pool of blood and the trail leading from it to the transport. He even looked past the naked, decomposed corpse of Nelson. His eyes followed the direction of Hague's thumb.

When he saw it, his shoulders slumped and he said, "Son of a bitch."

****

Thorpe reached the loft. He made no move toward Wright, not at first. He simply stood and stared, as if he wanted to relish the moment of triumph his efforts had brought him.

Wright remained at the workstation. His Adam's apple traveled up and down his throat. "Colonel, what's your answer?"

"We have a problem here, Wright." Hansen's voice was soft. "The hanger hatch is wide open. If you open the landing pad, you won't just decompress the hanger. You'll decompress this entire section of C-ring."

The corner of Wright's mouth curled up in a half-smile. "I'll decompress more than that, Colonel. I'm going to open every exterior hatch and airlock Armstrong has."

The intercom crackled silence.

Thorpe took his first steps toward Wright.

"Wright, you'll be killed." Hansen's statement was matter-of-fact.

"Better to die like that than the alternative." He pressed a few buttons on the engineering workstation. The monitor came to life. The GSA logo flashed and was replaced by a command prompt. Wright inputted his code. He glanced up, saw Thorpe close the distance between them. He inputted more commands. The image on the screen changed to:

Warning Warning Warning
All Exterior Hatches Armed
All Airlocks Armed
Landing Pad One Armed
Landing Pad Two Armed
Landing Pad Three Offline
Warning Warning Warning

Wright nodded at the screen, took another glance at the new arrival to the engineering loft. "Ready on this end, Colonel."

"Major Wright, don't you fucking DARE open those hatches! Stand down AT ONCE Major!" Wright did not need the intercom to hear Dwyer. She screamed so loudly the sound cut through the hatch. It was loud enough that Thorpe paused and turned in the direction of the sound.

"Wright, are you sure about this?" Hansen's voice was flat, emotionless.

Wright looked at Thorpe. The geologist had returned his attention to him. He moved around the engineering station. "Positive. Hang on, Colonel. Blowing the hatches now."

"*MAJOR WRIGHT—*"

Wright's finger hovered above the correct button.

Thorpe reached for him. "I need you," he said.

"I bet you do," Wright replied.

He hit the button.

****

It took the least amount of time for the command module to evacuate its atmosphere. The single exterior hatch on the south bulkhead flew open. The air inside the main control room became a gale. Empty seats at the various control stations were picked up and rocketed toward the front of the room. Some bounced off bulkheads and workstations on their way to the open hatch. Thorpe flew backwards as if he were on the victorious side in a tug-of-war. He sailed off the engineering loft and collided with the mainframe access station. His body disintegrated under the impact, and he became a dust devil that quickly evaporated within the gale.

Hasegawa followed him a split-second later. The wind shifted slightly, and she impacted the hatch to Wright's office. Her right arm and most of her torso vanished under the impact. She rebounded and gained altitude. She crashed into the main monitor. Sparks flew as the image on the screen wavered. Cracks appeared around her on the monitor's surface. A moment later it went dark. Hasegawa remained pinned in place until the wind shifted direction once again. It tore her from the monitor and shot her through the hatch leading to the airlock.

273

She left a smear of dust on the top of the hatch frame, but the wind quickly blasted that away, as well.

Wright managed to hang on to the engineering station for several more moments before he, too, lost his grip. He followed Hasegawa through the hatch. Sparks flew from several workstations and were carried away in a stream that seemed as continuous as a laser beam. The open hatch at the opposite end of the main control room offered no resistance, and the contents of the corridor that connected the central hub to A-ring quickly exploded into the room. But A-ring had problems of its own.

****

There were three airlocks within A-ring. They opened simultaneously. The most dramatic scene occurred in and around the infirmary.

Everything not bolted to the deck began to whip about the room. Trays and medical instruments became projectiles. They found their way out of the room either through the open hatch or the shattered window. They bounced off bulkheads and followed the air currents out the nearest airlock.

The Gemini quickly emptied its contents into the corridor. Bottles, tables, chairs and one ancient pinball machine careened through the corridors of A-ring. The moon rock sign above the hatch tore free; it impacted the bulkhead opposite the Gemini and shattered into small particles. One of the chess pieces, a white rook, embedded itself into one of the bulkheads. The pinball machine exited A-ring with enough momentum that it slammed into the exterior wall of B-ring. It shattered into its component pieces. Most were buried in the lunar dust.

The personnel quarters fared better. Their sealed hatches protected both the contents of the rooms and their atmosphere. Only Mikhailov's quarters voided its contents. The hatch, rarely locked due to her occupation, flew open. Furniture and keepsakes tumbled into the corridor and were carried away. The photograph of Mikhailov on her tricycle would end its journey somewhere in the dust between B- and C-rings.

Inside the generator room, Duncan's tool belt whipped off the chair and disappeared through the open hatch. The chair followed it out a moment later. The lights on the main control board all came alive at the same time. The generator red-lined as the mainframe computer ordered it to maintain heat, atmosphere and artificial gravity. Circuit breakers tripped and the lights went out everywhere but the central hub. The generators would maintain temperature and artificial gravity for several more moments before they, too, went down.

****

The two transports within hanger one were too heavy with too much mass to be affected by the gale. They remained in place, even when the landing pad opened above them. The control room windows cracked then shattered. Sparks flew from them and followed the broken glass through the open landing pad.

The isolation bulkheads, which had dropped around airlock three, retracted the same time as their airlock itself opened. The former passengers and crew of the *Sovereign of the Stars* were unable to capitalize on the open hatch in front of them. The atmosphere that evacuated through airlock three swept them back onto the lunar surface. Several of them were flung back inside the wreckage of the starliner. A few of them were caught in competing airstreams when they were blasted by the torrent that erupted from the open garage. They pirouetted several meters above the lunar surface before the air currents released them. The LSTs were flung from within the garage, followed by numerous tool chests and diagnostic computers. The lights inside the garage winked out.

Transport four-two-one did not react to the hurricane within hanger two. It simply sat as it always did. Nelson's headless, naked body vaporized under the sudden torrent. Millman was ripped from the deck and vanished out the open landing pad. Mason managed to hold onto the side of the transport's steps for a moment before he was airborne. He struck the cockpit windows on his journey to the lunar surface. His head all but exploded under the impact, and he left a rather large smear of dark blood behind him.

The hanger control room, with its hatch open, equalized rapidly enough that it remained mostly unaffected. The single seat inside the room fell over. Warning lights flashed on the console. They went dark a few moments later.

****

Hansen stared at the bloodstain that used to be the head of Dr. Mason. It took him a moment to wrench his eyes from it. He did so at the same time he realized his fingers had dug their way into the armrests of the co-pilot's seat. He pulled his hands away and flexed his fingers.

Hague likewise seemed to have difficulty pulling away from the blood on the cockpit window. Hansen placed a hand on Hague's shoulder. The pilot jumped a bit and then looked sheepish.

"Sorry." His voice was barely above a whisper.

"Don't be," Hansen said. "If ever there was an occasion to be in shock, I think this is it." He leaned forward and craned his neck. He caught sight of the open landing pad in the ceiling. The stars winked at him. Hansen looked away. "Can you make it out that opening?"

Hague shook his head to clear it. He blinked a few times. "Yeah, I can make it." He sat up in the seat, as if the act of speaking aloud had stiffened his spine. "No problem at all."

Hansen hit the intercom switch. "You two okay back there?"

It took a moment for Narita to reply. He sounded out of breath. "We're okay, Colonel."

Hansen nodded. "Good, because we're leaving. Stand by for take-off."

"Standing by," Narita replied.

Hansen turned to Hague. "Okay, let's do this."

Hague flipped a few switches on his panel. The hum of the transport's engines grew louder. "Roger that." Hague pulled back on the steering yoke.

The view from outside the cockpit windows shifted. The bulkheads of the hanger fell beneath them. A moment later, they cleared the open landing pad. The lunar surface and the whole of Armstrong base lay spread beneath them. Hansen could see lights flicker from windows throughout the base. All but those within the command module went dark in the few moments it took Hague to orient the transport.

Hansen got his first real look at the wreckage of the *Sovereign of the Stars*. It lay on its side next to pad three. Its entire port hull was ripped open, blown apart from within. He whispered, "Nix," and his voice was soft enough Hague did not hear him. Hansen saw what he first took to be flotsam from the wreck, until he noticed some of the flotsam seemed to move.

Hague steered the transport over and above Armstrong. As they grew closer to pad three, Hansen could see a few of the passengers and crew of the starliner shuffle their way to the open airlock next to pad three.

"Look at that," Hague said.

"I'm looking, but I've seen enough. Let's get out of here."

"No argument here." Hague leaned on the yoke. The transport lifted up and away from Armstrong. Hansen did not look back.

****

Once-Sanchez climbed slowly to his feet. Dust fell from his hair and his clothes, but he did not notice. His eyes fell on the smoldering wreckage of the *Sovereign of the Stars*, but it was the sight of the transport ascending into the lunar atmosphere that caught and held his attention. In a dark corner of his mind, he seemed happy to see the ship recede into the distance. He even smiled. He watched it until the pinpricks of light that were her engines were no longer distinguishable from the stars themselves.

From that same dark corner within his mind flashed an image of a different type of ship, one that had been of some importance to him in a different life. He could not remember the name of the ship or why it was important, only that it was. He turned his head slowly until something told him he faced the correct direction. He took one step, then another.

Forty-five minutes later he would reach the LST abandoned by Narita and Hague. He would regard the vehicle only for a moment, concluding it was of no importance to him. Three days after that he would reach the most famous of all shipwrecks. He would stand outside the vessel, and part of him would wonder why he had made the trek. He would, of course, never arrive at an answer.

Hours later it would occur to him to board the ship and fulfill the dream of a young man now dead. It would be years before once-Sanchez saw the stars again.

****

Dwyer crawled out from under the desk and looked about. Pure instinct had sent her under the desk in the first place. She was perfectly safe within the office. The hatch was sealed and locked, and it withstood the decompression easily enough. The air vent above the deck had sealed itself automatically when Wright stupidly opened the outer hatches. Throughout the ordeal, she had felt no more than a slight tremor in the deck plates.

She placed one hand on the desk and used it to haul herself to her feet. She felt the difference in gravity immediately. She was lighter on her feet. She straightened her skirt and walked around to the back of the desk. She took the chair and sat down. She took a deep breath, felt the tightness in her chest. Absently, she reached for the inhaler in her pocket. She took two long pulls from it and felt better. She replaced the inhaler and activated the desk monitor.

It showed nothing but snow. Its small speakers hissed static at her. She remained calm. She hit one of the buttons on the panel in front of her. The snow skipped a beat but remained in place. She hit the button again. More snow. "Cocksucker," she said softly.

She tried it again. The image wavered and changed. She saw the room on the other side of the hatch. The con was deserted. No dead base personnel, no Wright. The main monitor was dark and dead. The image blurred and traveled halfway up the screen. She hit the button again.

It took three more attempts before she found another functional camera. The bottom of the image was full of snow and static, and its location was unreadable. Fortunately, the rest of the image was clear enough. She saw the signage on the bulkhead. **C-3**, it read. The damaged airlock was down the corridor but near enough to the camera Dwyer could see it. It was wide open.

She was about to change the image again when something caught her eye. Her hand stopped an inch away from the button. She had seen something move on the monitor, she was certain of it. The movement had originated near the open airlock. Dwyer leaned in closer to the screen, until the tip of her nose nearly touched it.

A man stepped through the open airlock and entered the base. He moved slowly in the low gravity. He wore the burned remains of an engineer's uniform. Behind him, two more once-people followed him. They moved slowly past the camera. She changed the image twice more before she grew tired of the snow and gave up.

She sat back in the chair and let out a long, slow breath. This was a setback, nothing more. She had had her share of them, mostly due to the incompetence of others. This was no exception. She'd find a way through this, of course she would. All she had to do was beat the jamming signal and she'd be able to contact Earth. Even if that disloyal bastard Cromwell ignored her, she was certain her reputation alone would be enough to ensure a rescue. All she had to do was find a way around the goddamned jamming signal.

The lights flickered. Dwyer's breath caught in her throat. She looked at the ceiling lights. They were on and working properly. *Must have imaged it*, she thought. *Get a fucking grip, Lindsay*. She leaned forward again and pressed buttons on the monitor. The screen was dark, as dark as its much larger counterpart in the main control room. She hit the side of the monitor with her hand. Still dark. She laughed.

She hit buttons on the panel, slowly at first but with greater and greater speed. It took her several moments to realize the buttons and lights on the panel were as dead as the monitor. "This better be someone's idea of a fucking joke," she said to no one.

The lights flickered again. She ignored them. The lights went out completely. They came back on a moment later. Dwyer was all the way back in the chair. Her eyes were wide; her hands gripped the armrests until her knuckles went white. Her breath came in short, rapid gulps.

The lights went out and stayed out. Dwyer became aware of the sound of her breathing. It sounded much too loud. It was drowned out a moment later by blood pounding in her ears. Distantly, she became aware of another sound. It seemed far off, but grew closer. It sounded like someone pounding a war drum. It took her several moments to realize it was her own heartbeat.

She sat in the chair, hands white-knuckled on the armrests and chest heaving. The sound of her heartbeat filled the world. Until someone (some*thing*) pounded on the hatch.

Dwyer screamed.

Joseph J. Christiano

The author wishes to thank:

My parents, Joe and Donna

Kim

Sheldon Reid

Michael and Nancy

About The Author

Joe grew up in Connecticut's Naugatuck Valley. A voracious reader since he was old enough to hold a book in his hands, he surprised his second-grade teacher by using the word "invulnerable" (learned from a Superman comic book) in a sentence.

He wrote his first story at the ripe old age of 11. His favorite authors and influences include Richard Matheson, Rod Sterling, Agatha Christie, Stephen King, Alan Moore and Neil Gaiman.

Thank you for your purchase. If you would like to read more by Joseph or other fine TT author, please visit our website:

www.tell-talepublishing.com

www.ingramcontent.com/pod-product-compliance
Lightning Source LLC
Chambersburg PA
CBHW071236190726
48292CB00007B/2315